Copyright © 2023

All righttion may be reproduced, sitted, in any form, or by anotocopying, recording or opermission of the author.

This book is a work of fiction. Names, characters, places, organizations and incidents are either products of the author's imagination or used fictitiously. Any resemblance to actual events, places, organizations or persons, living or dead, is entirely coincidental.

First Published – July 30, 2023

Table of Contents

Chapter 1 1
Chapter 2 10
Chapter 3 19
Chapter 4 28
Chapter 5 36
Chapter 6 44
Chapter 7 52
Chapter 8 60
Chapter 9 68
Chapter 10 76
Chapter 11 84
Chapter 12 92
Chapter 13 100
Chapter 14 106
Chapter 15 114
Chapter 16 122
Chapter 17 131
Chapter 18 140
Chapter 19 149
Chapter 20 157
Chapter 21 165
Chapter 22 174
Chapter 23 183
Chapter 24 191
Chapter 25 199
Chapter 26 207
Chapter 27 215
Chapter 28 223
Chapter 29 233

Chapter 30	243
Chapter 31	251
Chapter 32	261
Recipe – Empire Fruit Cake	270
Acknowledgements	272
Join my Newsletter	273

MURDER AT CASTLE MORSE
By LEENA CLOVER

NOTE: This book uses British spelling.

THE EARLS OF BUXLEY

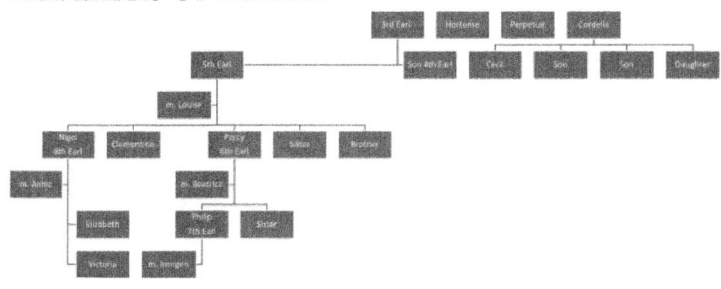

TEXT VERSION

Hortense

Perpetua

Cordelia

Cecil

3rd Earl

4th Earl

5th Earl - married to Louise

Clementine

6th earl - Married to Beatrice

Philip (7th Earl)

Nigel (8th earl) - married to Annie

Elizabeth

Victoria

RESIDENTS OF BUXLEY
At Buxley Manor
Upstairs –

Nigel Gaskins – 8th Earl of Buxley, second son of the 5th earl

Clementine Barton – Nigel's widowed sister. She runs the manor with a firm hand, or tries to.

Hortense and Perpetua Gaskins – Nigel's great aunts

Imogen, Lady Buxley or Momo – Youngest Dowager Countess, widow of Nigel's nephew Philip, the previous Earl.

Gertrude Ridley or Bubbles – Imogen's unmarried sister, more or less a permanent resident of the manor.

Elizabeth Gaskins or Bess – Nigel's daughter

Downstairs –

Barnes – butler

Mrs. Jones – housekeeper

Mrs. Bird – cook

Wilson – lady's maid

Marci – scullery maid

At the Dower House

Louise, Lady Buxley – Nigel's mother, Dowager Countess

At Primrose Cottage

Beatrice, Lady Buxley – Nigel's brother's widow, Dowager Countess

At the Vicarage

Cordelia Chilton – Nigel's great aunt

Cecil Chilton – local vicar and Cordelia's son

AT CASTLE MORSE

Clive Morse – Lord of the manor

Lady Morse – Lady of the manor

Winifred Morse or Pudding – daughter and school friend of Lady Bess

Richard Morse or Richie – son, accused of murder

Neville Morse – nephew

Alfred Nash – secretary to Lord Morse

Chapter 1

Lady Elizabeth Gaskins faced her twin Victoria across a scuffed wooden table at the Buxley Arms. The two sisters were on a mission.

"You think they are going to remember what happened twenty years ago, Bess?" Vicky bit her lip and looked away.

The proprietor Harvey arrived and wiped the table with a dubious cloth before setting two tankards of ale before them.

"We showed them, didn't we, my lady?" he crowed. "Buxley can hold its own against those ruffians from Ridley."

The annual cricket match between the villages of Buxley and Ridley had taken place after a long hiatus. Spirits were up since the home team of Buxley won the match by five wickets. It was all the locals could talk about. Bess knew the triumph on the pitch would be brought up time and again until next year.

"Nice catch," Bess complimented him. "You are the best wicket keeper in the Cotswolds, Harvey. Did you ever try playing for England?"

Harvey gave a good natured snort.

"Go on now, Lady Bess. His Lordship isn't bad either."

Mrs. Harvey bustled to their table, carrying a steaming pie and a crock of gravy, her cheeks pink. She set it on the table and cut generous wedges. Her steak pie was famous in the region but serving Bess gave her a stamp of approval she didn't get from hungry farm workers.

"How are you settling in then, Lady Vicky?" she asked.

The girls chatted with the woman, waiting for the pie to cool a bit. Bess took a bite and went into raptures.

"This is delicious, Mrs. Harvey. Birdie's a good cook but she can't make pie like this."

"Hush now." Mrs. Harvey blushed. "We know you eat real fancy at the manor. This is just plain cooking, my lady."

"Why don't you take a load off and join us?" Vicky invited the woman to sit with them. "Have a slice of pie."

Mrs. Harvey's bosom heaved and her lips quivered, overwhelmed by the honour.

"I couldn't ..."

Bess nodded at Harvey who was hovering behind his wife. He pulled out a chair for her.

"You can't say no to Lady Vicky," he told his wife. "No harm in joining them for a bite."

Vicky served her a piece of the pie and Bess poured gravy on it, urging her to eat. Mrs. Harvey picked up her knife and fork, took a deep breath and cut into the pie, unable to hold back a broad smile. They let her have a few bites before Bess embarked on her questioning.

"Do you remember Philip, Mrs. Harvey?"

"The young Lord?" Harvey asked before his missus could respond. "He was a lively one, riding hard and raising hell with his cronies. Not like your father, Lady Bess."

Nigel Gaskins, the current earl and the twins' father was a baa lamb. Bess certainly thought so. He was happiest spending the day by a stream, fishing for trout. His nephew Philip had been the earl before him for a brief time.

"So, his death was not a surprise?" Vicky asked. "He must have been overconfident. No wonder he got thrown off his horse and died."

MURDER AT CASTLE MORSE

Harvey opened his mouth to respond but his wife quelled him with a glance.

"Nobody knows what happened that day." She cleared her throat. "How is the pie, my lady?"

"If that's true, why do they say my Papa had a hand in his death?" Bess shot back. "Who started these rumours, Mrs. Harvey?"

Although the police had never found any evidence against Nigel, the seed of doubt had been planted. Twenty years later, the murmurs continued. Bess and Vicky had suffered the most, being separated at the tender age of one when their mother took Vicky and fled to America, unable to bear the backlash. A chance meeting on a battlefield in France brought the sisters face to face. Now they were determined to prove their father's innocence, ready to leave no stone unturned to solve the twenty year old crime.

Harvey hastened to make his position clear.

"Hard to say with these things, my lady. We know your father would never hurt anyone. Him and young Lord Philip got on like a house on fire. Why, there was talk of your father leaving Buxley and going to America."

"Why didn't they think it was an accident?" Vicky interrupted. "Aren't they common during hunting?"

"Lord Philip was a really good rider," Mrs. Harvey explained.

"But every rider has a bad day," Bess argued, remembering what Detective Inspector Gardener from Scotland Yard had concluded. "Maybe Philip was careless."

Mrs. Harvey snapped her fingers at the young girl standing by the kitchen door and asked her to bring the apple crumble.

She was determined to ply the girls with food until they let go of the uncomfortable topic.

"Tell me more about Philip," Bess invited. "Wasn't he awfully young to be earl?"

"The 6th earl caught a nasty cold," Harvey sighed. "By the time they sent for the doctor, he was gone. Had never been sick in his life."

The whole village had been shocked by the sudden death. Philip grew up overnight.

"He changed." Mrs. Harvey lifted a shoulder in a shrug. "Stood by his father's grave and vowed to be the best earl Buxley had seen. Told the tenants he would do right by them."

Bess and Vicky praised the crumble and thanked the Harveys.

"Weather's cooling a bit," Harvey observed. "You ready for the first hunt of the season, my lady?"

Bess gave him a nod, although her mind was far away.

"What a waste of time," she grumbled on the way back to Buxley Manor. "Frankly, Vicky, I don't think we got anywhere."

Vicky shared her gloomy outlook. They were quiet on the ride home, mulling over the impossible goal they had set for themselves.

"I don't see how Papa will ever be exonerated." Bess abandoned her car near the manor's front door, blithely assuming one of the servants would come and take care of it.

Barnes, the faithful old butler at Buxley Manor, came out and greeted them.

"Are you having a good day, my lady?"

"Could be better, Barnie," Bess muttered as she flew past him and stalked to the west wing. She was ready to admit she was stumped. Vicky guessed what she was thinking and agreed with her.

"The great aunts will know how to proceed," she soothed. "Shouldn't we wait for Grandma Louise though?"

They stumbled into a cosy parlour, coming face to face with three older women engrossed in a lively discussion.

"Grandmother!" Bess exclaimed. "Good. You are here."

The oldest Dowager Countess of Buxley greeted them with a warm smile and a twinkle in her eye. Her cheery countenance was at odds with the severe Victorian garb she favoured.

"Where have you been gallivanting today, girls? I missed you at lunch."

"We all did." Great Aunt Perpetua cleared her throat. "Were you off rendezvousing with some young man?"

The large mole on her cheek helped Vicky remember who she was.

"A disreputable one at that," Great Aunt Hortense sniggered, dabbing her face with a lace handkerchief soaked in lavender water. She was always hot.

Vicky told them they were doing no such thing.

"How are we ever going to prove anything?" Bess flung herself on a sofa and huffed. "Twenty years is too long a time to remember anything. The villagers just like to spread malicious gossip and Papa is an easy target."

"Why doesn't he retaliate?" Vicky wondered.

The aunts shared a knowing glance.

"What would you have him do, my dear? Flog them? Or throw them out of their homes?"

Louise told them some of the local families had been their tenants for over a hundred years.

"I suspect Philip's mother Beatrice is at the bottom of this nonsense. She instigates someone every few months, so the talk never dies down."

"We need a solid plan," Bess declared. "How do we find out what happened to Philip?"

Hortense rang for tea while the ladies put their heads together.

"I think you should avoid any direct questions," Louise suggested. "That puts their back up. Why don't you start by asking them about Philip?"

The twins didn't see how that was going to help. Most people thought Philip had been the cat's meow.

"He must have ruffled a few feathers," Bess argued. "Why else would someone kill him?"

"How can we come up with a list of his enemies?" Vicky wondered.

Louise opened her mouth to respond but clammed up when she spotted Barnes at the door. The ladies were quiet while the tea was served. Bess stirred her cup of Darjeeling, unable to hide her frown.

"Are you thinking of giving up so soon?" Louise was curt. "Chin up, my dear. We never said it was going to be easy."

They tossed a lot of ideas back and forth, nibbling on cucumber sandwiches and ginger biscuits. Finally, Hortense presented an unusual idea.

"Why don't you pretend you are writing his biography? That will give you the perfect excuse to ask any number of questions."

Louise and Perpetua thought it was an excellent idea.

MURDER AT CASTLE MORSE

"Just get people talking," Louise nodded. "You want them to lower their guard, not feel like they are under scrutiny."

"Tell them you are asking for quotes or something," Hortense added.

Vicky pulled out a small notebook from her purse and began taking notes. They agreed they would begin with his childhood and move up from there.

"Why don't we make a list of random questions, like his favourite dinner or the colour he wore most," she suggested. "They should sound really silly."

Bess caught on immediately.

"And we can sneak in the tough ones in there, like who his enemies were."

Louise cautioned they would need to be a bit more delicate than that.

"Why don't we think over this and regroup tomorrow?" Hortense stifled a yawn. "I would like to rest a bit before it's time to dress for dinner."

Bess apologized for losing track of time.

"Are you feeling well, Aunt Hortense? Should we send for Dr. Evans?"

The aunts declared they were fine and shooed the girls away. Louise accompanied them as they left the west wing, debating going for a drive or a walk in the rose garden.

They ran into her daughter Clementine in the hall.

"I say, Aunt Clem." Bess greeted her. "What ho!"

"Nobody told me you were still here, Mama." Clementine greeted Louise, her brows drawn together in a frown. "Tea will be served in fifteen minutes."

Louise informed her they had already imbibed, inciting her further. Clementine had returned to Buxley Manor after being widowed and had taken charge of the household. She had strict rules about everything but was often thwarted by the family.

"Ask the chauffer to bring the car around," Louise interrupted. "And stop acting like a school marm, Clementine. I am not going to live my life according to your schedule."

Bess and Vicky tiptoed out of the corridor and burst into the morning room, trying to hold back their laughter.

"Poor Aunt Clem!" Bess sighed. "She just can't let go."

"Don't be unkind," Vicky chided. "I am sure she has her work cut out for her."

Bess agreed that running a household the size of Buxley Manor was not easy. Discipline was required to keep it going like a well oiled machine.

There was a knock on the door and Barnes entered. There was a sense of urgency about him.

"What is it?" Bess sucked in a breath.

"You are wanted on the telephone, Lady Bess. It's Miss Winifred. She sounds tense."

"Pudding?" Bess rushed out of the room and down the hall, wondering what her old friend Winifred Morse wanted.

Maybe she was bored and was throwing an impromptu party.

"Hello? What ho, Pudding!"

She could barely make out the voice at the other end.

"I say, slow down a bit, will you? What's happened?"

Vicky saw her face turn white and squeezed her hand. Bess placed the receiver in the cradle and turned to her sister.

"You remember Joe Cooper?"

MURDER AT CASTLE MORSE

"That groom they found dead in the stables?" Vicky prompted.

"The police think Pudding's brother Richie killed him. We need to leave for Castle Morse at once."

Chapter 2

Bess wanted to rush out and get into her car right away but Clementine held her back.

"Hold on, my dear. It's going to be late by the time you get there. Surely you are not thinking of driving back after dark?"

"She has a point, Bess," Vicky agreed. "You think your friend Pudding will put us up for the night?"

Bess gave in. The twins rushed up to their rooms to pack an overnight bag. Barnes stood by the front door when they went down fifteen minutes later. The old Vauxhall had been brought around by the chauffer.

"You will telephone, my lady?" Barnes tried to sound nonchalant but failed.

"Don't fuss, Barnie!" Bess quipped. "I've got Vicky to keep an eye on me."

"You will tell our father?" Vicky asked Barnes. "Maybe we should look in on him?" she wondered.

Bess told her the clock was ticking.

"Who knows what's happening at Castle Morse? Pudding sounded beside herself."

Both girls tied scarves around their heads and pulled on goggles. Bess had a heavy foot on the accelerator so Vicky clutched the door and braced herself. They had to slow down when they drove through the village of Buxley. A bunch of children ran after them, waving and screaming at the top of their lungs.

"Can you tell me more now?" Vicky asked. "What's got your knickers in a twist?"

MURDER AT CASTLE MORSE

Bess told her Pudding wasn't the hysterical type.

"She sounded frantic on the phone. I wonder what Richie's done."

Vicky asked if he was like the typical aristocratic British male, bent on whiling away time getting into silly scrapes, spending his inheritance.

"Not even close," Bess interrupted. "Richie fought in the war and came back a Captain. I think he was recommended for the VC too."

They reached the village of Ridley forty minutes later and drove through it.

"And this man is a murder suspect?" Vicky frowned. "There must be a reason why the police think so."

Bess blew a raspberry and yanked the steering wheel to the left.

"Well, if they are anything like Constable Potts ..."

"All I'm saying is, don't go off half cocked, Bess. We don't know the facts yet."

They climbed a hill covered in towering oaks, casting low shadows on the road. Dense foliage surrounded them on all sides. Vicky looked around in awe as they crossed a stone bridge with swirling water below.

"That's the Severn," Bess pointed out. "This area is called the Forest of Dean. Morseford is pretty, surrounded by wooded hills. The timber's just a drop in the ocean though."

The Morses owned mines and had amassed a veritable fortune from coal. The current Lord Morse, being more industrious than his ancestors, had invested a lot of money in railroads in Britain and America, managing to quadruple his holdings. The apple hadn't fallen far from the tree. Richie was a hard working young man, determined to learn from his father and add to the coffers.

Vicky pulled a bottle of lemonade from a basket Barnes had handed them, courtesy Mrs. Bird the cook. She asked Bess to pull over by the side of the road.

"A few minutes won't hurt us."

"It will certainly be quicker than stopping at a pub. I am parched, Vicky. And I could use some sustenance."

The basket produced a lot more than they expected. Bess gobbled a few egg sandwiches and duly appreciated some jam biscuits. They got out to stretch their legs.

"Is it cooler here than at Buxley?" Vicky gave a deep yawn. "Must be all these trees."

They heard the roar of a motor in the distance and looked up, curious. A magnificent red automobile crested the hill before them and began its downward journey.

"Wait, is that ...?" Vicky laughed. "Looks like he beat us to it."

Bess was looking mutinous.

The car slowed and stopped and a familiar face waved at them.

"Lady Elizabeth, Lady Vicky? On your way to Castle Morse, no doubt? I should have known."

Bess asked the man what he was doing in the region.

"You do know this is my job?" Detective Inspector James Gardener of Scotland Yard replied. "Although I might be unemployed very soon if Detective Gaskins is on the trail."

Bess allowed herself a tiny smile.

"Call me Bess, Inspector. I think we know each other well enough by now."

MURDER AT CASTLE MORSE

Vicky asked him if he was investigating the murder at Castle Morse. James nodded. The Morses wielded a lot of influence in town. Scotland Yard wanted their top man on the job.

"Apparently, my job description has changed now," he grumbled. "I am to pander to these rich aristocrats, make sure they are handled with the right amount of delicacy."

Bess knew he was only half serious. He was called Bulldog Gardener for a reason.

"You think Richie did it?" she quirked an eyebrow.

"It is too soon to reach to any conclusions." He was deadpan. "May I remind you it is illegal to keep information from the police?"

Bess told him to relax. She was just answering a friend's cry for help. All she planned to do was be with Pudding in her time of crisis.

"You are saying you won't interfere in my investigation?"

Bess and Vicky shared a glance and shrugged.

"We might ask a few questions, just get a lay of the land."

James warned them to be careful, bringing up the time they had come to harm that summer while tracking down a killer.

"You may not be as fortunate this time."

"We will count on you to rescue us," Vicky grinned. "And now, I think we should get going, Detective Inspector."

James drove off with a look of resignation, an unspoken warning clear in his eyes. He could call off their truce any time he wanted.

They reached the village of Morse a few minutes later.

"It's Morseford, really, but it's always been shortened to Morse."

Bess pointed out the landmarks. Vicky took in the half timbered buildings on the main street. There was a pub and a clock tower and the spires of a church rose in the distance.

They drove on and entered the castle grounds, traversing an avenue of oaks to a big circular driveway. Turrets rose at one side of a central block made of local stone. Parts of the structure were Gothic and Vicky assumed some of it had been rebuilt in the recent past.

"There used to be a moat," Bess explained. "But they filled it in about fifty some years ago, when the current Lord Morse was a babe. Pudding can tell you a lot more about the history of the place."

"It's certainly imposing."

Bess parked before a set of steps leading up to a grand entrance. The door opened and the butler stepped out, followed by Pudding. She ran down to greet them, almost slipping in her haste.

"I say, old girl," Bess grabbed her by the arms. "Steady on."

"You are here." Pudding clasped her hands together. "I feel much better now, Bess."

They followed the butler inside, stepping into a spacious parlour decorated in hues of peach. Pudding's mother presided over a pot of tea.

"Good Evening, Lady Morse," Bess greeted her. "Aunt Clem sends her regards."

She gave them a welcoming smile and told Vicky the coffee was on its way.

A stout brown haired man of medium height sat in a spindly chair near Lady Morse, staring at the fireplace. Vicky nudged Bess, prompting her to introduce them.

MURDER AT CASTLE MORSE

"What ho, Neville!" Bess greeted the man in the chair. "Meet my sister Vicky."

There was no response.

"He barely speaks now, poor thing," Lady Morse clucked. "It's been like that since he came back from the war."

Vicky realized the poor man was suffering from shell shock. She had seen several patients like that when she worked as a wartime nurse.

"Why do the police suspect him?" she asked.

Pudding told her Neville was her cousin. Richie was out with Lord Morse, taking care of some business.

"Our kind has always been targeted by the working class," Lady Morse retorted. "They are jealous, of course."

Bess caught Pudding's eye and a silent message passed between them.

"Why don't I show you to your room?" she asked. "You don't mind sharing, I hope?"

Lady Morse reminded them dinner was at seven sharp.

The girls didn't say much until Bess closed the door of the chamber assigned to her and sat on the bed.

"Spill the beans, Pudding. How terrible a situation is Richie in?"

Pudding brought up the dead groom. Bess and Vicky were aware of his death.

"He died on the day of the cricket match." Vicky remembered. "But that was almost a week ago."

The local constable had no experience in dealing with murder. The verdict at the inquest had been murder by persons unknown.

"I think Papa must have called in Scotland Yard," Pudding sighed. "Says there is a killer on the loose at Morse and we cannot have that."

Bess remembered her own father had done something similar when a man had been murdered at Buxley. Calling in the detectives was a two edged sword. Once they arrived on the scene, nobody controlled their actions.

"Why does DI Gardener suspect Richie?" she asked.

Vicky interrupted and told Pudding to begin at the beginning.

"Did your brother know the victim?"

Pudding collapsed on the bed and punched a pillow.

"We all knew Joe. He has been head groom here since I was a child. He taught all of us to ride."

"Yes," Vicky pressed. "But how often did they meet? I mean, did they have a relationship beyond master and servant?"

Pudding nodded vigorously.

Joe Cooper had been Richard Morse's batman in the war.

"He promised Papa he would bring Richie back home safely. And he lived up to it."

Bess wasn't surprised to hear about the groom's loyalty. The servants at Buxley Manor had always been protective of her too, spoiling her with hugs and never letting her feel her mother's absence.

"I don't see what the problem is then, old girl." She patted Pudding. "Was it just a ruse to get us here?"

The girls had been known to play many pranks while growing up, resorting to extreme measures to spend time with each other.

MURDER AT CASTLE MORSE

"I wish!" Pudding cried. "No Bess, I need your help. Richie was the one who found the body, you see? He found old Joe bashed to death in the stables."

Vicky thought the police had a valid reason to suspect Richard Morse but she kept her opinion to herself.

"What was he doing there?" Bess mused. "Does he go there often?"

Pudding stared back, her eyes wide open.

"You do know Richie? He rides twice a day and he started some program to breed thoroughbreds. Of course he goes to the stables."

Bess thought it was the first question the police would ask and they would not stop there.

"How is Richie taking it?"

According to Pudding, her brother was unflappable.

"Ever since he got back from the war, he thinks he's invincible. But I am not taking any chances. Mother agrees."

They wanted Bess to find out who killed Joe Cooper.

"I will do anything to help Richie," Bess replied. "And so will Vicky. But we can't promise anything."

A bell rang, making them jump.

"Time to dress for dinner." Pudding scrambled to her feet. "Don't be late, girls. You know how temperamental Henri is."

Unlike the homely cook at Buxley Manor, a French chef reigned over the Castle Morse kitchen. Bess rubbed her hands, looking forward to one of his superlative offerings. She presumed they would also meet Richie.

"What have you told him?" she winked. "Am I supposed to be undercover?"

LEENA CLOVER

Pudding told them she had invited them to discuss the upcoming onion festival.

"It will give you a reason to meet all the villagers and talk to them."

Chapter 3

Dinner at Castle Morse stretched for an hour. Lord Morse was his jovial self, eager to talk about the upcoming hunt. Richie arrived five minutes late and received an earful from his mother. Bess thought he looked tired but didn't appear like someone who was worried about being arrested for murder.

The youngsters played some records after dinner and exchanged gossip about their friends. Vicky tried to broach the topic of the murder.

"Joe was the best groom a chap could ask for," Richie replied. "It's going to be hard to replace him."

He refused to say anything more, urging them to enjoy the evening.

"Life is for the living."

Bess wasn't sure if he was being callous or just putting on an act. She decided to take his advice, dancing with abandon for the next two hours. Richie excused himself when the tea arrived, claiming he had some work to do before he turned in.

Pudding handed Bess a cup of tea and urged her to sample the petit fours.

"You see why I am so worried, don't you?"

Vicky told them Richard was in denial. It was clear he was loathe to face what had happened.

"But that won't help," Bess sighed. "He will have to speak up at some point."

The girls went to bed after that, exhausted by their busy day. Morning arrived soon enough. A maid woke them with hot chocolate and rolls, assuring them a more elaborate meal was laid out in the morning room.

"Henri makes the best omelettes," Bess told Vicky. "But I am going to miss my kedgeree."

Vicky knew Bess did not like to start her day without the fish and rice dish. She herself had never taken a liking to the British penchant for eating fish at breakfast.

Pudding greeted them at the table. Bess wondered where the rest of the family was.

"Mother never comes down this early. Papa and Richie left an hour ago."

Bess and Vicky both opted for the chef's special omelette, buttering some toast while they waited.

"What's the plan, Bess?" Pudding was nervous and excited. "How do we go about this sleuthing business?"

"I am not sure." Bess looked at Vicky. "You thought of something?"

The butler came in and addressed Pudding.

"The festival committee meets in an hour, Miss. When shall I have the car brought around?"

"Oh no! The onion festival!" Pudding slapped her head. "There goes my entire morning."

Bess suggested regrouping in the evening.

"Gives us time to go home and pack a bag for a longer stay. You will have to put us up for a week or two, old girl."

"You can stay here till Christmas!" Pudding cried. "Why don't you telephone Barnes? He can send your maid along with whatever you need."

Vicky told her she was expecting something in the mail.

"Have it your way." Pudding flung her hands in the air. "But you better get ready to dig your heels in. Richie needs you, Bess."

They didn't linger over breakfast. Pudding left for her meeting and the twins drove back to Buxley.

"Why are we going back?" Vicky asked.

"Thanks for the quick save," Bess grinned. "I wracked my brain for ideas last night and hit a wall. A meeting of the Nightingales is in order."

"I will never underestimate Grandma Louise," Vicky laughed. "Or the great aunts." She was awed by how indefatigable the older ladies were. They had taken an active interest in solving a murder at Buxley Manor earlier that year, forming an impromptu sleuthing club of sorts in the process.

It was a pleasant day for a drive and they made quick time. Barnes greeted them with a raised eyebrow, generally the extent of any emotion he showed. Clementine was more vocal.

"Hello girls. We have curry for lunch."

She led them to a parlour where two more women sat having tea.

"What ho, Momo! Bubbles!" Bess greeted them with an abundance of bonhomie.

Momo or Imogen, Philip's wife, was the youngest dowager countess at Buxley. Bubbles or Gertrude Ridley, her sister, was almost a permanent resident of the manor. They were poles apart in personality but both doted on Bess.

"Have some cake," Bubbles offered, cutting two slices for the twins.

Momo handed Bess a cup of Darjeeling and ordered coffee for Vicky.

"How is Lady Morse?" she asked. "We haven't seen her since summer."

Bess provided enough updates to make her happy and stood up.

"We are going to see the great aunts."

The twins headed to the west wing, hoping their grandmother had arrived from the Dower House. Bess had telephoned her from Castle Morse that morning, promising a treat.

"We have a new case," she declared when they entered the aunts' chamber.

The three ladies occupied their favourite chairs, their backs ramrod straight and eyes alert. Vicky embraced each of them while Bess gave them a finger wave and collapsed on a sofa.

"Thwarted already?" Louise, the oldest Dowager Countess and grandmother of the twins laughed. "You are smarter than that, my dear."

"I presume this is about Joe Cooper?" Hortense asked, dabbing her brow with her lace hanky.

Bess and Vicky gave them a brief summary.

"The police suspect him just because he found the man," Bess scoffed. "How terrible."

Louise laughed. "Sadly, my dear, you are poorly informed."

"Horse," Perpetua grunted. "Motive."

Hortense launched into a detailed explanation, soaking her handkerchief in a silver basin filled with lavender water. Richie had a favourite horse, a thoroughbred, who was a champion racer. He was in high demand as a stud. Something went wrong and the horse died.

MURDER AT CASTLE MORSE

"He blamed Joe Cooper," Louise continued. "Richard accused him of poisoning the beast."

"But why would a groom do that?" Bess cried.

"That's what you will have to find out. Did Joe Cooper take any deliberate steps to kill that horse? And how much did it affect Richard?"

The dowager stressed the need to find more suspects. Did the groom have other enemies? It was obvious he had angered someone.

There was a knock at the door and Barnes glided in.

"Luncheon is about to be served, my lady."

There was a spirited exodus to the dining room. Curry was a much anticipated meal at Buxley Manor.

Nigel, the current earl of Buxley and the twins' father, sat at the head of the table, absently patting the poodle at his feet. The footmen began serving the meal.

"What ho, Papa!" Bess greeted her father. "Caught any trout this morning?"

"Where have you girls been?" He abandoned his soup and frowned, his glance hovering between the twins.

Vicky thought he sounded like a petulant child.

"Didn't Barnes tell you?" Bess sat back, allowing a footman to clear her plate. Her eyes lit up when a plate of steaming, fragrant mutton curry was set before her, resting on a mound of rice. "Pudding needed me. In fact, we are going back to Castle Morse after lunch. We won't be back for a few days."

"I say!" Nigel's frown deepened. "I bally well won't allow that."

Louise laughed and told him to stop being ridiculous.

"Does this have anything to do with Joe Cooper, Bessie?" Nigel asked. "You will not put yourself in danger again."

Bess was engrossed in relishing her favourite meal. Vicky promised they would be careful. Clementine sided with her brother, making her opinion clear.

"Lord Morse should call in Scotland Yard. I will talk to him."

Momo jumped in with her own reservations and the meal turned noisy, with everyone speaking at once. For the first time in the history of Buxley Manor, the cook's spotted dick was ignored.

The twins followed Nigel to his study.

"What would you have us do, Papa?" Bess sat on a sofa and punched a cushion.

"Whatever young girls do," Nigel shrugged. "Run up to London and shake your limbs in a dance club. Go to Paris on a shopping spree."

They knew what he was leaving unsaid. Nigel had just reunited with Vicky and was afraid of losing her again.

"What do you think of Richie?" Bess asked him. "Is he empty headed like other young men of his ilk?"

Nigel's eyes held a knowing gleam.

"He distinguished himself in the war. Any father would be proud to call him son. Say, you don't think ..."

Vicky laughed. Bess needed a minute to catch his meaning.

"What? No, Papa. Pudding's brother?"

Nigel argued he wasn't related to them by blood.

"Mad about horses, though. What? Was fit to be tied when that Arabian of his died. Vowed to murder whoever harmed him."

MURDER AT CASTLE MORSE

Bess thought it was just the sort of thing one said in the heat of the moment. Surely Richie didn't intend to act on it? She needed more information before she could say for sure.

Nigel rallied around after the girls spent an hour or so in his study. Vicky pulled Polo, the poodle from her lap and set it down gently.

"We need to leave now."

"I'd rather not drive in the dark," Bess added for good measure.

Nigel urged them to go to the police at the slightest sign of danger.

The drive to Castle Morse was uneventful. Pudding accosted them as soon as the butler Norton ushered them into the parlour.

"I thought you weren't coming."

Lady Morse poured tea and the girls replenished themselves with cucumber sandwiches and Empire fruit cake. It was a Castle Morse specialty, lovingly developed by their old cook. Bess made sure she took a hefty slice. The sun was close to the horizon when she suggested a walk in the garden.

"Take us to the stables," she told Pudding when they stepped out. "I suppose we should take a look at where they found him."

The smell of fresh hay greeted them, accompanied by the neighs and grunts of the horses. Two young stable hands went from stall to stall, filling the water troughs. Pudding led them to the end of the aisle, heading toward a polished wooden door that was slightly ajar. The stall was bigger than others, taking up thrice the space. A plaque announced the name of the star inhabitant.

A figure moved out of the darkness as they got closer, revealing himself.

"Richie!" Pudding exclaimed. "We missed you at tea. Mama was fretting."

Vicky noticed his red eyes and flushed cheeks. She glanced at Bess to make sure she had spotted them too.

"What ho, girls!" Richie asked brightly. "Going for a ride?"

Pudding told him they might do just that.

"You never rode Sindbad, did you, Bess?" Richie sighed. "He was faster than the wind."

In a wistful tone, he launched into a series of anecdotes about his beloved horse.

"What about Joe Cooper?" Vicky interrupted after a few minutes.

Bess could guess what she was thinking. Richie seemed to have forgotten the dead groom.

"He poisoned Sindbad." Richie clenched his jaw. "The bounder! Fed him something that killed him."

"Is this where you found him?" Bess probed.

Richie leaned against the door, his breath shallow.

"He was lying on his side, poor chap, eyes wide open, foaming at the mouth. I have nightmares about the fear I saw in his eyes." He closed his eyes. "I think he knew the end was near."

Bess tried to make sense of what he was saying. As far as she knew, Joe Cooper had been dead when Richie found him in the stall.

"Are you talking about your horse?" Vicky cut in, her voice sharp.

Richie gave a start.

"Of course. My poor Sindbad. Where will I find another like him?"

Pudding gave a snort.

"They want to know about the dead groom, you dolt."

Bess backed her up. She wanted to hear his account of how he had encountered Joe Cooper.

"I come and sit here sometimes." He gave a shrug. "Makes me feel close to him."

This time, they knew he was talking about Sindbad. Richie had arrived in the stables that afternoon, meaning to spend some time in the empty stall. He had come across Joe Cooper's body.

"Did you call the doctor?" Vicky asked. "Check for a pulse?"

Richie told them he had seen enough dead men on the battlefield to know when a person was gone.

"Kind of poetic, what?" He smirked. "Him dying on the same spot where Sindbad took his last breath?"

Chapter 4

Richard Morse watched his sister and her friends return to the house. He thought he had given them a convincing account of that fateful day. Had he managed to deceive Bess? She was smarter than Pudding and harder to fool. That's why he had pretended to be maudlin about Sindbad. Bess loved horses. Almost everyone of their kind who rode had a soft spot for them. Most communicated better with horses than humans.

Joe Cooper's death was good for everyone. Maybe they would finally resolve the long debate about building a war memorial and erect the darned thing. It would give the villagers something to exclaim over every time they passed the village green.

Richard had been shocked when he found Joe in Sindbad's stall that day. There was a pool of blood around his head, seeping into the earth. Clearly, the poor man had been dead for a while. Richard did all the appropriate things, asking the butler to call the local police. A tiny part of him had been relieved. He didn't have to fake his grief. Joe had been his mentor, had taught him to ride and fought shoulder to shoulder with him in France. But he had a bee in his bonnet about the memorial. Richard was sure that had caused the groom's untimely death.

Bess had been relentless in her questions. He made an effort to be accurate. Her eyebrows had shot up when he mentioned a peculiar scent lingering in the air, mixed with a faint metallic tang. She didn't believe him.

**

Pudding walked back to the main house with Bess and Vicky, lost in thought.

"How was your meeting?" Vicky asked, her amusement evident in her voice. "I have never heard of an onion festival before. Do you give a prize to the person who grows the largest onion?"

"It's a venerable tradition in these parts," Bess explained. "Not to be made fun of, old bean."

Vicky made a face when she learned what the contest was about.

"Eating a raw onion? That's vile."

Pudding couldn't hold back any longer.

"Did you believe him, Bess?"

"I say, has he lost his marbles?" she exclaimed. "That boy we just spoke to was nothing like the Richie I know."

Vicky asked if his personality had changed since he came back from the war.

"This could be his way of handling trauma. Some people withdraw into themselves, like your cousin. But some put on appearances to hide their true feelings."

"We are British, Vicky," Bess clucked. "We always hide our feelings." She stopped mid step and turned toward Pudding. "No, Richie's smarter than that. I say what we just saw was an act. He was lying through his teeth, the rascal."

"What?" Pudding's face coloured. "Do remember why you are here, Bess. I want you to save him."

Vicky told her they would not condone murder. If Richie was guilty of harming the groom, he would have to face the consequences.

"You stay out of it." Pudding's lower lip quivered.

Vicky realized Pudding saw her as an interloper.

"I don't want to come between you two friends, but Bess agrees with me."

"She's right, old girl," Bess sighed. "I have to do the right thing."

Pudding blanched. This was the first time Bess had sided with someone against her.

"That will not be necessary because Richie is innocent. I can vouch for him."

None of them uttered a word as they marched across a path lined by colourful flowers. Bess wanted to get in her car and drive home to Buxley Manor at once. What had got into Pudding? She wove her arm through Vicky's, flashing her an apologetic look. Vicky squeezed her hand, letting her know she was alright.

They heard some voices before they went around a corner and came across two men engaged in a lively conversation. A short, plump man was taking a groundskeeper to task. His face relaxed in a smile when he looked up and spotted them.

"Lady Bess!"

"You remember Mr. Nash?" Pudding prompted. "Papa's secretary."

Bess tried not to stare at the empty sleeve dangling from the man's shoulder. Another casualty of the war, she surmised.

"How do you do?" she greeted him. "Have you met my sister?"

He gave Vicky a brief bow, his eyes full of admiration.

"I heard you were a nurse during the war? You must be very brave."

MURDER AT CASTLE MORSE

Vicky told him she had followed her heart. She couldn't sit at home sipping coffee while men lost their lives, trying to do the right thing.

Bess thanked him for his service.

"Does it hurt much?" She nodded at his missing arm. "I suppose it couldn't have been avoided?"

Alfred Nash struggled to keep his emotions in check. He was glad to be home, although not entirely in one piece.

"They called us invincible, the Morse 13. And now look what has happened. We lost Raymond to gangrene and old Joe got himself killed."

He didn't need much prompting to launch into his story. Thirteen men from the village joined the army. Richie had been one of them. They defied many odds and fought in several battles before coming back home just before the war ended.

"It was no mean feat," he preened. "The war left its mark but at least I am alive, not lying in an unmarked grave in a foreign land."

Pudding invited him to dinner. He thanked her but declined, saying he wasn't fit to eat in polite company.

"So you knew Joe Cooper?" Bess asked.

Nash laughed. "We came to the castle around the same time. He was a cheeky young man, full of himself. But he knew his business. Nobody knows more about horses in these parts. In fact, I'm surprised Lord Buxley let him go."

Bess made a mental note to ask her father about it.

"Can you tell us more? Did he have any family, for instance, other than Constable Yates? I believe he was Joe's uncle."

Nash gave a shrug. "Not as far as I know. He spent every waking moment with his horses. Had never gone farther than the Cotswolds before we joined the army."

Vicky surmised he must have been a familiar figure in the village.

"That he was," Nash nodded and laughed. "Especially at The Crown. Joe was fond of a pint or two."

Bess promised to find him if she had any more questions about Joe.

"You never mentioned the Morse 13, Pudding?"

"Just some silly moniker the villagers came up with," she dismissed. "What a terrible bore."

They went to their rooms to rest a bit before dressing for dinner.

"Have you come up with any questions about Philip?" Vicky asked Bess when they were alone. "All I could think of was his favourite colour or favourite food. Sounds foolish."

"Maybe talking about something so trivial will jog their memories? We won't know until we try."

Vicky thought they had time. "We'll think of something else by the time we go home to Buxley."

Bess thought of Lord Morse. She told Vicky he had known Philip well.

"Why don't we start with him?"

The dressing bell rang, prompting the girls to change into their evening frocks. They went down and joined the Morses in the parlour for drinks. It was a sparse gathering.

"Why don't you invite Meredith for a visit, my dear?" Lord Morse nudged his wife, referring to his oldest daughter who lived in America. "We haven't seen her in years."

MURDER AT CASTLE MORSE

Neville sat in a chair by the fire, cradling a glass of whiskey. He looked up for a split second but said nothing. Richard was handing out drinks.

"How about a gin rickey, eh, Bess?"

Vicky opted for a glass of sherry.

"Boring!" Pudding muttered under her breath.

Norton arrived to announce dinner was served.

There was a clear fishy soup, escargots, a carrot soufflé, followed by coq au vin. Chef Henri came in to present the dish himself.

Vicky admitted the food was delicious and tucked in.

"Don't you ever miss British food?" Bess asked Lord Morse.

He told her he went to The Crown when he fancied a steak and kidney pie. Or invited himself to Buxley Manor.

"Philip teased me about it," he guffawed. "He knew I was hankering for an old fashioned English roast when I turned up unannounced."

Bess told him he was always welcome at Buxley.

"That's exactly what Philip used to say. Now his mother Beatrice ... you know how she is. Your Aunt Clementine is very generous though, I must say. And so was your mother Annie, of course."

He paused to dab his mouth with a napkin.

"I wonder why we never hired a French chef at Buxley," Bess mused.

"Philip was against it," Lord Morse replied. "He hated French food with a passion. Said it reminded him of something unpleasant. But he liked coffee. Drank it black, without adding any milk or sugar. Momo always teased him about it."

Twenty years had passed since Philip's death but the Buxley Manor kitchen had never welcomed a French chef. There had been a time when Clementine proposed it, encouraged by Bubbles, but Lord Buxley had put his foot down. He did not wish to disrespect his cousin's memory.

"Did Philip like kedgeree?" Vicky chimed in. "Bess throws a tantrum if she does not see it at the breakfast table."

Lord Morse nodded vigorously. "He was the same. His grandfather, the 4th earl, was fond of it. Kedgeree is a Buxley Manor tradition, my dear. Philip was a stickler for tradition, very conscious of his role as the earl. He was brought up that way, I suppose, being the heir."

"Unlike Papa," Bess spoke softly. "No wonder he struggles."

"Now, Bess," Lord Morse admonished her. "Nigel has done an excellent job as the 8th earl and you know it. No wonder he is so popular."

Bess didn't agree. If the villagers were so fond of her father, why did they suspect him of murdering Philip? Why did they talk behind his back and believe baseless rumours. She looked around the dinner table and decided it was not the time or place to express her feelings.

"How is dear Annie?" Lady Morse asked Vicky. "She has been so kind to our Meredith."

"I am expecting a letter from her any day now," Vicky smiled, thinking of her mother.

Lord Morse told them Richie was planning a trip to America to look at some race horses.

"When do you sail, my boy?" he asked as the footmen set a plate of cheese and fruit before him. "A change of scene will be good for you."

All eyes swung toward the scion of the Morse family. He tapped a spoon against the table, biting his lip.

"Not in the near future, Papa. That detective from Scotland Yard has forbidden me to travel."

"You don't say?" Lord Morse turned red. "Let me talk to the superintendent."

Clive Morse was one of the richest men in England and wielded a lot of power. But Bess knew it wouldn't be enough if Richie had really murdered Joe Cooper.

Chapter 5

Bess and Vicky sat in bed the next morning, eating the croissants the maid brought with their chocolate.

"This feels so decadent." Bess peeled a layer off the roll and popped it in her mouth. "France is calling, my dear. What do you say to popping over to Paris for a few days?"

Vicky wondered why they hadn't heard from Annie yet.

"What if Mom never talks to me again?"

Bess dismissed her concerns with a wave.

"You're home now, Vicky. Papa will take care of you." She sipped her chocolate, hesitating before her next question. "You did tell her about me?"

Vicky pointed out their mother had always known about Bess.

"And you have no idea if she ever misses Buxley, not even a bit?"

The two sisters were quiet, each lost in contemplating what their future held. They had grown up without one parent and both wanted to breach the gap at the earliest. But that would require some kind of truce between their parents.

"What are we doing today?" Vicky asked. "I think we need to meet more people, those not related to Richard Morse."

Bess agreed with her. A maid arrived to help them get ready but they sent her back. Both had cut their hair short in the style of the day. Vicky wore a summer frock that brushed her calves, loose fitting with a dropped waist. Bess wore a pant suit that was sure to invite comment.

MURDER AT CASTLE MORSE

Pudding was munching on toast when they entered the breakfast room. Lady Morse sipped a cup of tea. Her eyes opened wide when she greeted the girls.

"I say, Bess. How modern! It suits you."

They ordered omelettes and made plans for the day while they waited. Bess loaded her plate with kippers and beans from the side board.

Lady Morse wanted some buttons and asked if they could make a stop at the haberdashery.

"Of course, Mama," Pudding promised. "I was going to give them a tour of the village. It's been ages since Bess visited and Vicky has never been here."

They set off on foot after breakfast, deciding they needed to stretch their legs.

"Where's Richie?" Bess asked. "I hope he's not going to abscond, Pudding. That will put the fat in the fire."

The haberdashery was situated right in the centre of the village square, announcing itself with a prominent sign. Pudding led the way in.

A tall young man with tawny eyes and a firm jaw stood behind the counter. His greeting was polite but lacked warmth.

"Good morning, Ron." Pudding flashed a brilliant smile. "Got any new designs I can look at?" She turned toward Bess. "This is Ronald Griffin, the proprietor of this store. He's also a brilliant hat maker."

Bess turned toward the man with renewed interest.

"I have been trying to set up a meeting with Lord Morse, Miss." Ronald hailed Pudding. "Can you put in a word, please?"

"Sure!" she agreed. "Anything urgent?"

"I would say so." Ronald pinned her with his gaze. "The memorial has been delayed long enough. Now that Joe Cooper's gone, we just need your father's nod to begin construction."

Bess wanted to know more.

"Ron lost his brother Raymond," Pudding sighed. "It was hard luck."

"My brother died a hero." Ronald's eyes burned. "He gave his life for his country. All we are asking for is something to honour his memory."

Vicky wanted to know where he died.

"That's the hard part." His voice was heavy. "He was shot in the leg somewhere in France. They patched him up but the wound hadn't healed properly. He got gangrene and died a week after he came home."

Bess could feel his pain. She had heard similar stories. Sometimes, the hospitals were so full they had to release patients early. Raymond must have been one of them.

"We are sorry," Vicky commiserated. "At least you were able to meet him one last time."

"Barely," Ronald sighed but agreed. "It's been three years and we still don't have a war memorial."

Bess thought that was strange. Sadly enough, they had become a common feature across villages in the country.

"All thanks to Joe Cooper." Ronald's voice was bitter.

Pudding asked for the buttons Lady Morse wanted. They paid for their purchase and left soon after, walking two doors down to a tea room.

"I am tired of hearing about that silly memorial," Pudding exclaimed. "It's all anyone talks about in this village."

Vicky told her she was being callous.

"What about the poor souls who lost their lives? It's easy for you to be so dismissive."

Pudding turned red as a tomato.

"How dare you!"

"She's not wrong, old girl," Bess sided with her sister. "You didn't put your life on the line. There were a dozen jobs you might have volunteered for but you chose not to."

Pudding thought she had behaved like any well brought up girl of her class. She obeyed her parents and stayed home.

"It's like I thought, Bess. This is the second time you have taken her side."

Vicky sprang up and left without a word.

"What's wrong with you, Pudding?" Bess cried. "I just found her and she is my sister! I will bally well side with her against the whole world." She pushed her chair back so hard that it toppled. "You spent the war drinking tea in your parlour. No wonder you don't understand."

She swept out and walked away from the centre of the village, trying to curb her temper. She found Vicky by a pond, watching the ducks.

"Let's go home."

Vicky took her hand and smiled.

"Don't be silly. You are not going to abandon a friend in need over a juvenile contest. She's never had to share you with anyone."

"That doesn't mean she can be unkind. It's just not cricket."

Vicky wrapped her in a hug. Bess felt her anger evaporate. She had been surrounded by people as a child but the only warm embraces had come from the cook and the housekeeper.

Was her mother as affectionate as Vicky, she wondered for the umpteenth time.

They walked back to the village green, looking for Pudding. She stood outside the tearoom, looking sheepish.

"I say!" she rushed over, uncertain. "I am sorry, Bessie. Don't know what came over me." She turned to Vicky. "I acted like an idiot, didn't I?"

Vicky accepted the olive branch and they headed back to the castle.

"Tell us about this war memorial, Pudding," she prompted. "Why doesn't Morse have one yet?"

Bess admitted she was curious too. Why had the topic never come up between them?

"It's such a volatile subject," Pudding confessed. "I suppose we didn't want outsiders to know about it. By that, I mean, people who don't live here."

The Morse Thirteen had come back home in 1918, a few months before the armistice. They had been in a bad skirmish and had received an honourable discharge from the army after that.

"You heard what Ron said. His brother Raymond died a few days after they got home. So the Griffins were the first family to suggest we build a memorial."

Joe Cooper had been vehemently against it. He argued that a memorial was not relevant since they had all returned home. A plaque announcing their victory was more appropriate.

"Thirteen men left and thirteen came back, he used to say." Pudding frowned at the memory. "Building a memorial is almost an insult."

MURDER AT CASTLE MORSE

Vicky pointed out that wasn't exactly true since Raymond had succumbed to a wound acquired in the battle. He was a war hero and deserved to be hailed as such.

"But he did come home alive," Bess argued.

Pudding stopped in her tracks and whirled around.

"That right there. That's it. This is what the locals have been going back and forth over for the past three years. It's what men talk about in The Crown at the end of the day. And what the ladies discuss over tea."

Pudding told them the village was divided over the issue.

"Why not do both?" Bess mused. "Build the memorial and also have a plaque or whatever for the people who survived."

Apparently, that was an option nobody had thought about.

"What did Richie think?" Vicky asked. "He was a Captain in the army, right? All those men must have served under him."

Pudding told them he wanted the memorial. But Joe Cooper had prevailed. He declared he could not stay in the village if the memorial was built.

"You know how mad Richie is about his horses. He needed Joe to make a success of his racing operation. So he stayed neutral."

Bess thought they were finally beginning to learn something about the dead groom. He wielded a lot of power in the village of Morse and bent people to his will. She could imagine he was a thorn in Ronald Griffin's side.

"What about now?" Bess asked Pudding. "Has Richie changed his stance?"

She told them the village council was going to meet in a few days to discuss the topic. But most of the people who had opposed the memorial were coming around.

"So the Griffin family will finally get what they want," Vicky summed up. "Do you realize this gives Ronald a motive to kill Joe?"

"What?" Pudding burst out. "Sweet Ron? He can't say boo to a goose."

Bess told her the meekest person had the ability to commit violent acts when provoked. Ronald must have been at the end of his tether.

Pudding refused to believe her. Ronald wielded a needle and a thread, not an axe.

"If that's the case, Richie's the only one who looks guilty," Bess replied. "He clearly blamed Joe for killing Sindbad. And he was present at the spot."

They were tired and depressed by the time they reached the castle. Norton led them to the dining room where lunch was about to be served.

Lady Morse was aghast at their blotchy faces and ordered them up to their rooms to freshen up.

"You are not school girls any more, my dear," she scolded Pudding. "You could have taken the car."

She had calmed down by the time the girls returned to the dining room. Lunch was a green salad with cold chicken and truffles folded in the most delicate pastry. They had lavender ice cream with macarons, another specialty of Chef Henri's.

Bess asked after Lord Morse. She wanted to talk to him about the memorial. Lady Morse told them he was meeting Alfred Nash in his study and did not want to be disturbed.

The girls sat in the parlour, rifling through some magazines. Vicky was trying hard to stay awake.

"I am going up for a nap, Bess," she announced.

Pudding offered to ring for coffee. Vicky thanked her, insisting a brief rest was all she needed. Maybe she would have a long bath after that.

"I say!" Bess dropped the book she was holding. "Do you remember that pool we used to bathe in, Pudding? Is it still there?"

The two friends stared at each other, wide eyed.

"Why wouldn't it be?" Pudding breathed.

They told Vicky about a rock pool surrounded by dense trees. It was fed by natural springs and was large enough to swim in.

"We don't have bathing costumes," she pointed out, her lips spreading in a mischievous smile. "Unless you want to go skinny dipping."

"Don't think I won't," Bess shot back.

"I dare you!" Vicky laughed, just as Lord Morse came in.

"What devilish scheme are you plotting now, girls?" His eyes crinkled with humour.

Bess grew sober and asked him about the memorial.

Chapter 6

The Morse family liked to entertain. So Bess wasn't surprised to see new faces at dinner. The vicar was accompanied by his unmarried sister, there were two genteel spinsters who lived on their own in straitened circumstances and a lawyer who had come to visit the coal mines on behalf of his client.

The food was lavish as usual. Bess had the vicar on her left. He was quite vocal about the goodness of traditional British food. Richie sat on her right.

"We need to talk," she spoke under her breath. "I have many questions for you."

"Don't be such a bore, Bess," he replied with a smile. "I was hoping you would liven things up a bit on the home front, what?"

Not to be outdone, Bess pinched his thigh.

"Meet me in the garden later," she warned, eliciting a smile.

The ladies retired to the parlour after the meal. Lady Morse rang for tea and told Pudding to play some records on the gramophone.

"I dare say you want to dance."

Vicky found herself in demand with the spinsters who wanted her advice on treating various aches and pains.

"I am not a doctor yet," she protested. "But a gentle walk in the fresh air should not hurt."

Bess heard an owl hoot in the garden and slipped out. She crossed the terrace adjoining the dining room and climbed down a few steps to the meticulously maintained garden.

MURDER AT CASTLE MORSE

Richie was waiting for her behind a tall topiary resembling a chimp.

"What ho, Bess! This is not an assignation, is it?"

She planted a fist in his arm, making him howl in pain.

"You jolly well know it's not. I thought you would be more amenable to spilling the beans, away from everyone."

Richie stiffened.

"Golly, Bess. That sounds serious."

"You do realize you are suspected of murder?" she pressed. "I need facts if I am to be any help."

They plunged deeper into the darkness until the low hum of conversation from the dining room and parlour faded. Bess asked him about the day Joe Cooper died.

"Tell me how you found him and don't leave anything out."

Richie told her it had been a day like any other. He did something or the other with his father before joining the family for lunch.

"The pater's bent on teaching me about the business," he grumbled. "It's terrible, Bess."

She prodded him to continue. Richie had knocked some balls around in the billiards room after lunch. It had been a fine day and he thought of going for a ride.

"Did you go looking for Joe?"

"Not particularly. He was the only one who could saddle Sindbad but ..."

Bess understood what he wanted to say. With Sindbad gone, Richie would use another mount. Any other groom would be able to do that for him.

"I told him to make himself scarce when I was around," Richie admitted.

None of the grooms were around when he entered the stable. He headed to Sindbad's stall by force of habit. It was mucked and kept clean on his orders and fresh hay was put in even though no horse inhabited it at the moment. Richie often sat in there for a bit when he wanted to get away.

"I almost trod on him, Bess."

"Did you see anything out of the ordinary?"

His first reaction was shock. Then he must have rushed out and called for help. A man working in the garden nearby heard him and came running.

"Someone went for the police constable," Richie shrugged. "It's all a blur."

It had been a few minutes past two in the afternoon. Richie was sure the stable had been deserted. With a pang, Bess realized what that meant. There was no one to back him up.

"What about footprints? Any objects that didn't belong there or strangers?"

"Unfortunately, no, old girl." Richie was resigned. He began to say something but hesitated. "No. That can't be right."

Bess was patient.

"I smelt something. It felt out of place at the time."

"Was it blood?" After being an ambulance driver on the battlefield, Bess was anything but squeamish. "Hay, perhaps?"

Richie shook his head. He meant something other than that, something that did not belong in a stable.

"Not the usual hay or manure, Bess." He scratched a spot near his eye. "Flowers, maybe."

Bess thought the wind might have picked up the scent of flowers growing in the garden.

"No," Richie insisted. "It was inside the stall. Very faint and barely discernible but nothing to do with horses."

They took a circuitous route back to the house.

"Do you miss Joe Cooper?" Bess asked him. "Pudding said you were around him a lot while growing up."

Richie admitted the man had been a large part of his life. But the dynamics had shifted when he became an adult. There was a lot of water under the bridge.

"I realize he was not the man I believed him to be. His cavalier treatment of Sindbad was the last straw."

Bess assumed the groom must have been apologetic.

"That's just it, Bess. He told me there would be other horses. I was rich enough to buy a whole stable full of thoroughbreds and not feel the pinch. It was the way he said it, as if he begrudged me my wealth."

"What about the memorial everyone is talking about. Did you really oppose it, Richie?"

He refused to say anything on the subject. They went in different directions once they entered the house from the terrace. Richie headed toward the billiards room and Bess went back to the parlour. Lady Morse noted her arrival but said nothing.

"Where have you been, Bess?" Pudding called out. "The tea's gone cold."

They rang for another pot and Bess helped herself to some Empire fruit cake the housekeeper had sent up. She knew it was Lord Morse's favourite and their old cook made it especially for him. The woman had a cottage on their land and had been forced into retirement when Lady Morse hired the fancy

French chef. But she provided the kitchen with a steady supply of the cakes and pies Lord Morse had a hankering for.

Vicky was yawning her head off. The twins excused themselves soon after Bess finished her cup of tea and retired to their room.

"Any luck with Richie?" Vicky asked Bess as they undressed.

"He said nothing about the war memorial," she replied.

"And you think that's important?" Vicky quizzed.

Bess gave a shrug. They were in the information finding phase. Inferences could be drawn later.

Vicky wanted to know if they had a war memorial at Buxley.

"Of course! Right outside the Buxley Arms in the middle of the village. Haven't I pointed it out?"

It had been built in record time. Although not very imposing, it was symbolic. It showed the village cared about the men who had lost their lives in the war.

"So it's a bit unusual that the village of Morse does not have one?" Vicky asked.

It was obvious that Joe Cooper had wielded a lot of influence.

"Papa and Lord Morse talk about everything," Bess told her. "They must have discussed the war memorial at Buxley. In fact …" she broke off for a minute, her face set in a frown. "I believe Lord Morse was present at the little ceremony we had to inaugurate ours."

They went back and forth over why Lord Morse had delayed building the memorial as they drifted off to sleep.

MURDER AT CASTLE MORSE

Vicky sat in the window seat when Bess woke the next morning. Dawn was just breaking over the fields.

"Did I wake you, honey?" Vicky asked.

Bess flung off the covers and joined her sister at the window. The sun was barely visible behind the dense tree cover, unlike at Buxley where they could see it rising above the horizon in the distance.

"Let's telephone Barnes after breakfast." Bess placed a hand on Vicky's back. "The mail should be in by then."

There was a knock on the door and the maid brought croissants with blackberry jam, accompanied by the rich chocolate.

Vicky's expression was wistful as she tore a piece off the roll.

"You miss them, don't you?" Bess laughed. "Momo, Bubbles, Aunt Clem ... and Papa?"

Vicky nodded, her lips stretching into a grudging smile. Bess promised to drive back to Buxley in a day or two. The Nightingales would have plenty of questions and she wanted to have something substantial to tell them.

Pudding came in, wanting to know their plans for the day.

"Shall we go for a swim later? It's going to be particularly hot today."

Richie had gone to London on the morning train. Bess wondered if the servants would open up knowing he was not around.

Lord Morse presided over the breakfast table, engrossed in reading the newspaper. There was a twinkle in his eye when he greeted the girls. Vicky realized he was very different from

Nigel who always looked like he had the weight of the world on his shoulders.

"What are your thoughts on the war memorial, my lord?" Bess cut into her fluffy omelette, wishing it was kedgeree.

Lady Morse set her fork down with a thud.

"I am so sick and tired of hearing about that blasted memorial."

"Language, my dear," Lord Morse chuckled.

"No, really Clive. The whole thing has become a terrible farce. I think I am going to pick up a spade one of these days and start digging myself."

The girls looked at each other, aghast at this display of emotion from the usually composed Lady Morse.

"We have one at Buxley," Bess prompted.

Lord Morse gave a nod but said nothing. That seemed to irk his wife more.

"That poor boy died, didn't he?" Her cheeks had turned pink. "Richie saw him getting shot with his own eyes."

Bess confirmed they were talking about Raymond.

"What is the point of contention?" She stepped in. "His brother believes his war wound was the cause of his death."

Lord Morse gave a deep sigh.

"Nobody is arguing that, Bess. There is no doubt the wound festered and led to his unfortunate demise."

Lady Morse stood up.

"God knows why you sided with Joe Cooper on this. Poor Mrs. Griffin cries her eyes out every day, wondering why we won't give her son his due. She will never forgive us, Clive."

MURDER AT CASTLE MORSE

Lord Morse told her there would be a vote soon. Most people who had sided with Joe Cooper were bound to give up their opposition.

"The only reason they dared to do that was because you stood by Joe. You and Richie."

Lady Morse stomped out of the room without another word. Pudding gave a low whistle.

"You are in hot water now, Papa."

"Marvellous," Lord Morse muttered under his breath and put his newspaper down.

Neville Morse sat a few seats away from them, calmly eating his omelette, completely oblivious to the drama unfolding next to him.

Bess thought of meeting all the people who had been in favour of building the war memorial. Who among them had the disposition to commit bodily harm? Maybe this person had tried to convince Joe Cooper to change his opinion. They got into an argument that did not end well.

"What kind of man was Joe Cooper?" she wondered out loud. "Would you say he was a hero?"

"The bravest kind." Lord Morse was terse. "He made sure Richie came home safe and sound. The least I could do was support him."

Chapter 7

The meeting of the onion festival committee was in full swing. Bess and Vicky were there at Pudding's insistence. The previous day had not yielded much, a large part of it spent frolicking in the pool, followed by a scrumptious picnic by the water and a nap in the shade of some chestnut trees. Dinner was another extravagant affair. Chef Henri produced a rich meal and Bess had been too languid to tackle a new member of the Morse family and ask any unpleasant questions.

They were assembled at the vicarage, presided over by Miss Hastings, the vicar's formidable sister. The detritus of a large fruit cake from Castle Morse lay on a sideboard, along with crumbs of biscuits. The conversation had gone downhill after a broad shouldered woman with thick arms and legs and a plait of black hair that fell to her hips arrived. Bess marvelled at the rosy hue of her cheeks which were beginning to resemble two ripe red apples. A not so fine layer of peach fuzz graced her upper lip. She stood in the middle of the room, arms akimbo, rotating like the hands of a clock, glaring at everyone in turn.

"You have to choose, Eileen." Miss Hastings laid down the rules. "Either you join the committee as secretary or you be a participant. You simply cannot do both."

"And why not?" The woman pulled herself up, trying to look more intimidating. "I have been the women's champion since I was sixteen. Why should I let anyone beat my record?"

Miss Hastings assured her nobody came close.

"There is a conflict of interest, my dear. Don't you see?"

MURDER AT CASTLE MORSE

Bess tapped Vicky's knee and stood up, looking for a way out of the room. She headed toward a dark nook which turned out to be a small passage. It led to the garden at the back. Vicky was right behind her, followed by Pudding.

They didn't say a word until they tiptoed across a tiny path through a vegetable patch and entered the church yard. Pudding couldn't hold back her giggles any longer.

"This is like playing truant at school, Bess. Be ready to face consequences."

"Miss Hastings won't spank you, will she?" Vicky was aghast. "She reminds me of a nanny I had when I was five."

She would mention their transgression to Lady Morse who in turn would let Pudding know how disappointed she was.

They reached the lychgate and stepped out.

"Who was that battle axe though?" Bess wanted to know. "One of the old ladies was shaking with fright."

Pudding laughed again.

"Oh, Eileen. Her bark's worse than her bite. She's our butcher. Her brother owns the shop now, to be accurate, but she lends a hand."

Vicky thought that was quite progressive.

"I have never heard of a woman doing that sort of work. Must need a lot of upper body strength."

"Have you seen her arms?" Bess asked. "Thick as tree trunks."

They debated what to do next. Pudding suggested visiting their old cook.

"Let's not go home yet. Mama will give us an earful for walking out of that meeting."

They drove the short distance to the edge of a grove. Bess parked the car and they went down a well trodden path, glad to be out of the sun. Smoke rose from a chimney and it wasn't long before they came across a cottage in a small clearing, nestled against a copse of beech. Pink roses climbed over the windows and ivy covered one wall.

A grey haired woman of ample proportions came out, wiping her hands on a white apron.

"Miss Winifred!" she beamed. "I haven't laid eyes on you since Easter. Come in, come in."

Cook darted glances at Vicky while she ushered them into a cozy room.

"You finally met your match, Lady Bess," she chortled. "You both favour your mother."

Bess had lost count of the number of people who had known about Vicky but kept it from her. The past was the past and could not be undone.

There was a rich, savoury aroma in the cottage, making Vicky's mouth water.

"Do I smell tarragon?" she asked.

"Right you are," Cook beamed. "The pie should be out in ten minutes. We can talk about what mischief you are up to, Miss Winifred. Shouldn't you be at the vicarage right now?"

Bess marvelled at how well informed the woman was. But there were hardly any secrets in a small village.

"Eileen and Miss Hastings were fighting like cats and dogs," Pudding replied.

Cook went into the kitchen to pull the pie out.

"That Eileen likes to pick a fight. She hasn't been right since she got jilted, poor girl."

MURDER AT CASTLE MORSE

They trooped into a cozy kitchen and sat around a scuffed wooden table. Bess thought Eileen looked older. Cook told her she was right. Eileen had turned thirty earlier that year.

The pigeon pie was dished out and the girls tucked in. Cook hovered over them, making sure they had enough gravy, urging them to sample some of her homemade elderberry wine. Pudding insisted she join them and have a bite.

"Tell us about Eileen," Vicky prompted after Cook had taken a few bites. "Has she always been so belligerent?"

The girls sat back in awe as the story unfolded. Eileen had been a shy girl who loved playing the flute.

"You could find her by the river on a fine day," Cook sighed. "She has a gift, you know. She barely learned to read but the music somehow flowed from her."

Eileen was wooed by many local young lads but she only had eyes for one.

"The whole village knew, of course, and her brother tried to hurry the boy to the altar. But he wanted to give her the best."

They waited until the man worked his way up to better wages and saved money to give her the grand wedding she wanted.

Bess wondered neither of them had strayed.

"They were in love," Cook shrugged. "At least everyone thought so. He became head groom and prepared to ask for her hand in marriage. The village waited with bated breath for the banns to be read. But things fell apart."

"Why?" Vicky dropped her fork, engrossed in the story.

"Wait a bit," Bess nudged her. "Did you say head groom? Was Joe Cooper the boy Eileen was in love with?"

Cook nodded.

"Why did I not know that?" Pudding cried.

"You were at that fancy school, Miss. And you were too young to know this kind of gossip."

Bess steered them back to Joe Cooper.

"So Joe Cooper was married?"

Vicky told her she was missing the point. She asked Cook to continue.

"Where was I?" Cook paused for a bit. "Oh yes, Joe met Eileen's brother and got his blessing. Then he took her for a picnic by the river and asked her to marry him."

She stopped to check their plates and served each of them another slice. Bess poured gravy over hers and took a large bite, barely tasting it.

"Go on, Cook," she prompted.

"It was the war, you see." Cook shrugged. "Eileen must have lost her mind or something. Joe Cooper and others from the village were going to join the army with Master Richie."

Bess thought it had been a good time to get married. Didn't most engaged couples marry before the man went off to war?

Apparently, Eileen did not want that. She was twenty three with her whole life ahead of her. What if Joe never came back from the war? She did not wish to spend the rest of her life as a widow.

"But that's absurd!" Vicky exclaimed.

Joe thought the same, so did Eileen's family. They tried hard to make her see sense but she would not budge.

"Did they at least get engaged?" Bess asked.

Eileen made no promises and told Joe they could talk when he came back.

MURDER AT CASTLE MORSE

Bess felt sorry for the groom. He must have been devastated.

Cook put the kettle on and pulled out a batch of warm biscuits from the oven. Eileen realized she had been hasty a week after the men left but it had been too late by then. Joe was gone and Eileen had four long years to repent at leisure.

"So she let him go, then pined for him?" Bess frowned. "What a foolish girl she must be."

Vicky asked what happened after the war. Cook poured three cups of tea and apologized to Vicky.

"I don't have any coffee, my dear. Mrs. Bird told me you don't like tea."

"That's okay," she rushed to reassure her. "I don't want any now."

She picked up a biscuit at Cook's urging and bit into it. They waited until Cook stirred some milk and sugar into her own tea and took a sip.

"Joe barely spoke to Eileen after he came back. Maybe he had time to think during those long years and decided she had been unkind."

"So she grew more in love and he fell out of love," Pudding gasped. "How sad."

Bess thought it was dramatic. Maybe Joe just wanted to make her suffer. In a way, he was justified.

"Eileen's brother spoke to Joe, reminding him of his intentions. He had an unmarried sister who wasn't getting any younger. But Joe declared he did not want to marry anyone."

Three years had passed since the men came back. Most of the young men in the village were already married. Others were afraid of her. So Eileen stayed single and grew bitter by the day.

"She breaks into a fight for silly reasons," Cook sighed. "Nobody dares to contradict her."

The butcher shop was doing good business since Eileen charged exorbitant prices and got away with it.

Bess asked if Eileen and Joe had been on speaking terms.

"Barely. They had a public spat a couple of years ago. Eileen told Joe she would make him pay."

They had never been seen together after that. Cook was sure they made every effort to avoid being in the same place. Eileen's younger brother was one of the Morse 13 and had gone to war with Joe.

"When Joe began that whole nonsense with the memorial, he chose to be in the opposite camp and sided with Ronald Griffin. That had further driven a wedge between Joe Cooper and Eileen's family."

Bess wanted to know exactly how many people had sided with Joe Cooper and why.

"Raymond Griffin was a good man." Cook's eyes filled up. "He deserves a tribute from all of us." Her eyes swung toward Pudding. "Lord Morse is a generous landlord and I am indebted to him, Miss. But I have never minced my words."

Vicky patted Cook's hand, encouraging her.

"Most of the Morse 13 want the memorial. But Lord Morse and the young master sided with Joe Cooper. Some of the people working on the estate felt they should support their lord."

"I don't think you have to worry about that now, Cook," Pudding replied.

Vicky asked if Cook had ever participated in the onion festival.

"I am not daft, dear." Cook shuddered. "Never ate a raw onion in my life. It's vile."

The girls decided they had imposed long enough. Cook accompanied them to the motor and waved until they went around a bend.

Bess drove back to the castle, humming a tune she had heard at a dance club in London.

"I say, Bess." Pudding huffed. "That's another day gone. Fat lot of good you are doing for Richie."

"You poor thing," Bess laughed. "Haven't you heard? Hell hath no fury like a woman scorned."

Pudding folded her arms and blew out her breath.

"Will you stop talking in riddles? It's a terrible bore."

"Eileen," Vicky explained. "We found another person who had a reason to hurt Joe."

Chapter 8

Her nerves had been frayed since she boarded the ship in New York. Things did not improve as the days passed although she tried to keep herself busy, catching up with the pile of paperwork she had brought along. The captain invited her to dine at his table a few times. There was the mandatory small talk to endure but her thoughts were occupied with what would happen when she came face to face with him. What was she going to say after all these years?

The crossing was choppy at times but she scarcely noticed. She made a split second decision when she set foot on land. She would spend a few days in London, visit some familiar sites, get her bearings. Three days later, she realized nothing would quell the burgeoning anxiety in her chest. A car was hired and she finally set off to confront her past.

Autumn was making itself known across the countryside but some remnants of summer were still visible. She had forgotten how beautiful the fields looked, dotted with sheep. Her heart thudded in her chest when they reached the rolling hills of the Cotswolds. Soon she was crossing the village, turning into the gates to traverse the vast parkland that would take her to the manor.

It was as if time stood still. Annie Rhodes Gaskins squared her shoulders and prepared to face the music.

**

Bess and Vicky proceeded to the dining room at Castle Morse for breakfast the next morning. Bess was rubbing her eyes while

MURDER AT CASTLE MORSE

Vicky stifled a yawn. They had stayed up late, Pudding and Bess regaling Vicky with their escapades at the posh boarding school they had attended. Lady Morse greeted them curtly and glanced at a clock on the wall.

Bess apologized for being late, longing for a plate of kedgeree. The chef's French omelette was beginning to lose its appeal. Norton arrived, looking grave.

"You are wanted on the telephone, Lady Bess."

She sprang up and followed him to the hall where the Morses kept their telephone.

"Hello? This is ..."

Aunt Clem cut her off.

"Come home at once, Bess." She used her special tone, the one that did not encourage any arguments or questions. "At once."

"What's wrong?" Bess asked. "Is it Papa? Or Grandmother?"

"Don't waste a minute." Clementine ended the call.

A myriad scenarios flashed through Bess's mind in a second. Was someone ill or had the police come to arrest Nigel? There was only one way to find out.

She hurried back to the dining room and took Vicky's arm.

"We have been summoned back home. Aunt Clem wouldn't say anything more."

Pudding was bewildered but Lady Morse handled the situation with aplomb. Norton was ordered to locate the chauffer and have the car brought around. Henri was asked to pack a meal for them so they could eat on the way.

"No time to pack," Bess decided. "We are just going home."

Lady Morse nodded her approval. Their room would be waiting for them whenever they were able to return.

"You won't forget about Richie?" Pudding did not hide her dismay.

Bess assured her they would be back after handling whatever crisis had risen at Buxley Manor.

"Aunt Clem likes to fuss. She's probably riled up because we disobeyed one of her silly rules."

They thanked Lady Morse and promised to telephone when they reached Buxley. The chef had provided finger sandwiches made with ham, cheese and bits of omelette. Bess found she was ravenous and both sisters ate every crumb.

"You will drive slowly, won't you, Bess?" Vicky urged. "We do not want another mishap on our hands."

They speculated about what might have happened at Buxley, producing one bizarre scenario after another, ending in gales of laughter. Bess handled the motor well, reaching the village a few hours later. They grew quiet as they entered the manor's grounds.

"Whatever it is, we will handle it." Bess drew up before the front steps.

The door opened and the butler Barnes stepped out to receive them. Bess and Vicky started up the steps, hand in hand.

"Good Morning, ladies," Barnes greeted. "They are waiting for you in the morning room."

"How bad is it?" Bess asked. "Give me the scoop, Barnes."

He refused to say anything.

"I say, this is getting serious!" Bess exclaimed and rushed inside.

Vicky was not surprised when they headed to Nigel's study instead of the morning room. They needed to reassure themselves that he was alright.

Bess flung open the study door and barged in, heading to the sofa where he liked to sit.

"What ho, Papa!" her words died on her lips.

Polo danced around her ankles, barking with abandon as Bess gawked at the woman who sat in a chair next to the window. She was a complete stranger.

Vicky rushed toward the woman and embraced her.

"This is a surprise! You could have told us you were coming, Mom. Sent a telegram or something."

Bess felt her knees buckle. So this was the woman who had given birth to her, then abandoned her when she was a year old. She had tried to imagine this moment hundreds of times since she met Vicky on a battlefield in France. Would she instinctively recognize her mother? Would some sixth sense alert her that this was the woman whose womb she had sprung from? Vicky had told her many things about their mother but nothing compared to coming face to face with her.

She barely noticed walking to the sofa and sitting down beside her father.

Nigel cleared his throat, looking more lost than usual.

"Clem was supposed to break the news gently."

Bess told him they had bypassed the morning room and come straight to the study, depriving her of the pleasure.

"You never play by the rules, Bessie," he grumbled. "My dear, this is your mother, Annie. She arrived last night."

All eyes were on her, waiting for her to say something but Bess was tongue tied. There was an awkward silence. Nigel suggested ringing for tea. The door opened immediately and Barnes glided in, bearing a tray loaded with tea things. He set it on a table and picked up a crystal decanter filled with amber fluid.

"Perhaps a little brandy, my lord?"

"What? What?" Nigel's neck swung between Bess and Annie. "Jolly good, Barnes."

Vicky perched on the arm of Annie's chair, her eyes wide.

"Did you get my letter?" she asked.

Annie gave a silent nod.

Bess took the brandy Barnes handed her and drank it one gulp, feeling it burn down her throat. Her upbringing kicked in, allowing her to maintain a stiff upper lip.

"I trust you had a pleasant journey, Lady Buxley?" she inquired.

Annie turned white.

"Now, now, my dear," Nigel protested. "That's no way to talk to your mother."

The study door flung open again and Clementine swept in.

"Can't you do what you are told for once, Bess?" she thundered, darting a glance at Annie.

Bess walked out. Vicky followed her without a word to some stairs in the back the servants used. Neither said a word until they entered their bedroom and locked the door.

"You could've warned me!" Bess cried.

"I swear, Bess, I didn't know. But she's here now. Isn't that what you wanted?"

Bess collapsed on the bed and buried her face in a pillow. She hated to admit she was stunned. Nigel seemed to be handling the situation better than her.

MURDER AT CASTLE MORSE

"Papa seemed calm," she observed. "That is so unlike him."

There was a knock on the door. Annie came in, accompanied by Nigel.

"I owe you an apology, Bess." She held her arms out. "Will you forgive me?"

"We are both at fault," Nigel added. "Annie and I realize we should not have split you up, girls. But we cannot change the past."

Bess took the high road, trying to appear nonchalant.

"All water under the bridge, Papa. We should have a party, invite all our friends. Everyone will want to meet Annie."

The name just rolled off her tongue. If Annie had any objections, she was welcome to speak up. But she just flashed a beatific smile and told them she would see them at lunch.

Nigel stood there after she left, looking uncertain.

"It's a fine day, Papa," Bess said. "Why don't you go fishing?"

"But your mother ..." his eyes grew wide. "Clem ..." "Mama ..."

With an ease that came from practice, Bess managed to read between the lines and set him at ease.

"Annie will stay for a while. I can handle Aunt Clem, don't you worry. And Grandma Louise won't mind if you go fishing. I will make sure she is invited for dinner."

She took his arm and led him out of her room. Barnes waited outside, ready to take over.

Vicky stood by the window, staring out over the formal gardens that stretched for half a mile. Bess joined her and laid her head on her shoulder.

"She is here to meet you," Vicky spoke under her breath. "And our father."

Bess would not allow herself to hope. She announced she was taking a bath. Vicky sighed but said nothing.

Lunch was a boisterous affair as expected. Louise arrived from the Dower House wearing a monstrous new hat and sat facing Annie, flanked by the great aunts. Momo and Bubbles sat on either side of her and would not stop asking questions. Bess and Vicky were at the other end of the table, near Aunt Clem.

"Cecil and Cordelia will be here for dinner," Clementine announced. "I have ordered a rack of lamb for us. Mrs. Bird promised to make something American for you, Annie."

Nigel was conspicuous by his absence. The meal dragged and Bess kept herself busy by eating two helpings of everything.

"We need to catch up, Grandma." She gave the older ladies a meaningful look. "Plenty of new information has come to light."

They headed to the west wing and took their usual seats.

Vicky told them about Eileen.

"So we have three suspects with a motive," Louise summed up. "Richie, Eileen and that poor boy's brother."

"Ronald," Vicky supplied.

Perpetua asked where the others had been that day.

"Did they go anywhere near the stables?" she asked, rubbing her mole. "That's what you have to find out next, girls."

Hortense suggested getting in touch with the Detective Inspector.

"He can tell you about the post mortem report."

"I doubt it," Bess dismissed. "He already warned us to stay away from his investigation."

Louise didn't agree. It wouldn't hurt to ask.

"Now stop beating around the bush, young Bess," she boomed.

Bess understood what she meant. She wanted to know if she had made Annie feel welcome.

"I don't know, Grandmother."

"Annie is the Countess of Buxley and also your mother," Louise railed.

Vicky spoke for Bess.

"Mom will have to be patient, Grandmother. Where was she for the past twenty years?"

Chapter 9

Bess headed below stairs to the kitchen, her mind in turmoil. Why was everyone making such a fuss over Annie's arrival? Aunt Clem was on the telephone, inviting their friends and neighbours for an impromptu dinner, barking orders to Mrs. Jones, the housekeeper at the same time. Vicky was charged with making sure that Annie was comfortable in the room assigned to her.

The cook was rolling a pie crust and the maids were peeling potatoes, dicing vegetables. She dropped the rolling pin when she saw Bess and opened her arms wide.

"Now, now, my lady. This is a happy day for all of us. She's as pretty as ever, your mother."

Bess measured and sifted flour in a bowl and poured milk in it. She began kneading the dough without a word, pounding it with all her might, trying to release her pent up frustration. She had been a wilful child, often at odds with her aunt who liked to control everyone. The kitchen was her safe haven. Mrs. Bird had offered solace and taught her to direct her anger at a lump of dough. The habit stuck. Mrs. Bird said nothing, letting her blow off steam.

"Pudding will be mad." Bess resolved to talk about anything but Annie. "She thinks Richie might be arrested any day now."

Mrs. Bird was well aware of what she was talking about. She nodded along, encouraging Bess to speak.

"Did you know Joe Cooper?"

MURDER AT CASTLE MORSE

"Why wouldn't I?" Mrs. Bird shook her head. "Was in and out of my kitchen since he was a lad of ten, wasn't he?"

Bess noted her smile and the warmth in her voice.

"You were fond of him. Would you say he was a good man?"

Mrs. Bird lifted a shoulder in a shrug, lining a tin with pie crust. She had not seen much of him since he came back from the war.

"He never shied from hard work," she told Bess. "Always boasted he would be head groom one day. That's why he left for Morse after spending ten years at Buxley."

Joe Cooper had continued to visit his old friends in the Buxley stables even after he left for Morse. He always dropped into the kitchen to say hello to Mrs. Bird and eat her pies and cakes. She had prayed for him when he went off to war and heaved a sigh of relief when he came back whole.

"Why would someone kill him?" Bess asked. "Was he the kind to pick fights or make enemies?"

Mrs. Bird stiffened. She had been shocked when she learned he was against building a war memorial at Morse.

"I told him he was no longer welcome in my kitchen, Lady Bess. And that was it. Never laid eyes on him again."

Bess was not surprised. How many people had Joe Cooper managed to alienate by opposing the memorial?

She decided to skip having tea with everyone and slunk upstairs to her room, clutching a plate heaped with sandwiches and cake, managing to avoid her aunt Clementine. She paced across the room, wolfing down the food, unable to hold a thought. The shadows lengthened outside and she accepted she could not skip dinner. A long bath improved her mood a bit and she dressed in a red sleeveless frock Pudding had brought for her from Paris. Aunt Clem was of the firm opinion that debutantes should not wear red.

Vicky arrived, wearing a demure frock in a pastel shade. A large diamond hung on a thin gold chain around her neck. She clapped her hands when she saw Bess.

"Why don't you wear the rubies? They will be perfect with that dress."

Bess was tempted but held back. After all, she had not decided if the dinner was a happy occasion.

They headed to the parlour where everyone was assembled for drinks. Annie was surrounded by a horde of women. Lady Ridley, Bubbles and Momo's mother, stood on her left while Aunt Clem flanked her other side. They were both engrossed in hearing Annie's account of dinner on the ocean liner.

"I could never dare to attempt it," Lady Ridley shuddered. "But look at you, Lady Buxley, taking the trip multiple times." She stole a glance at her daughter. "What a pity you will have to brave the journey again when you return to America."

Momo joined them and took Annie's arm.

"She won't have to, Mama. We hope Annie has come home for good."

Bess smirked when Annie gave no response. She spotted Nigel at the far end of the room, nursing a glass of whiskey. His eyes were trained on Annie, filled with a sense of longing.

Louise and the great aunts sat close to a roaring fireplace, sipping sherry. Bess knew they would be watching her for the slightest sign of impudence.

A hearty voice startled Bess from her thoughts. Lord Ridley entered, accompanied by a barrel chested man who was shorter than Bess. Most of the assembled company appeared astonished to see him.

"Welcome to Buxley Manor, Sir Lawrence," Aunt Clem gushed. "I didn't know you were back home."

He guffawed and kissed her hand, twirling his luxuriant moustaches.

"Couldn't stay away from you, Clem. Not many pretty ladies in the bush, what?"

A German Shepherd trailed after him, making Bess gasp in surprise. Aunt Clem usually made a big fuss when Polo entered the dining room but she didn't utter a word of protest against the big, mangy dog.

"Who is he, Bubbles?" she asked. "One of your father's cronies?"

"Sir Lawrence Watkins. Big game hunter from Africa. Papa went to school with him."

Bess did not have to ask any more questions. Sir Lawrence was vocal enough. He slapped Nigel on the back and gave him a knowing look, glancing at Annie.

"He has a false eye." Vicky nudged Bess, coming to stand next to her. "Do you know him?"

Bess shook her head, walking over to greet Cecil Chilton, the vicar, and his mother who had just arrived.

"Good evening, Aunt Cordelia," she greeted Nigel's aunt. "Nice weather for a walk."

Barnes announced dinner and the company proceeded to the dining room, talking at the top of their voices. Nigel sat at the head of the table with Annie on his right and Louise on his left. Bess and Vicky sat next to Annie while Sir Dorian Ridley was placed next to Louise. The hunter Sir Lawrence sat beside him, directly opposite Bess. Dr. Evans sat at the far end of the table near the vicar. Bess realized that apart from the big game hunter from Africa, most of the assembled company were family.

Clementine provided an explanation.

"The Carringtons are in London and the Morses ... they are otherwise engaged. So it's just us, Annie. But we are most sincere in welcoming you back home."

Bess rolled her eyes as Annie thanked everyone, saying she was glad to be at Buxley.

"Feels like I was here just yesterday," she smiled. "Nothing has changed here."

Bess bristled as everyone at the table fawned over her mother. Had they forgotten she had been absent for twenty years? She hadn't just deserted her husband and young baby. She had also shunned the responsibilities she had as Lady Buxley.

The footmen cleared the soup and Barnes supervised the serving of the next course.

"Trout from our stream, grilled as you like it, my lady." He hovered near Annie and Nigel. "Cook has also prepared roast leg of lamb with mint jelly."

"That's excellent, Barnes," Annie smiled. "Will you thank Mrs. Bird for me?"

There was a pleasant buzz of conversation around the table, accompanied by the clank of silver against fine China.

"Say, Nigel." Sir Lawrence licked butter off his knife and laughed. "Are you and Annie going to make a go of it this time?"

MURDER AT CASTLE MORSE

Bess bit back an exclamation when she noticed his eyes for the first time. One of them was amber while the other was green.

"Glass," Vicky whispered under her breath, averting her gaze when both rested on her.

"The green is a fake," Sir Lawrence supplied. "Lost it when I was mauled by a lion six years ago. They call me One Eye Watkins."

He launched into a fantastic tale of how he had been attacked by a lion on his way back from a party one night. He wrestled the beast and subdued him but had lost his eye in the scuffle.

"Isn't it time you gave it all up, old boy?" Nigel asked. "You are not getting any younger."

"Never!" Sir Lawrence shuddered. "But I do need an heir. If you know any suitable young ladies, do send them my way." He leered at Clementine. "I would marry you in a heartbeat, my dear, but I'm afraid your breeding years are behind you."

There was a stunned silence around the table. Sir Dorian cleared his throat, looking uncomfortable.

"I say, a lot of unwed ladies here, what?"

"Unwed, maybe," Sir Lawrence continued, unperturbed. "But not naïve, eh, Bubbles?" He darted a sly glance at her.

Bess thought the man had lost his manners after spending most of his life in the jungle. What was this buffoon doing at their table?

"Come on, Lawrence," Nigel chuckled. "You must be sixty if you are a day. Why would a girl as young as my Bess want to marry you?"

"Love, old boy!" he boasted. "I might be a dusty old curmudgeon but I still believe in it. And if that's not enough, an estate in Kent and millions in the bank should pave the way." His eyes narrowed at Annie. "You must have married for money. That's why you couldn't make her stay."

Sir Dorian cleared his throat again, his eyes almost bulging out of their sockets. Lawrence cut into his lamb and carried on as if nothing had happened.

"Philip loved a good roast," he boomed. "Lamb was his favourite. Isn't that right, my dear?" He swung his eye toward the middle of the table.

Bess wondered if he was looking at Momo or Bubbles.

"You are right, Sir Lawrence," Momo replied. "Philip never tired of lamb. Even liked the stew Mrs. Bird makes for the servants. He often had it sent up."

"Miles hated lamb," Sir Lawrence laughed. "Those were the days, huh? You, me, Philip, Annie, Miles, Bubbles, Nigel ... and Trips, of course. How long has it been, my dear?"

Vicky saved Momo from a response.

"Have you only killed lions, Sir Lawrence?"

He drained his glass of wine and slammed it on the table, looking around for a footman to refill it.

"Lions, camels, zebras, elephants and deer ... lots of deer. And rhinos, of course." He puffed up, taking a loud sip from his full glass. "One time, I killed a lion and an elephant in a single day. Right 303?" He dunked his head under the table to pat his dog.

A magnificent jelly arrived, accompanied by ice cream and Mrs. Bird's apple pie. Nigel and Vicky took the jelly while Annie wanted to sample all three.

MURDER AT CASTLE MORSE

"We're kicking off the hunting season soon," Nigel announced. "You will stick around until then?"

Sir Lawrence gave a nod, spooning some jelly in his mouth. A bit of it got stuck in his moustache. Bess debated pointing it out.

"It won't be the same without Philip though, chaps."

Chapter 10

Bess woke early after a restless night. She decided to slip out while she had a chance and drive to Morse. Vicky would probably want to catch up with their mother. There was no point making her feel bad about it.

Barnes stood at the foot of the stairs, holding her coat and a thermos of tea. Bess wondered how he knew she was up since she had not rung for her maid.

"Have a safe trip, my lady. You are sure you will not wait for breakfast?"

The vision of a steaming plate of kedgeree swam before her eyes. For a second, she contemplated going down to the kitchen to eat but she fought the temptation.

"No rest for the wicked, Barnes," she sighed. "Better leave before the natives wake up."

Since Vicky was not present to caution her to lay off the accelerator, she made good time and reached Castle Morse as the family were arriving for breakfast.

"What ho, Neville!" she greeted, pulling out a chair beside him. "Sleep well?"

He tapped open his egg without a word and dipped his toast in it.

"You are back!" Pudding embraced her. "I feel terrible, Bess. Pulling you away from your mother."

Lady Morse inquired after Annie. Bess avoided saying anything impolite. She opted for a boiled egg and toast and worked through them at a solid pace. Pudding peppered her with questions the moment they stepped out into the garden on the pretext of taking a walk.

"How does she look? How are you holding up, old girl?"

Bess told her it was all a big palaver.

"Richie needs me." She squared her shoulders. "Has anything new happened while I was gone?"

Pudding assured her they had managed to avoid trouble in the past twenty four hours. Bess wanted to go to the stables and look around.

"What do you expect to find?" Pudding asked.

Bess wasn't sure. She just hoped that looking around the place might give her some ideas or lead to questions she could ask Richie.

A stableboy came running when he saw them, wanting to know if they needed the horses saddled. Pudding told him to take it easy.

"Do you saddle everyone's horse for them?" Bess asked.

The boy touched his cap and cowered before her, mumbling that he just mucked the stalls and filled the water troughs.

"The grooms saddle the horses, silly," Pudding laughed. "And Joe always took care of Richie or Papa."

The boy scampered off and Bess checked some of the empty stalls, noting they were a lot smaller than the one that had been reserved for Sindbad. She sniffed the air, checking to see if the wind carried the perfume of the flowers growing outside. The only scent that filled her nostrils was a mixture of manure mixed with fresh hay. Was Richie fibbing about the flowers? Or was the breeze flowing in a different direction the day Joe was killed?

"Have you thought about the onion festival?" Pudding asked. "I can finally participate if you agree to be the judge."

Bess shook her head in wonder.

"You really wish to gobble an onion before the whole village?"

Pudding had discussed it with her mother. Lady Morse thought it would be good for morale. The judging was just a formality, in case there was a tie.

They fed sugar to some of the mares and headed back to the house for refreshment. The morning room was deserted, Lady Morse having left for a meeting in the village. Pudding rang for tea, looking bored.

"What now?" she asked Bess. "Do you have a solid plan?"

The housekeeper arrived with the tea and gave directions to a young maid. Bess was glad to see slices of fruit cake on a plate along with some colourful macarons.

"Did Cook send that?" Pudding cried, going for the cake. "Jolly good."

"Shouldn't you practise eating onions?" Bess teased.

The housekeeper agreed with her.

"You cannot beat that Eileen, Miss. Treats it like an apple, she does."

Bess was surprised. "You know her too, Mrs. Hadley?"

"And why not?" the housekeeper frowned. "She runs the only butcher shop in the village. Has a spot of tea with me in the kitchen sometimes. That poor girl!"

Pudding was surprised to know the girl visited the castle.

"She delivers the meat when the boy is out sick or too busy," the housekeeper explained. "Gives her a chance to get out of the shop, away from that awful smell."

MURDER AT CASTLE MORSE

Bess surmised the housekeeper was a lot older than Eileen so she was surprised at the unlikely friendship between the two. Mrs. Hadley sounded protective, almost like an older sister.

"That rascal Joe!" she fumed. "He didn't treat her well."

Pudding asked if Eileen came to the castle hoping to get a glimpse of Joe.

"It sounds romantic, doesn't it, Bess?" she sighed. "Were you helping them make up, Mrs. Hadley?"

The housekeeper shook her head vigorously. Joe Cooper might have been a good lad when he first came to the castle but success had gone to his head.

"She was better off without him, and that's what I told her the last time we had tea."

"And when was that?" Bess struggled to be calm.

The housekeeper counted the days on her hand, sitting up straight, her eyes growing wide.

"Why! It was the day they found him dead."

Pudding jumped up and began pacing the room.

"Do you mean to say Eileen came to the castle on the day Joe Cooper died, Mrs. Hadley?"

The housekeeper hesitated slightly before nodding her head. She had never made the connection before but her shocked look meant she realized the importance of it. Bess asked her to think carefully and write down the exact time when Eileen had arrived and when she had left the kitchen. Mrs. Hadley promised to get back to them soon.

Lord Morse arrived just after they ate the last bit of cake.

"Hello Papa!" Pudding greeted him. "Shall I ring for more tea?"

Bess noted the jovial man was more exuberant than ever.

"Tea! It's time to pop the champagne, girls."

They glanced at each other, befuddled.

"Have you made a new business deal, Papa?" Pudding asked.

Lord Morse was famous for having the Midas touch. He had a brilliant mind and any venture he took up generally ended in profit.

"This is far beyond any monetary profit, my dear." He rubbed his hands with glee. "If all goes well, we might have bagged ourselves a place in history."

They watched as he mumbled under his breath and laughed, looking around the room.

"Where is your mother?" he asked Pudding. "She thought it was a terrible idea, you know."

Pudding threatened to leave.

"You are not making any sense, Papa!"

He finally sat and asked her to pour him a cup of tea. "Ballard thinks he found something."

Bess thought he was as cryptic as ever. "And who is this Ballard?" she played along.

"You don't mean that man with the weird hump who's digging holes on the north side of our property?" Pudding asked.

"None other, my dear," Lord Morse beamed. "That digging has now borne fruit."

Bess asked if the man they were talking about was an archaeologist. Lord Morse told her she was right.

"So is it some ancient burial site?" she was curious. "How do I not know this?"

Lord Morse launched into an explanation.

MURDER AT CASTLE MORSE

"You were in France when I was first approached by Stephen Ballard, my dear. He and his crew have been digging here off and on since then. I suppose we all forgot about it."

Bess wanted to know if they had found something.

"He is hopeful. He is going to send it to some experts at the British Museum for validation."

Pudding was sceptical.

"I have seen the bits and pieces they have dug up, Papa. They barely qualify as pottery."

Lord Morse was indulgent. "That's what I thought. But I scarcely paid any attention to him the past few months, other than inviting him for dinner once in a while. I had no idea when they found some significant shards that could be pieced together to form a complete object."

Bess wanted to know which era they were talking about.

"Vikings, Normans?"

Lord Morse beamed. "Romans. But mum's the word about this, girls. We don't want a stampede here."

Bess realized every amateur archaeologist in England would head to Morse to try their luck and get their hands on a piece of history.

"Where do these people live?" she was curious.

Lord Morse had invited Stephen Ballard to live at the castle but the man had politely declined.

"Something about keeping odd hours. They live in the Dower house because it is close to the dig site. There is a secretary, a researcher who is a woman in her late twenties and his older sister. It's all above board. And there are students who work on a temporary basis."

Bess assumed that Lord Morse provided the funds for the project.

"Is there any record of this?" Pudding wanted to know. "Why choose this particular site?"

Lord Morse thought the archaeologist was better equipped to answer them.

"There have been so many conquests on our land. You dig around long enough, you are bound to find something."

Bess wondered if anyone had ever thought of digging on Buxley land. She would have to ask Nigel about it.

"What do you hope to find though?"

Pudding wanted to head to the dig immediately and look around.

"Now, now, my dear. I have insisted they all take the day off. Where is your mother anyway? I want her to invite Ballard and those two women to dinner tonight. And make sure Chef Henri presents a nice roast of beef in one of his fancy sauces."

Lady Morse arrived in time for lunch. Bess wondered what Vicky was up to as she cut her ham, trying not to be jealous. Aunt Clem had given her an earful when she telephoned from the castle. Maybe she shouldn't have rushed over without saying anything.

Pudding convinced her to go swimming again in the afternoon. The girls ran into Alfred Nash on their way out of the castle. He had just been with Lord Morse.

"You don't look so good," Bess observed. "Should we take you to the doctor?"

He gave a weak smile and assured her he was fine.

"Lord Morse invited me to dinner. I don't like turning him down."

"Then don't," Pudding urged. "You have to start having dinner with us again, you know. Just like old times."

Nash turned red. "I don't mind the family, Miss. But I cannot bear to embarrass myself before visitors."

Bess reminded him she had seen far worse. She was not going to make fun of him if he spilled some soup.

"You must think I am horrible."

"Not you, my lady." He bit his lip. "It's that charlatan Ballard. I can't stand the sight of him."

Chapter 11

Dinner was a disaster. Stephen Ballard arrived with two women, one clearly his sister. He was a middle aged man, younger than Nigel, Bess guessed, but looked a lot older. His brown hair was sun bleached and flecked with grey. There were cuts on his face in two or three places. Apparently, the man did not have a valet and could not be trusted to shave himself. The hump Pudding had referred to was quite prominent, causing him to stoop and stare at the floor.

Lady Morse was a gracious hostess, sensing the discomfort of her guests. The assistant was brash and did all the talking for the trio. Miss Ballard was a mousy woman who shrank at the slightest sound and was afraid of her own shadow.

Chef Henri provided a rich meal of a clear seafood soup followed by fricassee of chicken and leg of mutton in a rich wine sauce. It was clear the party was overwhelmed.

"I have broth for supper on most days," Miss Ballard admitted. "A rich meal before bed is not good for the constitution."

Stephen Ballard ate with gusto, talking about the various countries he had visited.

"Digs are generally situated in the middle of nowhere," he blabbed. "So there is no choice but to eat the local food."

Bess expressed a desire to visit the dig.

"By all means, my lady. Shall we say, tomorrow morning at nine?"

Pudding gave a slight shake of her head and Bess proposed the hour of ten.

MURDER AT CASTLE MORSE

"Wear a proper hat," he advised. "The sun can be quite warm for someone not used to roughing it. We don't want you fainting and falling into the pit, do we?" He laughed at his own joke, jabbing an elbow into Neville who sat beside him.

Neville scarcely looked up, intent on the meal.

"Have you tried cold showers?" the assistant thundered, addressing him. "Time to forget the past and move on, my man."

Bess thought the woman had crossed a line, proving how vulgar she was.

The Ballards did not linger after the meal, the primary reason being Princess, Lady Morse's Persian cat. Stephen Ballard turned pale when the men came into the parlour after port, pointing a bony finger at the feline.

"Say, does that creature have to be here?"

Lady Morse, having done everything to please her unappreciative guests, was at the end of her tether.

"Afraid so. Princess can't sleep if I don't cuddle her often."

Bess and Pudding dissolved into giggles at the outrage on Ballard's face. Richie proposed a game of cards after the guests left.

"Would you like to join us, old boy?" he asked Neville.

None of them were surprised when he picked up a book and settled in a chair by the fire to read. Bess thought it was a good sign that he at least wanted to be around the family.

"What do you think of Eileen?" she asked Richie after they had played a round or two.

"Is she one of your London set?" He threw down the cards he was holding and stretched his arms above his head. "They all look the same, Bess."

Pudding told him Eileen was the local butcher.

"Why would I know a bally butcher?" he grumbled. "And when did women get into the game?"

Bess told him he probably knew her brother. He was one of the Morse 13.

"Harris? Of course I know him. Jolly good with a rifle, don't you know? But why would I know his sister?"

Bess gave up. They retired to their rooms, Pudding suggesting a ride before breakfast. Bess agreed, itching to do something. Nothing eventful had happened since she came back to the castle and the past two days had been a colossal waste of time.

She fell into a dreamless sleep the moment she closed her eyes and didn't stir until Pudding shook her awake. The ride put them both in a good mood, which was further enhanced by a hearty breakfast. Bess drove to the north end of the property to a point closest to the dig.

"I say, do we have to go?" Pudding asked after they had trudged across a barren patch for ten minutes, the sun beating down their backs.

Bess wiped the sweat on her brow with a lace handkerchief.

"At least we got hats."

Pudding thought Stephen Ballard was a big bore.

"Show me a dashing man, I say. One who is not afraid of cats!"

They spotted a few heads near the ground in the distance and picked up their pace. Ballard looked happy to see them.

"What a fine dinner Lady Morse gave us last night," he beamed.

MURDER AT CASTLE MORSE

There were a lot of holes in the ground, showing evidence of digging. Ballard led them to a square plot where his assistant sat six feet below the ground, engrossed in dusting a shard with a brush.

"We think this was a Roman villa," he gushed, waving his arm in one direction. "This here was a bath complex and there is evidence of an amphitheatre over there." He pointed at a clump of bushes a few hundred meters away. "And the mosaic, my lady. In mint condition, as much as an object several hundred years old can be, of course."

Bess found herself getting excited.

"Amphitheatre? They could hold hundreds of spectators, I believe."

"Thousands!" Stephen's jaw quivered. "Just imagine the possibilities. A Roman town with villas, bath houses and whatnot. They were an advanced race, you know. They had heated floors."

Bess congratulated him.

"It must be gratifying to see your hard work bear fruit. I believe it rarely happens in your line of work."

Pudding asked what he thought of Egypt.

"Isn't that where a lot of work is happening, in the Valley of Kings?"

It was the wrong thing to say. Stephen Ballard turned crimson and his glasses slid off his sweaty nose. He grabbed them and wiped them with the hem of his shirt.

"That's where the big money is of course. Men like Carter have wasted years, lured by tales of the ancient pharaohs. Greed makes people go to great lengths."

"What do you mean?" Bess was puzzled.

"They are digging for treasure, of course. I was there too, you know, in the beginning. But I came to my senses after four years of burning in the Egyptian sun."

England had a rich history, he said, one that was often overlooked by academics in search of the more exotic. That's what papers were written about and presented at the Royal Society.

"If you ask me, there is too much brouhaha about Egypt."

Bess lauded him for doing something different.

"You have taken the road less travelled, I suppose," she smiled. "Will your discovery make Morse famous?"

Stephen didn't want to count his chickens before they were hatched.

"It all depends, Lady Bess. We are on tenterhooks while the mosaic we found is proven to be Roman era."

Pudding asked if they were taking some time off until then. They could ride or visit nearby attractions.

"Have you been to the caves?" she asked. "Surely they are of interest to someone with your background?"

"I am not very familiar with the area," he admitted. "My sister would like a bit of a change, I suppose."

Bess offered to take her with them for a ride or for a spin in her motor.

"She would love that," Stephen's eyes brightened. "Neither of us ride though, I am afraid."

Pudding glanced at Bess, unable to hide her smirk.

"How have you been getting around then?" she probed. "I thought Joe must have set you up with a mount when you first got here."

"Lord Morse offered something like that." Stephen wiped his glasses again. "But going to the stables was out of question since I don't ride. We just walk over from the Dower House."

So he had no reason to know Joe Cooper, Bess realized.

"Joe was found dead a few days ago," she informed him. "I don't suppose you knew him."

Stephen laughed, looking sheepish.

"No, no. Say, what happened to him was terrible, what? Alfred Nash had an axe to grind with him."

Bess asked what he meant, alert.

"I don't know the details. But Nash blames this Joe Cooper for his wound. Says he would have the use of both his hands if it hadn't been for that turncoat."

Pudding wanted to confirm he was talking about Alfred Nash, Lord Morse's secretary.

"Of course!" he exclaimed. "The man with one arm."

Bess and Pudding spent some time admiring a few shards of pottery Stephen presented, along with a line of three stones in the ground which he thought had once been a wall.

"I say, that was punishing!" Pudding exclaimed as they dragged themselves back to the car. "It was your idea, Bess."

"Did Alfred Nash and Joe get along?" she asked.

Pudding had no idea. She suggested talking to Richie.

"You think he'd be more forthcoming, considering his life is on the line," Bess complained. "I think he's holding back, Pudding. And that's not cricket."

**

Vicky and Annie sat on a bench in Eden. It was a wild garden nestled in the Buxley grounds, not too far from the manor house.

"Did she say when she will be back?" Annie asked.

Vicky had realized Bess wasn't around the moment she went down for breakfast. Barnes confirmed her suspicion. She remembered her first few days at Buxley. Talking to Nigel had been hard and she had scarcely known what to say. Bess must feel the same, if not more.

"We are the ones who left, Mom."

Annie told her not to blame herself.

"You did not have a choice, sweetheart." She took Vicky's hand in hers. "Nobody blames you."

That meant they blamed Annie. Vicky thought they were justified. She had been shocked to see her mother arrive at Buxley.

"Why are you here? And why didn't you write or telephone? Don't you trust me at all, Mom?"

Annie sighed. She had not wanted to give Bess the opportunity to abscond.

"I wanted to meet her, see her with my own eyes."

"She's beautiful, isn't she?" Vicky grinned. "And she takes after you, Mom. There is no dare she won't accept, no scrape she won't get into. All the servants love her!"

Vicky was beginning to realize she herself was more like Nigel. They both had a tendency to stay in the background.

"Isn't it weird?" she laughed. "She takes after you while I favour our father."

They watched a pair of swans glide around in a pond.

MURDER AT CASTLE MORSE

"Papa comes here often, Mom. He showed me this place, told me all about it. How he had it planted for his young bride who hated the formal gardens."

Annie admitted she still hated them.

"I can't stand those topiaries."

Vicky believed Nigel still cared for Annie. The garden was a testament to his hope, his belief that she would be back one day.

"What really happened all those years ago, Mom?"

Annie couldn't meet her eyes. Vicky wanted to know what had driven her mother away from a loving husband and an infant child.

"Was this too much for you? Buxley? The role of countess?" Vicky pressed. "Or did you fall in love with someone else?" She did not need to mention any names.

"Of course not." Annie shrank back. "I was loyal to your father."

"Then what, Mom?" Vicky raised her voice. "Do you believe he murdered Philip?"

Chapter 12

Bess spent another day at Castle Morse before being ordered back home again. This time, her grandmother telephoned.

"I have always supported your madcap ventures," she began. "So you listen to me now, young lady."

Bess had no choice but to surrender. The drive home gave her plenty of time to think. Part of her was eager to connect with Annie but a survival instinct held her back. What if her mother left again? How many years would she stay away this time?

Vicky greeted her with a hug. Clementine ordered her favourite railway mutton curry for lunch. Mrs. Bird made rice pudding scented with cardamom and loaded with sultanas. Nigel regaled her with plans of the upcoming hunt. Everyone at Buxley was trying to make her smile.

"Buck up, my dear," Nigel whispered on his way to the library. "Chin up."

She gave him a watery smile and debated going to the pub.

"Not so fast, young lady." Hortense planted her cane in her path, smelling of lavender. "We have something to say."

Sighing deeply, Bess followed the great aunts and her grandmother to the west wing. The Nightingales asked for an update about Joe Cooper's murder. Bess told them about the archaeologist.

"Clive Morse is a smart man." Louise nodded approvingly. "He has quadrupled the family fortune but money can only take you so far."

Bess and Vicky asked her to explain.

"He wants a place in the history books," Hortense marvelled, patting a cheek with her handkerchief.

Perpetua nodded with her sister. Finding Roman ruins at Morse would make news. Lord Morse would be hailed for sponsoring the dig and lauded as a patron of the arts.

"Stephen Ballard is a terrible bore but he sounded quite confident," Bess replied. "You should have been there, Vicky."

Louise admonished her for leaving without a word. They expected more from a young woman.

"You are going to talk to your mother now, Bess. No dillydallying." She pressed her lips, her brow settling in a frown. "I trust two intelligent women like you and Annie can clear the air and move forward."

Bess knew Louise had always been her champion, especially when it came to breaking barriers and going against the norm. She could never say no to her grandmother.

"What's the plan, Granny dearest?" She rested her elbow on the arm of the chair she was sitting in, running a hand through her hair. "Have you prepared any talking points?"

"Cheeky." Perpetua huffed.

Louise ignored the sarcasm and told her Annie was waiting for her in the rose garden. Bess rose to her feet, darting a glance at Vicky.

"She stays right here," Louise thundered. "Two is trouble."

Bess left the room without another word and stalked out of the west wing. Her mind was numb as she traversed the corridor that ran along the length of the house and stepped out of a door to enter the grounds. She walked down a path lined with neatly trimmed bushes and spotted her Vauxhall under a tree. Her feet moved toward it and a few minutes later, she had started the motor and was off. She drove through the grounds at a sedate pace, telling herself she would stop if she saw Annie on the way. Soon she reached the village and pulled up outside the Buxley Arms.

The pub was dark and cool and the familiar smell of hops mingled with butter and thyme greeted her. Harvey, the proprietor greeted her with a wide smile.

"The missus was talking about you, Lady Bess." He placed a tumbler of ale before her.

Bess climbed up on a stool at the bar and took a hearty swig, letting the bar man prattle on, only half listening. Her ears perked up when he mentioned Annie.

"The hunt always dredges up memories. And with Lady Buxley here, there is plenty of loose talk, my lady," he warned.

Bess felt helpless.

"I think Papa's too kind to his tenants. Do they realize they are biting the hand that feeds them?"

"Some might say you have the wrong end of the stick." A voice drawled.

Bess noticed the man sitting in a dark corner. Built like a tank, one side of his face was disfigured from being burnt during an air raid.

"You! Have you been eavesdropping on us all this time?"

Detective Inspector James Gardener smiled and asked Harvey to serve him another pint.

"Is this how you spend your days, Inspector? No wonder you haven't found poor Joe's killer yet."

"It's Detective Inspector, Miss," he corrected her. "I mean, your Highness."

MURDER AT CASTLE MORSE

Bess refused to take the bait, knowing a truce would serve her better.

"Have you thought about sharing what you have learned?" she cajoled. "I don't mind letting you take all the credit, like last time. It's just that Richie is worried and I would rather clear his name at the soonest."

The DI told her to let the police do their job. He would follow procedure rather than go haring about the countryside, harassing people.

"And how many suspects do you have so far?" Bess challenged. "Latching on to Richie just because he found the body is horrible."

"You were lucky last time." He gave her a slight bow. "But your ill advised antics almost cost you your life. Be warned, my lady."

He walked out of the bar without giving her time to respond.

"Insufferable ass," Bess muttered under her breath.

She waved goodbye to Harvey and left. Going back to the manor meant facing the Nightingales so she pointed her car west and drove to Morse. A few clouds marred the sky and the wind picked up. The leaves were beginning to change colour as the cool autumn breezes battled with remnants of the lingering summer. Bess mulled over all they had learned, wondering about something Stephen Ballard had mentioned.

Pudding was nowhere to be seen when she arrived at the Castle. Norton informed her the ladies were spending the afternoon in Ridley.

"But I just drove through there!"

Bess decided she would choose a book to while away the time. She requested Norton to send a pot of tea to the library.

Alfred Nash sat at a heavy walnut desk, his head buried in a thick ledger. He struggled to his feet when Bess walked in, placing his only palm on the table for support.

"Good afternoon, my lady. I think the family has gone to Ridley."

Norton arrived with a maid carrying a tray loaded with a fat kettle along with a plate piled high with sandwiches and cake.

"Splendid!" Bess thanked the butler and offered to pour for Nash. "You and I can have a nice little chat."

If Nash was bemused at this declaration, he did not show it. Bess carefully placed a cup of tea on the desk, hoping he would be able to manage it with one hand.

"Pudding and I went and saw the dig site yesterday," she began. "That man Ballard said you were at odds with Joe."

Nash ate a cucumber sandwich and calmly waited for her to continue.

"Do you have a question, my lady?" he asked after there was a long pause.

Bess sipped her tea, deciding the blend the Morses used was not as fine as the Darjeeling served at Buxley.

"He implied you and Joe did not get along at all. So tell me honestly, Mr. Nash, how do I know you did not bash him on the head in the stables and leave him to die?"

Nash swallowed too soon and dissolved into a fit of coughing. His genial tone had turned bitter.

"I hated Joe Cooper, Lady Bess. Hated him with a passion. I have never tried to hide the fact."

MURDER AT CASTLE MORSE

Bess wondered why no one had mentioned it yet.

"I presume there was a reason for these strong emotions?"

Nash's hand shook as he set his cup down. He pointed at the empty sleeve dangling from his shoulder. Joe Cooper had been responsible for crippling him for life.

Bess leaned forward, intrigued. Her mouth hung open in shock when she heard the story he told.

"The Allies were having a bad day. Bullets whizzed past us as we tried to get back in the trenches."

Joe had lunged behind him at the last minute, causing him to take a bullet, then run back without sparing him a second glance. Nash fell and Raymond Griffin rushed to rescue him, getting hit in the process.

"Raymond and I were both struck, lying there in the middle of the field. We could barely move, my lady."

Richie had jumped into the line of fire and hauled them back one by one, without a thought for his own safety.

"The Captain risked his life for us that day. And Joe Cooper! He was a coward who abandoned us and left us to die."

Bess thought of Richie, Pudding's easy going older brother who joked and laughed with everyone, playing the fool. She felt a warm glow inside, knowing he had not shirked from his duty when push came to shove.

"But this means you have a strong motive to kill Joe," she blurted, scarcely aware she was alone in the room with him.

Nash laughed and asked if she would pour him another cup of tea.

"I hated the man. Did I not say that before. I have cursed him since that fateful day in France and yes, I admit I wanted to kill him." He stared into her eyes. "Wouldn't you?"

Bess admitted Joe had done him a grave injustice.

"But that doesn't mean I did," he sighed. "There were plenty of opportunities in the past three years when I might have done away with the bounder. And who would blame me?"

But he was not a murderer.

"How many people know this?" Bess asked.

Nash reminded her that Richie had been awarded a medal for bravery. The powers that be were aware of what had happened that night. And the Morse 13 knew, of course.

"Ronald?"

Alfred was not sure if Raymond had lived long enough to tell the tale after they came back to Morse. But the others would not stay quiet.

"So Ronald knew that Joe Cooper was the reason his brother got shot?"

"We all knew," Nash reiterated.

But only Ronald had lost his brother. Surely he must have blamed Joe. As if that was not enough, Joe had been steadfast against the war memorial. Raymond Griffin had not been given the honour he deserved.

"What were you doing the day Joe Cooper died?" she asked, wondering if he and Ronald might have teamed up.

"I was right here, my lady. I spent the day in the castle, reading some letters and going over the accounts."

Bess asked if he had learned to write with his left hand. Nash told her he was trying, making a little progress each day.

"I might even master holding a bat and play cricket again. It's all a matter of training your body to work in a different manner."

Bess watched him stand and pick up the heavy ledger and take it to a shelf. She believed he was capable of wielding a weapon and striking a blow with his only hand. But had he?

Chapter 13

Bess went up to her room and realized she had forgotten to choose a book from the library. She sprawled on the bed and closed her eyes, trying to martial her thoughts. Soon, she had succumbed to slumber. The sun hung low in the sky when Pudding woke her.

"Time to dress for dinner. Chef is making Coq Au Vin."

"Chicken in wine?" Bess yawned, sitting up in bed. "Aren't you tired of eating this bland French food?"

Pudding told her to hurry up. Bess took one look at her and sat down again, folding her arms.

"Spill the beans, old girl. I can see you are bursting to tell me something."

"I met the most interesting man just now, Bessie." Pudding had a silly smile on her face and a faraway look in her eyes. "He's killed a hundred lions in a year."

Bess remembered where Pudding had spent her afternoon.

"Are you talking about that obnoxious hunter who is visiting Ridley Hall?"

Pudding told her his name was Sir Lawrence Watkins.

"He's everything a man should be."

"Rude, overbearing and insufferable?" Bess scoffed. "What's the matter with you, old bean? He was at Buxley a few nights ago and I think he's just terrible."

Pudding's face fell but she didn't counter Bess. They did not talk much during dinner. Lady Morse had invited the usual crowd, the vicar and his sister, the local doctor and an impoverished squire and his wife. Bess did her duty and encouraged them to eat well, nodding along politely as they discussed the onion festival.

"Our Winifred wants to participate this year," Lady Morse told the assembled guests. "I think she's brave."

Richie answered with a snort but said nothing. Bess wondered if Lady Morse had any idea of what took place on a battlefield.

They escaped before Lady Morse roped them into playing cards with her guests. Pudding headed for a pergola situated amidst a walled garden, beside a big marble fountain with cherubs in it.

"I say, Bess. You haven't forgotten why you are here?"

It was certainly not to eat rich, buttery meals that added to her waistline, Bess retorted.

"Richie is not helping. He spins some faradiddle every time I ask him something."

They sat down, barely out of reach of the spray from the fountain. Pudding had brought a bar of chocolate with her. They broke it in two and reminisced over midnight feasts at boarding school.

"I know I am not clever like you, but I can listen."

"Thank you, old bean."

Bess decided to summarize everything she had learned. How many people had a motive to kill Joe and where had they been when he died?

She started with Ronald Griffin.

"He wants a war memorial but Joe opposed it. What's more, he convinced other important people like Lord Morse to support him."

Pudding supported Ron. He was mild mannered and polite and she had never seen him raise his voice. But he was also tenacious. Ron had spent three years trying to convince Joe but he hadn't given up.

"He was in the haberdashery that day, Bess, nowhere near the stables."

Bess asked if he could have sneaked out of the store for some time.

"Not without someone in the village spotting him," Pudding argued.

Bess moved on to Eileen. She was easily provoked and had the temper and physique needed to physically attack a man.

"Cook told us she picks fights. Have you actually seen her beat anyone up?"

Pudding giggled and shook her head.

"You think she's just putting on an act? Must be hard, running that butcher shop. Men laugh behind her back, you know. And make lewd comments. Richie told me so."

Bess wasn't surprised. Eileen was probably the only female butcher in the whole country.

"Act or not, she has the strength needed to cosh someone on the head."

They knew Eileen had come to the castle that day.

"But that was in the morning," Pudding pointed out. "Mrs. Hadley might have given her a cup of tea but I doubt she would be allowed to loiter."

Bess thought of Alfred Nash and his version of what had happened in France. She wondered if Pudding knew. If Richie wanted to keep it secret for some reason, she did not want to be the person who let the cat out of the bag.

MURDER AT CASTLE MORSE

"Alfred Nash hated Joe. At least according to the resident archaeologist."

"Oh him! He should meet Sir Lawrence. Learn a thing or two from him."

"I say, are you planning to go on about that old fogey again?"

Pudding shrank back as if the insult had been hurled at her body.

"Don't be cross, Bess. And I told you to take poor Mr. Nash off your list. He's been here for yonks. It's almost as if he's part of the furniture."

A gibbous moon appeared in the distance and they lapsed into memories of the night they had climbed over the school gate and gone for a dip in the river. An unfortunate mate of theirs had caught her skirt on a finial before she jumped. The entire thing had come apart, bearing her generous glutes to the elements.

"She had the hardest time explaining it to Matron," Bess laughed. "Poor Freckles."

"Oh, no, that was Fanny. Freckles was really skinny and a head taller. Fanny and Freckles were inseparable."

Bess popped the last bit of chocolate in her mouth, smiling at the memory.

"Why didn't you go back, old girl?"

Pudding had shunned school after Bess ran away from home to join the war effort. Her extended family had tried hard to make her see sense but for once, Pudding persisted.

"It wasn't the same without you."

They clasped their hands together and smiled. Until Vicky came into her life, Pudding was the sister Bess never had. They shared an unshakeable bond but being brought up to appear phlegmatic and composed in every dire situation life threw at them, neither saw the need to put their feelings in words.

Bess thought Nash was a viable suspect but she did not want to contradict Pudding.

"And we come to Richie," she sighed. "How fond was he of this dead horse, really?"

"Sindbad. The sun rose and set with him, Bessie. I mean, Richie's mad about horses. We all are. But I have never seen him so attached to anything."

Bess remembered a day in the summer of 1919. Richie had been quiet since he came back from the war. The Morses feared he was a victim of shell shock, just like Neville. He had suddenly announced he was tired of sitting around and was going to breed racehorses. The search for a winner had begun. Two months later, he brought Sindbad home.

"Did he let you ride him?"

"Never," Pudding shook her head. "Old Joe was the only one who was allowed to put his saddle on or muck his stall. Richie brushed him down himself. He said they were kindred souls."

Bess didn't like what she was hearing. The aristocracy had a long history of being attached to their animals. Nigel didn't go anywhere without Polo. Lady Morse doted on Princess and fed her fish with her own hands. Even the madcap hunter Sir Lawrence seemed besotted with his German Shepherd. No, there was nothing amiss in Richie being enamoured of a mere horse. But it gave him a strong motive.

"Do you know how Sindbad died?"

MURDER AT CASTLE MORSE

Pudding shook her head. It happened when they were in France. Richie had reluctantly agreed to join them for a fortnight. A cable arrived at their villa one afternoon, informing him of the sad incident.

"He rushed back to Morse but it was too late, of course."

Joe was held responsible since the horse had been in his care. Richie put on a good show but mourned in private.

"Did you see Richie that day?" Bess asked. "Before he raised the alarm about Joe?"

"He had lunch with us, of course. Wait a minute. He was wanted on the telephone so he left us for a bit. I don't remember if he came back."

So he could have gone anywhere, even to the stables. A footman or stable boy might have seen him but Bess doubted the servants would speak up. They were loyal to a fault and none of them would utter a word against their future master.

"Let's face it. Richie has a motive and he found Joe's body. Isn't it possible he went out to the stables at lunch, got into an argument and hit him? He came back to the castle, waited until some time had passed before going back to discover the body."

Pudding stared at her, white with shock.

"Here, that's absurd!"

"I know it and you know it but this is what that bally Inspector will say."

Bess decided she was missing a vital clue. She needed to construct a timeline again.

"My head's ready to burst, old girl. Can we tackle this tomorrow?"

Chapter 14

"She wants to make amends, Bess."

Vicky and Bess set off across the grounds after breakfast, eager to catch up. Bess had come back after spending two restless days at Castle Morse. She was nowhere close to finding any new information. And she missed Vicky. Bess wondered how she had survived all those years without her. If Vicky went off to learn medicine in Edinburgh, they would have to live apart again.

"Have you talked to Papa?"

He had gone up to London to meet someone for a day. Although his routine had not varied much, she thought there was a spring in his step.

"I heard him humming at breakfast."

"See? This is what I am afraid of." Bess headed toward the folly, biting her lower lip.

Vicky said nothing. Bess knew that neither of them had an inkling of what Annie planned to do. Nor did they have an idea what Nigel wanted.

"Let's go to the pub," Bess suggested after some time. "I have a hankering for Mrs. Harvey's pie."

It was almost noon by the time they walked back to the manor and drove into the village. Harvey greeted them with a big smile.

"Fine day," Bess nodded, asking for the usual.

He placed two pints of ale before them. Business had been good and he was happy.

MURDER AT CASTLE MORSE

"Sir Lawrence is back. He tells a good story, that one. Buys rounds for everyone too."

"You mean that hunter? What is he doing in Buxley?" Bess frowned.

Harvey told them he had been a regular visitor back when the 6th earl was alive and Philip and Nigel were at school. Sir Lawrence was very fond of Philip.

"Taught him to shoot, didn't he? And ... begging your pardon, my lady, also to appreciate a fine ale."

Bess wondered what other vices Sir Lawrence had introduced Philip to.

"Sir Lawrence wanted to take young Lord Philip to Africa." Harvey was clearly besotted with the big game hunter. "Hunt lions and elephants."

Philip married Momo and settled into the role of earl. There was no chance of dropping everything and going to Africa then. But they still made big plans and Sir Lawrence never stopped trying to convince Philip to go with him.

"He hasn't been here in twenty years." Harvey's eyes widened. "Not since young Lord Philip had that accident."

They all knew what he was referring to. Philip's death.

"He must miss him," Vicky murmured, remembering how Sir Lawrence had mentioned the good old days at dinner. "I think Philip was like a son to him."

Mrs. Harvey came out with a steaming pie and began serving them. Bess poured a good amount of gravy on her slice and thanked her.

"Trouble's brewing, my lady." She gave her husband a sharp look and went inside.

Harvey looked uncomfortable.

"There's talk, my lady."

With hunting season coming up, people were giving in to memories. All it took was one person mentioning that fatal hunt all those years ago. Some old fogey launched into a memory of Philip and the others pitched in. It did not take much time for the conversation to derail and turn into an argument around Philip's death.

"There's them as believe it was an accident."

But it was more salacious to think it was foul play, Bess knew. When she was a child, Bess had sensed Nigel dreaded the harvest season. Now she knew why.

The villagers did not dare to say anything but there were sly glances and murmurs. Harvey told them Lady Buxley's arrival had sent tongues wagging. Men were already incensed, beginning to demand justice for Philip. Sir Lawrence was making things worse.

"Isn't there a pub at Ridley?" Vicky asked. "Why does he keep coming here?"

Bess wondered if he was angling for an invitation to stay at the manor.

"He's a lot older than Papa."

"But Aunt Clem seems charmed by him." Vicky continued her line of thought.

Mrs. Harvey brought out an apple crumble.

"Who cares if he killed a hundred lions?" she fumed. "Lady Buxley has finally come home. He better not drive her away."

Bess wondered if it was possible. Would Annie run off at the slightest sign of trouble, her tail between her legs?

MURDER AT CASTLE MORSE

"Gosh, Bess! She's not an impressionable young woman anymore," Vicky defended her mother. "Have some faith, will ya?"

A group of farm laborers came in and settled at a table near the window. They were a noisy lot. One of the men kept darting glances at the girls, muttering under his breath. Harvey set their ale down and tackled him.

"Isn't your rent overdue, Tobias? Six months, was it?"

The man clammed up and glared at Harvey.

"And who paid for the doctor when your missus had a breech birth?"

"That don't mean he can get away with murder."

Bess jumped down from her stool, itching to plant a fist in his face. Vicky held her back.

"Don't make it worse."

They left the pub and drove back to the manor, incensed.

"I feel so helpless. Let's go and see Momo, Vicky."

Barnes met them at the door and read Bess like a book.

"Tea in the library, my lady?"

"Where's Momo, Barnes? I need to speak to her now."

Imogen Ridley or Momo had married Philip to become Lady Buxley. After Philip's death, she had the dubious honour of being the youngest dowager at the manor.

Barnes informed them she had retired to her rooms after lunch. Clementine accosted them as they headed to the section of the manor occupied by Momo.

"You missed lunch."

"Not now, Aunt Clem!"

Bess was in a mood. Vicky mouthed a quick apology and rushed after her.

Momo sat alone in her sitting room, flipping the pages of a fashion magazine. Her sister Gertrude, better known as Bubbles, was absent.

"Where's Bubbles?" Bess asked, knowing she spent more time at Buxley than her own home of Ridley Hall.

"Papa sent the chauffer for her. They are having a dinner party for Sir Lawrence and her presence is mandatory."

Bess told her she was sick of hearing about the man.

"Why is he suddenly popping up like a bad penny?"

Momo told them he was a kind man beneath all the bluster.

"He doted on Philip. Said he was the closest thing to a son etcetera etcetera."

Bess reclined on a chaise and put her feet up. Vicky hovered behind it, concerned.

"You never talk about him," Bess charged. "Why, Momo?"

Vicky finally chose a chair and sat down, crossing one leg over the other in a demure fashion. She would save her own questions for later.

Momo told them his death had been a big shock. The investigation did not give any of them the chance to mourn. Allegations were made and wild theories were floated.

"I stood by Nigel, Bess. Father wanted me to go back home to Ridley but I chose to stay here at Buxley Manor."

She wanted to send a message. She completely trusted Nigel and did not believe he had anything to do with Philip's death. Then Annie had taken Vicky and left for America.

"It became a sore topic," Momo sighed. "I suppose Nigel and I both avoided it for fear of hurting the other."

MURDER AT CASTLE MORSE

They were a broken household. Clementine, who was also recently widowed, arrived and took charge of the manor. Bubbles arrived to keep Momo company.

"All that is history," Bess dismissed. "Tell me about Philip, Momo. What kind of a man was he?"

Philip was the heir to an earldom and had been brought up with certain expectations.

"He led a wild life as a youth," Momo told them. "But he left all that behind when his father died and he came into the title. It was quite a transformation, actually."

Vicky asked when she fell in love with him.

Momo gave a shrug, admitting she had admired him from afar. He was gregarious, always surrounded by a gaggle of friends. She had never expected him to pay her any heed.

"How did he get on with the tenants?" Bess was curious. "Was he harsh with them?"

"They worshipped him, Bess. Little girls brought him posies and the young women giggled and stared at him from behind doors. The matrons blushed when he paid them a compliment. He was their young lord and he could do no wrong."

Bess thought no man could be that perfect. He must have had some enemies.

Momo admitted Philip could be a bit conceited at times but that added to his charm. He had a certain magnetism that drew people to him.

"Why would someone murder him, in that case?" Bess plunged ahead. "You were blinded by love, Momo."

Vicky wished Bess would simmer down. Momo's eyes were brimming with tears. The tea arrived, providing a welcome diversion.

Bess poured the tea, adding milk and sugar and handed a cup to Momo.

"I say, I got a bit carried away. Will you forgive me?"

Momo blinked back her tears and nodded, taking a bracing sip. Vicky never drank tea so she occupied herself with a slice of lemon cake.

"Philip died in an accident." Momo put her cup down and reached for a slice of bread and butter. "I have gone back and forth over this, Bess. Philip got thrown by his horse, hit his head and died."

Bess wondered why the people in the village did not believe it.

"What does Bubbles think?"

"She agrees with me. No use dwelling over the past, like you say. It's history."

They finished the tea and left. Vicky went off to write some letters and Bess headed for the library, hoping to run into Nigel. She hadn't spent much time with him lately and she wanted to reassure herself that he was fine.

The library seemed deserted. She hesitated, debating going up to her room or taking a nap on the ancient leather sofa by the window. Polo came running toward her. Bess picked him up and went further in, looking for Nigel behind a bookshelf.

"Papa? Hello?"

Annie sat on the leather sofa under the window, a threadbare shawl on her lap.

"Say, where did you get that?" Bess exclaimed.

MURDER AT CASTLE MORSE

Annie smiled and patted the spot next to her. Bess ignored her and chose a chair farthest from her. Polo jumped up on the sofa and snuggled into Annie's lap.

"I think your father's gone fishing."

Bess had guessed as much. She couldn't stop glaring at Polo who seemed to have switched loyalties and entered the enemy camp.

"When are you leaving?"

Annie chose to stay quiet. Bess tried to tamp down the emotions that rose in her throat.

"Did you have an affair with Miles?" she blurted. "That's what they all say." She saw Annie's eyes harden and delivered the final blow. "It's what he said. Miles."

"That's a lie," Annie cried.

"Well, we'll never know."

"You do know because I am telling you so. I was never unfaithful to your father."

Bess asked her the burning question.

"Then why did you leave?"

Annie told her it had all been too much. She had been unable to handle all the innuendos.

"So you fled at the slightest sign of trouble. Did you not believe in Papa?"

Annie told her Nigel did not have an alibi for the day. He told them he had spent the day with Miles Carrington. But there was a chunk of time when he was alone.

"Did you ever consider Miles lied?" Bess asked her. "Why did you take a neighbour's word over Papa's?"

Chapter 15

Bess whirled around, her eyes wide at the opulence she saw around her. She was in awe. Bubbles had dragged her and Vicky to London that day, to have a look at the flat she had rented in Grosvenor Square. She had made several trips to the city, visiting furniture stores and drapers, carefully choosing the pieces she wanted in her new home.

"This is marvellous! You say you did all this on your own?"

Bubbles patted her bob and preened. She loved adulation, especially coming from Bess who was the most modern young woman she knew.

"Papa was scandalized." She laughed with glee. "He thinks it looks like a bordello."

Never on board with his daughter renting a flat in London to live on her own, Sir Dorian had paid it an impromptu visit.

"He asked if I aspired to be a courtesan, then told me I was too old."

There were striped sofas and chairs in the main drawing room, with sheer curtains made from silk imported from China. Oriental carpets lined the floors. The bedroom held a large round bed, upholstered in red velvet. Everything else was white, except for a chaise lounge in a floral print.

"Are you actually going to live here, Bubbles?" Bess asked.

Bubbles told her she planned to shift there in the new year. That gave her a few months to finish decorating all the rooms.

"You can choose the fabric for yours, Bess. We are going to the draper after this."

MURDER AT CASTLE MORSE

They went to the Savoy for lunch and ordered champagne and oysters. Bess insisted on taking the train back to Buxley.

"I suppose you don't need me around, now that your mother is here." Bubbles sulked the entire journey back home, refusing to say a word.

Vicky closed her eyes and dozed off. She thought Bubbles was a spoilt and selfish woman who had never grown up.

They reached Buxley Manor a few minutes before five.

"You missed tea." Clementine glanced at the clock in the hall. "We had the last strawberries of the season." She relented. "Don't worry. Mrs. Bird saved some for you."

They went to the parlour to greet Momo. The tea arrived with a large platter of cucumber sandwiches and a sponge cake layered with strawberries and cream. Clementine joined them, eager to hear about the flat.

"You are lucky," she sighed. "Women have more opportunities now, especially after the war."

Bess was surprised to hear the longing in her aunt's voice.

"Say, Aunt Clem, are we keeping you here against your will?"

"Don't be silly. We have company for dinner so make sure you wear something decent."

Bess was mystified. Clementine was rarely frazzled by anything, let alone a few guests.

"My parents are coming to dinner," Momo told her. "With our esteemed guest, of course."

Barnes waylaid Bess and Vicky on their way back to their rooms.

"The Dowager telephoned, my lady. She has requested your presence immediately."

Bess felt a burst of excitement. Louise must have some new information.

"Isn't Grandma coming to dinner?" Vicky blurted as they rushed out and got into the car. "What could be so urgent?"

Louise stood at her parlour window, waiting for them.

"You are late."

"We came as soon as Barnes gave us the message, Grandmother." Bess raised her eyebrows in anticipation. "Well?"

She was not surprised to see Hortense and Perpetua were already there. A full fledged unplanned meeting of the Nightingales meant they had made a momentous discovery.

"We have the post mortem results," Louise announced, looking jubilant. "At least, we are now in possession of the time Joe Cooper died."

"Changes everything," Hortense muttered, twirling her handkerchief to fan herself.

"Rather," Perpetua replied.

Bess was not surprised because she knew how resourceful the older ladies were. But she wanted to know how they had managed this feat.

"I say! How did you get your hands on the report? Surely that Inspector did not help you?"

Louise smiled. She had been feeling under the weather for a day or two and had telephoned Dr. Evans. He had rushed to examine her and make sure she was fine.

"He stayed for lunch. I insisted."

Vicky smiled. "Gee, Grandma!"

Bess asked Louise to continue.

"Well, we got talking about Joe. Dr. Evans knew him as a young boy, you know. He was smarter than the average stable boy. Joe Cooper, I mean."

Louise had asked a few questions like the time it took for a body to grow cold, wondering how long Joe Cooper lay there without anyone finding him. With a twinkle in his eye, Dr. Evans promised to let her know.

"He knows the doctor in Morse," she reasoned. "Must have talked to him."

According to the post mortem report, Joe Cooper had died that morning, some time between 10 and 12.

Bess realized they had made a big error. They had tried to find out what all the suspects were doing around noon.

"We have no idea what Richie was doing at ten in the morning," she cried. "Or Ronald or Alfred Nash for that matter."

Vicky pointed out that Eileen was the only one who seemed to be accounted for. She had visited the Castle Morse kitchen and had been having tea with the cook. But they did not know when she left. It would not take much time to reach the stables from the castle.

The older ladies were aghast when Bess told them Alfred Nash's account of how Joe had behaved on the battlefield.

"That turncoat!" Perpetua exclaimed, rubbing her mole.

"Not quite," Louise reasoned. "It is easy to pass judgement, sitting here in our parlours. Who knows what passes through a man's mind when bullets are flying around and he might be struck down any second. The survival instinct must take over."

Bess and Vicky exchanged a glance. Truer words had never been spoken. Mere words were not enough to describe the situation one faced on a battlefield in the middle of a raging war. Thankfully, they had both come through without any lasting effects and had not let the side down.

Hortense asked what they knew about Alfred Nash. Did he have a family, for instance?

"He might have had a sweetheart waiting for him. Are you sure you are not overlooking another possible suspect, Bess?"

"He's a lot older, almost Papa's age," she replied. "Richie or Pudding might know, although he's been Lord Morse's secretary since as far back as I remember."

Louise wanted to know if Richie was really mourning the dead horse or it was just an act. She wondered how Lord Morse put up with it.

Vicky explained it could be an aftermath of all the loss he had seen on the battlefield. Maybe he felt guilty about Raymond.

"Grieving for Sindbad might be good for him. Better than keeping it all bottled up like Neville."

Hortense pointed out the time. They needed to dress for dinner. The group broke up and Bess ferried the aunts back to the manor, promising to send the chauffer to collect her grandmother.

Hortense advised the girls on what they needed to do next.

"You will have to talk to all these people again, girls. Come up with some unobtrusive questions if possible."

"Rather," Perpetua agreed. "We don't want to tip off the killer."

The aunts headed to the west wing while Bess and Vicky ran up the main stairs to their room, hoping to evade Clementine. They were not successful.

"Still not dressed? You know how particular Sir Dorian is." Bess planted a kiss on her cheek.

"Relax, Aunt Clem. He already thinks I am beyond redemption."

They held back their laughter until she left them, her mouth set in a grim line, her head shaking at their impertinence.

"Was that necessary?" Vicky groaned as they dissolved into giggles in their room. "I think she means well."

"Oh, Aunt Clem is the bee's knees," Bess laughed. "And I am fond of the old dear. But she's wound up too tight."

"But still ..." Vicky collapsed in a chair. "You are terrible, Bess."

"I was a handful, growing up. Aunt Clem meted out punishments, Bubbles laughed and encouraged me to be worse and Momo cried, afraid to say anything."

They chatted about their respective childhoods as they waited for the maid Wilson. Bess had picked out a dark maroon sleeveless frock that barely skimmed her knees and had a plunging neckline exposing a large part of her back. She wanted to have it pressed. Vicky chose a demure black.

The guests were enjoying predinner drinks when they went down. Sir Dorian stood beside his friend, the hunter, who held a bunch of photos in his hand. Every picture showed him with a foot on a dead animal, holding a rifle in his hand. Most of them were lions but there was an elephant or two and a zebra in the stack. There was a story about how each of the poor critters had succumbed to Sir Lawrence's bullet, holding the audience enthralled. Bubbles stifled a yawn and sidled closer to Bess.

"What an insufferable bore."

Bess noticed Annie sat in a chair, lost in thought. Louise arrived and asked Bess for a cocktail. She had scarcely taken a sip when Barnes announced dinner.

They carried their drinks to the dining room, expecting Clementine to make a fuss. But she was too engrossed in listening to Sir Lawrence.

"I say, Aunt Clem is acting out of character."

"Besotted by that buffoon," Louise grumbled. "A daughter of mine should have more sense."

Momo sat next to Louise and the great aunts, away from the head of the table from Sir Dorian. Bess wondered if she had asked Barnes to switch the place cards, hoping to be away from Sir Lawrence and his probing questions.

Nigel seemed distracted as his guests talked about the upcoming hunt. The soup and partridge were consumed and cleared away. The footmen brought out a roasted leg of lamb, accompanied by fried potatoes and a cherry sauce.

Sir Lawrence declared he was looking for a good mount.

"I hear they have started a breeding program at Castle Morse. But it got nipped in the bud, unfortunately."

Nigel offered him the use of his stables. "Why don't I take you for a tour of our stables tomorrow? You can pick any horse you like, take him for a few rides."

Sir Lawrence thought it was a capital idea. It would give him a chance to get acquainted with the beast.

"You must find all this very lame," Clementine gushed. "I mean, we are not really in any danger, going after the fox. Not like what you face in the jungles of Africa, Sir Lawrence."

"Ah, but there is always an element of uncertainty, my dear. Look what happened to Philip."

MURDER AT CASTLE MORSE

A hush fell over the table.

"What was the name of that black stallion he rode, Momo?" he asked. "I wonder if you have any of his offspring."

"Diamond," Momo mumbled from the far end of the table.

"What's that? Speak up, will you?" Sir Lawrence turned toward her, his brown eye following while the green one stared straight ahead at Bess.

Clementine answered. The horse went lame during Philip's accident and had been shot.

"So the horse and poor Philip died at the same time," Sir Lawrence chuckled. "Well, Miles had an excellent Andalusian. What was his name, Annie?"

Bess bristled with anger as another embarrassed silence engulfed the diners. Annie ignored him, taking a sip of her wine.

"Was it Apollo?" Sir Lawrence persisted. "Captain something ... no, it was something shorter."

The footmen began clearing the plates.

"Shall I see you for lunch at the Dower House tomorrow, Annie?" Louise asked. "Just you and me." She pinned Bess and Vicky with a stern gaze.

"Confound it!" Sir Lawrence banged a fist on the table. "Zeus. It was Zeus! I am surprised you don't remember, Annie. You went on so many rides with Miles."

Chapter 16

"Aren't you tired of all this motoring?" Pudding asked Bess.

The girls were back in Morse and walking to the village to meet Eileen. After her disastrous attempt at trying to eat a raw onion, Pudding had taken it upon herself to master the so called art. She wanted to consult Eileen for some expert advice.

"I say, how does she do it every year?"

Bess told her Eileen probably ate raw onions every day of her life.

"Can you imagine doing that, old bean? Eating raw onions at the table while the family feasts on Chef Henri's delicate sauces? And having that malodorous breath all day long?"

Pudding refused to listen to reason.

"Why do you have to go back to Buxley again and again?"

Vicky reminded her they had a family too.

"Mom has come here to meet Bess. The only reason we are here is because she can't say no to you."

Bess knew Vicky was right so she said nothing. They reached the butcher shop and lingered outside until one or two people who were buying meat left. If Eileen was surprised to see them, she didn't show it.

"Mrs. Hadley want something more?"

Pudding was suddenly tongue tied. She stared at Bess, her eyes wide, imploring her to say something.

Bess cleared her throat and summoned her sweetest smile.

"Hello Eileen. We are here to get some advice."

MURDER AT CASTLE MORSE

There was a spark of interest in her green eyes. She folded her arms over her stained apron, feet planted apart, in her best aggressive stance. Bess wondered how much of it was bluster.

"Here now, you making fun of me?"

"Oh no!" Pudding finally found her voice. "It's for the onion festival, see? Mama thought it would be nice if I tried my hand at it this year."

Lady Morse had no idea what her daughter had signed up for. She would likely have a fainting spell at the sight of her precious daughter standing in line with the villagers, sinking her teeth into raw onions.

"Huh!" Eileen gave them a vacant stare.

"Can you show her how to eat an onion?" Bess stepped in. "You don't have to give away all your secrets. We know you will want to maintain your winning streak."

Eileen's shoulders shook as she dissolved into laughter.

"I am not worried about that. Are you prepared to cry?"

Pudding shrank back.

"Please ... it was just a thought. We are leaving now."

Eileen clasped her shoulder, resigned.

"I am not going to hurt you, Miss."

"Onions make your eyes water, Pudding," Vicky sighed. "The sulphur in them causes a chemical reaction. I think that's what Eileen is referring to."

Pudding relaxed and pulled a large onion out of her hand bag.

"Where do I begin? Do they give you a knife to peel it?"

Eileen came out of the store and walked a few paces to the village green, pointing at some stone benches where they could sit.

"I can keep an eye on the shop from here. Can't afford to lose any business."

Then she positioned the onion in Pudding's hand, coaching her on how to hold it. She had mastered a technique over the years, one she was willing to share.

"Most of the butcher shop's business comes from the castle, Miss. We owe Lord Morse. So I don't mind even if you win." She grinned, showing evenly formed, perfectly white teeth.

Bess asked if she delivered to the neighbouring villages.

"The quality of meat we ate here has been exceptional. I wonder if you would consider delivering to Buxley."

Eileen had never been out of the village.

"How long will it take to get there in my cart?" she asked.

She balked when Bess told her the distance. "So you just make deliveries around Morse, then?"

Eileen told her there was a certain schedule. The boy took the cart to the castle and one or two houses of the gentry. Most of the villagers came to the shop.

"But Mrs. Hadley told us she gave you tea."

Eileen shrugged. Sometimes, she took the cart out herself if the boy played truant or was sick.

"Do you remember the time you were there? It was the day they found Joe Cooper dead."

Eileen stood up and placed her hands on her hips.

"What you getting at, Miss? Has someone been talkin' 'bout me and Joe?"

Bess told her they were just trying to establish where everyone at the castle was that day. Anything she remembered would go a long way in helping Richie.

Eileen's gaze softened at the mention of Richie.

"Master Richard is kind, just like his Pa. But I didn't lay eyes on him that morning."

She had set off from the village after nine and spent some time having tea with Mrs. Hadley.

"She is not really a missus. We single women ought to stick together."

Bess nodded, mentioning the vicar's sister.

"Too high and mighty for the likes of me." Eileen's rosy cheeks turned darker.

"What did you do after that?" Vicky stepped in, determined to make some headway. "Came back to the butcher shop, I suppose?"

Eileen stole a glance at Pudding and continued. She had walked to a spot by the river and sat down to play the flute. It was on the castle's grounds but away from the main house. Hardly anyone went there and nobody minded.

"And then?" Vicky spurred her on. "Did you run into anyone?"

"I came back to fetch my cart, keeping my head down. Saw that Alfred Nash, the one that got his arm ripped off in the war." She hid behind a tree until he passed. "He can be a fusspot."

Bess felt a burst of excitement.

"And where was he going, could you tell?"

"Toward the stables, I reckon." Eileen shrugged. "Or taking a walk in the grounds. Why don't you ask him?"

Bess thanked her and told her she would.

"You didn't go to the stables yourself then?"

"And why would I?" Eileen told them she avoided the stables like the plague because she did not want to run into Joe.

"Never wanted to lay eyes on that scoundrel. If you knew how he treated me ..."

Bess noticed her eyes burn with unshed tears. The hatred Eileen felt for Joe Cooper had not abated with his death.

Vicky reminded them it was getting late.

"Lady Morse is expecting us for lunch."

Pudding thanked Eileen and promised to follow her instructions.

"Can I come to you again if I need more help?"

Eileen beamed at her, urging her to eat at least five or six onions every day.

"Start small, Miss. Walk before you can run."

Bess and Vicky let Pudding walk a few steps ahead of them on the way back to the castle, hoping to avoid the noxious fumes they were subjected to every time she opened her mouth. Pudding was in high form.

"She's a sport, that Eileen. I wonder why Joe didn't want to marry her."

Bess thought Joe Cooper had decided to be contrary. There was no logical reason why he had been against the war memorial.

Lunch was being served in the dining room and Lady Morse welcomed them back. Chef Henri presented steamed trout with a lemon butter sauce and a green salad, along with croquettes of beef and stuffed tomatoes.

"Your father has invited the Ridleys to dinner tonight, Winifred," Lady Morse announced. "Do you have anything nice to wear?"

Pudding's fork slipped as she turned bright eyes toward her mother.

MURDER AT CASTLE MORSE

"You don't say! Don't worry, Mama. I have the perfect thing. That little ecru number we got from Paris, with the matching brocade jacket."

Lady Morse gave an approving smile.

"Demure. Sir Dorian is a bit Victorian in his outlook."

Bess wasn't pleased with this new development and debated going back to Buxley. Vicky shook her head vehemently.

"Not again, Bess." She murmured under her breath. "We just got here."

Pudding wanted to know who Sir Dorian was bringing with him.

"Lady Ridley, of course. And Sir Lawrence." Lady Morse turned to Bess. "I don't suppose Bubbles will come with them?"

The girls headed to their rooms after lunch, at a loose end. Vicky took up a book on anatomy and Bess paced the room, trying to make sense of her cluttered brain. Joe Cooper's murder fought for attention with Annie and lost.

"She could have denied it, Vicky."

"But why should she?" Vicky understood Bess was talking about the insinuations Sir Lawrence had made about Miles Carrington and their mother Annie. "Mom has always been a subject of gossip. You know how hard it is, being a rich, separated business woman in New York? People make all kinds of assumptions about her and talk behind her back."

Bess flung herself on the bed and pulled the covers over her head, refusing to agree with Vicky. But some doubts had started creeping in. Was it possible the past twenty years had been hard on her mother too?

There was no elaborate tea ritual at Castle Morse, everyone choosing to order it according to their convenience. Bess and Vicky rang for the maid at five, longing for some refreshments. Pudding arrived with the tea, her eyes blotchy and swollen.

"What's wrong, old bean?" Bess cried.

"Onions!" Vicky rolled her eyes. "Too much of anything is not good, you know."

The twins recoiled as soon as Pudding opened her mouth. She had spent the afternoon following Eileen's instructions, practising on small onions. It had taken her the better part of an hour to eat just one.

"Eileen's record is four minutes twenty one seconds," she groaned. "For a half pound onion. I am nowhere close."

Bess urged Pudding to eat some cake to cool the fire in her mouth.

"I say, that's enough for today. Why don't you take a nice bath and it will be time to dress for dinner."

She wore a dark emerald pant suit with long rows of pearls around her neck. Vicky chose a simple black dress made by Coco Chanel, a designer from Paris.

They heard Sir Lawrence before they reached the parlour where drinks were being served. Vicky nudged Bess and a silent signal passed between them.

Pudding was already there, standing in a circle with Lord Morse and Sir Lawrence, nodding and laughing at one of his exploits. The German Shepherd sat on a table, his tongue hanging out, panting. Lady Morse sat in a far corner with Lady Ridley, staring at the dog in shock.

Richie came forward to welcome them.

MURDER AT CASTLE MORSE

"What will you have, my dear?" He kissed each sister on the cheek. "How about a gin rickey?"

He handed them their drinks with a flourish.

"A word of warning. Keep a safe distance from Pudding. She has the most atrocious breath."

Bess thought they were safe as long as Sir Lawrence was in the room. Pudding had not left his side.

"Those were the days, of course. Eh, Clive?" He dug an elbow in Lord Morse's side. "Philip was intrepid, my dear. Always ready for the next adventure. I do miss him so."

"Not as brave as you, Sir Lawrence," Pudding gushed. "He never killed a lion."

"Philip would have made a first class hunter," he clucked. "Maybe if the old earl hadn't died so early ... it was all planned, you see? He was going to join me in Africa."

"Life can be unpredictable," Pudding commiserated. "Was Momo going to join him in Africa too?"

Sir Lawrence hesitated.

"This was before he got married, of course. And before he became earl."

Lord Morse cleared his throat.

"Philip's death was a tragedy alright. But you must admit he could be reckless, Sir Lawrence. He just took one risk too many."

"Riding on his own land, across woods he knew every inch of?" Sir Lawrence twirled his moustache and patted 303. "I could never digest that, old chap."

Bess could not contain herself any longer.

"Why are you here, Sir Lawrence?" she demanded. "To stir up a hornet's nest?"

Sir Dorian began muttering under his breath. Pudding looked stricken. 303 began to growl.

Sir Lawrence, the bane of lions in Africa, role model of big game hunters across the world, pinned his one sharp eye on Bess.

"And what if it needs to be stirred, young lady? The Philip I knew would never be thrown off his horse."

Chapter 17

Bess gazed out of her window over the expansive grounds of Castle Morse the next morning, sipping her hot chocolate, contemplating skipping breakfast. She did not care to face Lady Morse.

She had given Sir Lawrence a piece of her mind the previous night. Vicky had been frantic, trying to calm her down. Most of the assembled party had been struck dumb. Richie was gazing at her in awe, Lord Morse chuckled while Sir Dorian Ridley sputtered and turned red, calling her a spoilt brat who was clearly out of control.

To everyone's surprise, Sir Lawrence laughed and called her a spitfire, just like her mother.

Norton came and announced dinner was ready, saving everyone more embarrassment. Chef Henri had provided an excellent meal as usual, and the food kept everyone busy. Nobody wanted to linger after dinner and Lady Morse heaved a sigh of relief when the Ridleys and Sir Lawrence left, citing some nominal reason.

Vicky told Bess they were going up to their room. They were getting undressed for bed when Pudding barged in, her eyes red, flashing fire.

"How could you, Bess! You vilified the poor man, for no reason!"

She slammed the door on her way out. Vicky gave a sympathetic smile and buried her head in a book. Bess collapsed on the bed and fell fast asleep.

"Should we leave?" Vicky's voice bore into her thoughts.

"Not yet. The Morses are used to my tantrums."

Lady Morse was buttering toast when they entered the breakfast room. Bess began to apologize.

"I don't know what came over me."

Pudding let out a snort, letting them know she was sulking. But Lady Morse patted Bess on the shoulder.

"He was asking for it, my dear. Lawrence has always been a stuffed shirt. He likes to hear the sound of his own voice."

Lord Morse chuckled behind his paper.

Bess filled her plate from the buffet, choosing eggs, bacon and grilled tomatoes. She had barely taken her first bite of toast when a loud banging started.

"Say, what's that?" Lord Morse put his paper down and bellowed. "Norton!"

The butler arrived, looking bewildered.

"A group of people from the village are outside, my lord. They wish to speak to you."

Lord Morse told him to direct them to Alfred Nash. Norton cleared his throat, informing him they would not budge.

"They insist on an audience with you, Sir."

Lord Morse took a last bite of toast and stood up.

"Come on, Richie. Do you have any idea what this is about?"

Richie had been staring out of the window from behind some drapes.

"Ron Griffin is leading them so this must be about the memorial, Papa."

Father and son strode out, unruffled. Lord Morse was known for being amicable and generous. He in turn put a lot of trust in his people. Bess hoped the mob outside was not riled up. She was surprised when Neville stood up and followed Richie. Would he be any help if fists began to fly?

Lady Morse talked about a party to welcome Annie.

"The annual hunt ball is coming up, of course. She can be the guest of honour."

Bess wondered if her mother would stick around that long. Not if that buffoon Sir Lawrence continued to pester her.

"She will love that, Lady Morse." Vicky looked at Bess, answering her question. "Tell me about this ball, Pudding."

None of them had realized when she left the room.

"I think Pudding is besotted with One Eye Watkins." Bess spread a generous amount of jam on her toast.

"Surely not!" Lady Morse pressed her lips. "Why do you say that, dear?"

Bess read the alarm in her eyes and tried to make light of it. "Just a hunch."

She was sipping her tea, considering a second cup when Lord Morse peeped in.

"Nothing to worry about, my dear." He flashed a smile at Lady Morse. "We are to begin work on the memorial tomorrow. Richie and Nash are hashing out the details with the men."

Lady Morse left for a meeting with the housekeeper. Bess nodded at Vicky and stood up. She had been waiting for a chance to speak to Lord Morse.

"No time like the present," Vicky agreed.

They walked down the corridor and knocked on the door of his office. A hearty voice invited them to come in.

"Bess, Vicky ..." He gave them a bemused smile. "To what do I owe the pleasure?"

The room was cavernous, with large bay windows along one wall, looking out on parkland. Lord Morse sat in a leather armchair by the fireplace. Bess smoothed her skirt and sat down before him, pulling Vicky along with her.

"Can we talk about the war memorial? I think it might have something to do with Joe Cooper's death."

Lord Morse told them the village of Morse owed a lot to the dead groom.

"He was a hero, girls. He brought my boy home safe and sound."

Bess was quiet as he went on to sing Joe's praises. Finally, she could take it no more.

"I don't mean to contradict you, Lord Morse. But that's not the real story."

She told him Alfred Nash's version, watching his mouth fall open when he heard how Joe Cooper had pushed the man in the line of fire, then abandoned his mates.

"Richie is the real hero."

Lord Morse was pacing the room, his hands clasped behind his back.

"If what you are saying is true, my dear, I have wronged the Morse 13. All of them were in favour of the memorial, except Joe. And I sided with him because I felt I was under his debt."

He rang for the butler and asked him to summon Richie at once.

"And get Nash too while you are at it."

MURDER AT CASTLE MORSE

Two minutes later, the door burst open and Richie himself rushed in, his face wreathed in smiles. Nash was right behind him.

"It's all done, Papa. We begin work tomorrow morning at 0800 hours. The Morse 13, or Morse 11, rather, shall offer an 11 gun salute to kick off the event. I shall join my men, of course."

Nash added that the villagers were appeased and looking forward to the next day.

"There is an atmosphere of celebration, my lord. Perhaps we might buy a round for everyone tonight at The Crown?"

Lord Morse held Richie by the shoulders and stared into his eyes.

"Tell me something, my boy. Was Joe Cooper a hero?" He watched Richie squirm and clenched his jaw. "Don't lie to me now."

Nash narrated what he had told Bess. Richie backed him up.

"So the man was a coward." Lord Morse curled his fists. "Why on earth would you let me think otherwise, son?"

Bess leaned forward, eager to learn why Richie had played along with Joe Cooper's subterfuge.

"I was a bit shook up after that day, Papa." Richie was contrite. "The horse program I wanted to develop was the only thing holding me together."

Fighting his own demons, afraid he would end up like Neville, Richie plunged himself into building the stud farm. Joe Cooper may not be virtuous but when it came to caring for thoroughbreds, his expertise was incomparable.

"He talked of leaving us, Papa. Going to the Highlands, starting out in a new place. But I needed him." Richie bit his lip. "Sindbad was attached to him too."

When Joe decided there would be no memorial, Richie went along with it.

"And you let me think he saved your life," Lord Morse thundered. "When it was the other way round."

Richie collapsed on a chair and gave a deep sigh.

"I have apologized to my men. And I am saying sorry to you now, Papa. Can you please forgive me?"

Lord Morse patted his back but said nothing.

Bess was busy analysing everything again. Although most of the Morse 13 wanted the memorial built, they could not be as desperate as Ronald Griffin. Ron had lost his brother and needed something tangible that would honour his memory.

"So Joe Cooper's death paved the way for building the memorial?" she asked abruptly. "I think Ronald's our man, Richie. Now if we could find some evidence."

Lord Morse did not agree.

"The Griffin boys were brought up in a good family, Bess. And young Ron? He's a bit of a namby pamby, to be honest with you. I really do not believe he is capable of hurting anyone."

"Not even to avenge his brother?" Vicky asked. "Grief can make people act out of character."

Richie and Lord Morse paused for a minute and shook their heads.

"You will have to believe someone other than you is guilty, Richie!" Bess cried.

He told her he could not condemn an innocent man just to save his own hide.

Vicky's knee crammed into hers and Bess got the message. They wished the father and son a good day and left the study.

"We are going to the village right now, Vicky. Let's talk to Ron again. See if he comes up with something new."

Norton was handing out their hats and coats when Pudding emerged from the depths of the castle, tears streaming down her face. Bess assumed they were caused by the vile chemicals residing in onions.

"What do you know about living in the wild, huh? Knowing a beast might rip you open any minute?" She began to sob. "That poor man!"

Bess and Vicky shrank back as a wall of onion breath hit them, watching Pudding run up a flight of stairs.

"Keep an eye on her, Norton," Vicky warned. "The bird's ready to fly."

The drive to the village did not take long. A mother and daughter duo were buying lace when Bess and Vicky entered the haberdashery. Ron gave them a friendly wave and promised to be with them soon.

"Good day to you," he beamed after the store emptied. "Have you heard the news? We begin work on the memorial tomorrow. Ma is going to be pleased."

Vicky congratulated him and commended his efforts.

"Must have taken guts. Going up to the castle and demanding to be heard."

Ron blushed. He knew Lord Morse would never turn them away.

"Joe Cooper's death is working out for you, Ron," Bess began. "Some might say you eliminated the one obstacle to the memorial."

Ron gave a shrug but said nothing.

"Where were you that morning?" Bess pounced. "You never told us."

"You think I bumped him off?" Ron's eyebrows shot up as he finally made the connection. "And I waited three years to do that?"

Bess provided her reasoning. He had tried to come to terms with his grief but failed miserably. Finally, he worked himself into a frenzy and decided to confront the person responsible for his brother's death.

"Maybe it was an accident," Bess cajoled. "Lord Morse might ask the judge to go easy on you."

Ron's hands trembled as he put some buttons back into their boxes. Vicky saw his chest rise and fall rapidly and urged Bess to calm down.

"Were you in the store that day, Ron?" she asked gently. "Do you remember anything?"

Ron pulled out a handkerchief and blew his nose. He had been in the store all day. Plenty of customers could vouch for him.

"I was holding a special sale so the store was always full."

He had ordered some sandwiches from the pub but never got time to eat them.

Vicky asked if he had noticed anything out of the ordinary.

Ronald began to shake his head, then stopped, his mouth falling open.

"Eileen came in around eleven. But I couldn't help her."

She claimed she lost a button from her dress somewhere in the woods. It had caught in a hair clip that morning and come loose. He had noticed the scratches on her arms and the tendrils of hair that had escaped from her braid.

"She gets into these fights, you know," he explained. "I didn't want to embarrass her so I said nothing."

They did not find a matching button so she got one that looked similar and left. Ron's eyes brightened.

"She can confirm I was right here, my lady."

Bess nodded and stomped out, ready to cry out in frustration. Vicky took her hand as they walked to the car.

"We don't know why she lied."

Chapter 18

Vicky and Bess sat in a window booth at the village pub later that evening. Lord and Lady Morse had been invited for a dinner party at a neighbouring estate. Richie was in London and Pudding had chosen to lock herself in her room. Bess wanted to get away from the castle.

"We might have gone home," Vicky sighed, holding aloft her spoon.

The lamb stew they had ordered did not look very appetizing. Bess told her she was tired of all the drama.

"Don't you feel too much is happening too soon? There is someone nagging us or expecting something from us every waking moment. Let's run away. Maybe we can go to Edinburgh, kill two birds with a stone."

Bess had guessed why her twin was despondent. Vicky had not received any positive news regarding her application for joining the university.

"There's another man who is not happy with his life," Vicky noted.

Bess whirled around on a reflex and saw Alfred Nash sitting alone in a dark corner, nursing a pint of ale. The man was clearly in his cups.

"Let's ask him to join us."

Nash was eager for company. He had a hard job. The tenants kept things from him fearing he would report them to the lord. And he was not really gentry so the Morse family kept their distance.

"Rum business this ... the blasted memorial." He burped. "I beg your pardon, ladies. Joe Cooper might be dead and buried but he still haunts me." The empty sleeve dangling from his right shoulder moved with his torso. "I remember him every time I look in the mirror."

Bess tried to commiserate. The battlefield was unpredictable at best. He might have been injured anyway.

"I was ready to die for the country, my lady. But to be slaughtered by a brother in arms ..."

"What kind of a person was he?" Bess was curious. "Did he have friends in the village?"

Alfred shook his head. "High in the instep. Lord Morse thought a lot of him."

Vicky thought he must have been good with the horses. He had risen fast in the ranks and become the stable master.

"Success went to his head." Alfred laughed. "Or he changed when that Eileen refused to marry him. Didn't take much to rile him up."

Had Joe loved Eileen, Bess wondered. Why had he refused to marry her after coming back from the war?

"There isn't a man in the village Joe Cooper did not have a problem with. Why, he was rowing with that bone digger one night."

"You mean the archaeologist?" Vicky prompted, trying to recollect his name.

"Ballard," Bess supplied.

Nash's eyes closed and he sagged in his chair, leaning to one side. Bess slammed her hand on the table, making him sit up with a start.

"Are you sure? We talked to Ballard the other day and according to him, he never had any conversation with Joe. In fact, he wasn't aware who Joe Cooper was."

Nash closed his eyes again.

"Do you know Princess doesn't like him, my lady? Hisses and spits every time she sees him. Scratched his arm once."

Bess remembered the fuss Ballard had raised over Lady Morse's cat. Nash was calling him a liar. Clearly, they needed to talk to Ballard again.

Vicky tried to force down a bite or two of the stew and gave up. Nash had fallen asleep with his head on the table. They crept past him and went out into the cool night. By the time they reached the castle, both realized they had barely eaten anything.

Bess was familiar with the kitchen and larder. She led Vicky downstairs and began foraging.

"Bingo!" Vicky pointed at a platter of sliced ham while Bess brandished a loaf of bread.

There was half a fruit cake and cold roasted chicken. They gathered everything and went up to their room. Bess thought of Pudding and decided to check on her. Half a dozen strong raps produced no response. Bess gave up. The thought of a feast in her room had made her nostalgic, bringing forth memories of midnight feasts they had shared at boarding school. But apparently, Pudding was not ready to forgive her yet.

Vicky stood by the window, staring out, when Bess entered their room.

"She's being a beast."

"Shhhh ..." Vicky placed a finger on her mouth and summoned her to the window.

MURDER AT CASTLE MORSE

Bess got the shock of her life. Pudding stood in the garden, illuminated by a bright moon, talking to a man.

"What on earth!" she exclaimed.

It was hard to make out the man's features in the dark but there was a third figure nearby, sealing his identity. Bess stared at Vicky, their mouths hanging open.

"One Eye Watkins. I was right!"

Bess wanted to go down at once but Vicky held her back.

"But ... you don't know. Pudding has a tendency to get carried away."

Vicky pulled her away from the window and told her to trust her friend. Appearances could be deceptive. Maybe Sir Lawrence had come to visit Lord Morse on the spur of the moment and Pudding was just being a good hostess.

Bess gave a wide yawn and decided she was too tired to go and confront her friend. She just hoped Pudding wasn't beyond redemption.

The entire Morse clan was present at the breakfast table the next morning. Although Pudding's eyes were swollen, hinting at another attempt at slaying a raw onion, there was a big smile on her face.

"Why don't you girls take a break from all this sleuthing?" Lord Morse suggested. "Go up to London and spend the night at our town house. I am sure the autumn collections must have arrived at the boutiques."

Richie backed him up. He was not worried at all which did not make sense to Bess. She still thought he was hiding something.

Pudding claimed she was already engaged. Bess told him they were going to visit the dig.

"That Mr. Ballard told us we could visit any time and watch his group in action."

Bess assumed Pudding would come along but she had not counted on her silence. She sat in the back seat, arms folded, her gaze fixed on the foliage.

"Do stop sulking, old girl, and tell us why that old buffoon was here last night."

Pudding's cheeks flamed and her wide eyes made it clear she was caught unaware.

"I am entitled to my secrets, Bessie, just like you." She shot a dark look at Vicky.

Bess did not respond. They reached the dig site and jumped out. Stephen Ballard stood surrounded by a group of youngsters who were listening to him with rapt attention. He lifted his hand and waved when he spotted Bess.

"Ladies! To what do we owe the pleasure?"

Bess asked if he had found anything new.

"A few bits and pieces." He sounded eager. "My assistants are going to try and piece them together today. We think they may have come from a vase."

He walked a few paces toward a patch of land that looked like it had been turned recently.

"We just began digging here. The entire square mile is very promising, like I told Lord Morse."

Bess asked if he didn't get tired of doing to same thing for days on end.

"Don't you take any breaks? Go for a walk or something?"

"My dear, I am so engrossed I barely look up."

MURDER AT CASTLE MORSE

Bess noted the fresh cuts on his face and believed him. Stephen Ballard was a man who did not have time for the mundane.

Vicky started talking about the river flowing through the property. It was very peaceful there, and a lot cooler because of the shade from the trees.

"You pass by the stables to go there," Pudding spoke up. "I think I saw you walk past there the morning Joe died."

Ballard insisted he had never left the dig site. He hardly ever did.

One of the assistants opened his mouth to say something but shut it again. Bess noticed the sharp look in his eyes and acted immediately.

"Would you mind if we treated all of your assistants to lunch at The Crown today?" Bess flashed her most charming smile. "I want to hear what they think about all this." She held her arms out. "So exciting, Mr. Ballard. I am going to tell Papa about it. Maybe you can come dig at Buxley next."

"By all means," Ballard's eyes gleamed with interest. "They have earned a break, I suppose."

The assistants thanked him profusely and agreed to meet the girls at the pub at noon. Vicky suggested visiting some of the area's attractions. Pudding told them they were on their own.

"Toodles." She jumped out as soon as Bess stopped the car in front of the castle.

"Any guesses where she is going?" Bess murmured.

Norton came out of the front door to give them a message.

"Lady Buxley was on the phone, my lady," he informed Bess. "Your grandmother, that is. Your presence is requested at the manor."

Bess thanked him, wondering what Louise wanted. Was it something to do with Annie?

"Hold your horses," Vicky advised. "We'll know soon enough."

Bess regretted inviting Ballard's assistants for lunch. They would have to spend an hour or two with them at the pub. Vicky suggested going down to the river to while away the time. They sat on the banks on a pile of rocks, surrounded by towering beeches. It was cool in the shade and the flowing water managed to calm Bess. They were ready for a hearty meal by the time they reached The Crown.

The group of youngsters were engrossed in a lively discussion. Bess and Vicky joined them.

"Do you eat here often?" she asked, knowing it was the only pub in the village.

None of them owned a motor so they did not have a lot of choice.

"It's pretty much what Cook puts before us," a pimply faced boy with an errant lock of hair shrugged. "Most nights, we are so exhausted we can barely stay awake to eat."

They agreed the work was tough but they loved it. All of them hoped to further their studies and make some big discovery one day.

"So the mosaic must be big news." Bess smiled. "Ballard is convinced it is Roman?"

They nodded vigorously, singing his praises. Stephen Ballard was one of the brightest minds in the field of archaeology. He was bound to be accepted to the Royal Society any day.

Bess had ordered meat pies for everyone. The food arrived, with rich gravy and boiled potatoes tossed in butter. She waited until the meal was underway before directing her gaze on a youth wearing horn rimmed spectacles. He was the one who had flinched when Ballard gave them his alibi.

"John, is it?" she asked. "What do you think about the murder? Do you feel safe at the Dower house?"

He agreed it was unexpected. But they rarely interacted with anyone at the castle so it had not affected them.

Had they seen or heard anything untoward that day, Bess asked.

"Not a word." John speared a potato. "We found some interesting pieces that morning and were engrossed in cleaning them. They turned out to be part of a comb."

"And Ballard could tell that just by looking at the pieces?" Vicky feigned surprise.

"Actually, he wasn't there that morning," John admitted.

Bess let him go on, barely listening. Why had Stephen Ballard lied to them? The other assistants giggled, sharing knowing looks. His assistant had also been missing and they suspected a lovers' tryst.

"In broad daylight?" Vicky exclaimed.

By the time the pudding was consumed, they were all great chums. The girl promised to keep them updated on the latest gossip about Ballard.

An hour later, Vicky and Bess were headed to Buxley Manor, Vicky reluctantly taking the wheel.

"I am not used to driving on the left, Bess."

"Isn't it time you learned, old girl?"

Vicky sidestepped the question.

"He can barely shave without cutting himself, Bess. I doubt Stephen Ballard has the patience to plan a murder."

Chapter 19

Tea was in full swing on the lawn at Buxley Manor. Platters of cucumber sandwiches, scones and apple cake adorned the table. Barnes stood by, directing the footmen as needed while Clementine had charge of the teapot. Bess and Vicky greeted her, expecting to be rebuked for being late.

"Sorry Aunt Clem. But we are famished."

Bess took the cup of tea her aunt handed her and took a bracing sip, savouring the particular flavour which was spicy with a hint of citrus.

"What ho, everyone!" She popped a cucumber sandwich in her mouth, trying to locate the Nightingales among the assembled crowd. "I say, where are the aunts? And Grandmother?"

Clementine huffed, giving a roll of her eyes.

"In the west wing. They claimed they were too busy to come down here. Up to no good, I tell you."

Bubbles gave a hearty laugh.

"You are mad because they are not under your thumb, Aunt Clem."

Nigel brushed some crumbs off his knee and asked the girls what they had been up to.

"Oh Papa! This motoring to and fro between Buxley and Morse is a big bore. Sometimes it feels like I am in perpetual motion."

"Now, Bess." Nigel smiled. "Let the chauffer take you next time."

Vicky thought that was a good idea.

"Capital," she smiled. "Isn't that what you say, Pops?"

Bess realized Annie was not among the group. She summoned Barnes with a silent nod and spoke softly in his ear.

"Where is she, Barnie?"

The butler did not have to be told who she was referring to.

"Your mother is in the kitchen with Mrs. Bird. I believe they are making apple pie."

Bess gulped another cup of tea and ate until she was full. Vicky was already up and heading toward the manor.

"Don't be late for dinner, girls," Aunt Clem called out. "The Ridleys will be here and I would rather not annoy Sir Dorian again."

Nigel being a generous host, Bess was used to seeing a crowd at the dinner table. She had long ceased to be afraid of Sir Dorian and had learned to ignore him.

"As long as they don't bring their guests …"

She did not wait for Clementine's response, setting a brisk pace for the west wing along with Vicky. The shadows had lengthened and it was growing dark, thanks to a thick cloud cover. Louise sat in her usual chair wearing her favourite hat, debating something with Hortense and Perpetua. The remnants of a generous tea lay before them and the fire crackled merrily, bathing the room in golden light.

"It's about time." Louise grumbled when she saw them. "Unless you already cracked the case."

Bess flopped down on the sofa and stared at the ceiling.

"No such luck, Grandmother. I want to forget all this and go on a holiday."

MURDER AT CASTLE MORSE

"And what about helping Richard Morse?" Hortense questioned, dabbing her forehead with the ever present handkerchief.

Vicky told them how they seemed to be hitting a wall everywhere they looked. Richie himself was no help since he refused to be honest with them.

Louise told them to calm down.

"Begin at the beginning," Perpetua nodded.

Hortense began summing up everything that had happened since Joe Cooper's death. She invited the ladies to interrupt her in case she made an error.

"Have I missed anything?" she asked when she was done.

"That's about it, Aunt Hortense," Bess groaned. "But I don't see a light at the end of the tunnel."

Louise suggested going through all the suspects one by one.

"Let us begin with Richie. He is, after all, the reason we are doing this."

They discussed if Richie had a strong enough motive to take a man's life. All the older ladies had been excellent horsewomen in their youth. Only the ravages of time had produced ailments that made it impossible for them to mount a horse. So they understood the emotions one might attach to their beasts.

"We have all had a Sindbad one time or other in our lives," Louise began. "And I could imagine wanting to kill anyone who harmed my old mare Jonquil. But I would never go through with it."

What did that mean, they pondered. Was Richie making much ado about nothing? Did he just want to sully Joe Cooper for some reason and hence went on about how Sindbad was poisoned? Or did he want to gain something else by exaggerating his grief?

"One might say he was angling for more funds to buy another thoroughbred. But the Morses are rolling in money. In fact, Lord Morse mentioned he is in touch with the top breeders in the country, even in America, to get a new foal." Bess scratched a spot on her hand until it turned red.

Vicky brought up the war memorial.

"Joe Cooper bent Richie to his will, in a way. And we know he was no hero. Richie must have been seething inside when he had to oppose the memorial. It cannot have endeared him to the villagers. Ron Griffin mentioned how none of them understood why the Morses sided with Joe."

"And Sindbad died," Perpetua reminded them. "That must have been a double blow."

Louise herded their thoughts. Whatever the reason, Richard Morse did have some motive to harm Joe. Now they needed to check where he was that morning.

"We never asked him that." Bess cried out in frustration. "He was at lunch with the family. Pudding told me he got a telephone call and went out. But that was all in the afternoon."

Vicky wrote it down. They would ask him where he was the next time they met him.

Hortense moved on to Ron Griffin. They thought he had a strong motive because Joe opposed the memorial. He had deprived the Griffins of the opportunity to honour Raymond's memory.

"It seems Joe Cooper was guilty of a lot more. In a way, he caused Raymond's death. I wonder if the brother knew that."

Bess was thoughtful. Ron had never mentioned it.

MURDER AT CASTLE MORSE

"All the Morse 13 knew the truth about Joe Cooper. Do you think they might have hidden it from Ron?"

Why would they, the aunts mused. Raymond might have wanted to protect his brother and urged them to stay quiet about what really happened on the battlefield.

"Can thirteen people really keep a secret?" Louise challenged. "One of them was bound to speak up."

"Like Nash did, you mean," Vicky nodded. "One or the other would have eventually spoken up."

Bess wondered if that is what had happened. Someone had told Ron the truth.

"Pudding says he wouldn't hurt a fly. But anyone might crack under extreme provocation."

Louise asked about his alibi. Her shoulders slumped when Vicky told her he had been in the haberdashery all day. A steady stream of visitors meant he had not had a chance to step out at all.

Bess put her hands behind her head, deep in thought, swinging her legs in a nervous rhythm. Was Ron a wolf in sheep's clothing, just biding his time to avenge his brother? How had he done it, then.

"Does the post mortem report have any wiggle room?" she thought out loud. "What if the window of death is nine to noon instead of ten to noon. Would that allow Ron to visit the castle grounds and get rid of Joe?"

Vicky thought it was worth following up. Dr. Evans would know. Or they would have to put it before the Inspector.

Louise thought they should move on to Alfred Nash. She had spoken to the man once or twice. Lord Morse depended on him and praised his diligence many a time.

"He is a sensible man but losing a limb can be earth shattering, I suppose."

Vicky had a lot of first hand experience working with wounded soldiers.

"There is a period of shock, followed by anger and then finally, acceptance. But some never reach that point, Grandma. The anger consumes them, leading them to drink or melancholia."

Bess thought Nash was trying to live a normal life despite his injury. But he did nurse a grudge toward Joe Cooper.

"I think he bore a lot of ill will toward Joe. Wished him to perdition. And what's more, even considered acting on it." She shook her head. "The obstacle here is physical. Joe Cooper was a strapping man in good health. Could a man with one arm have overpowered him and managed to deliver a fatal blow?"

Hortense pressed her mouth, considering the question.

"Rather," Perpetua shrugged.

"He had the last three years to plan and prepare," Hortense explained.

They were all silent as they digested this. Louise stretched her legs before her and sighed.

"And finally, the woman scorned. Let us not forget Eileen. Joe Cooper spurned her, shattering her dreams."

"Not really," Bess argued. "She rejected him first. I don't see how Joe Cooper was wrong in this case. He is allowed to have some self respect."

Hortense and Perpetua agreed with her. If Eileen found herself facing a life of spinsterhood, it was her own fault.

"Tell them about the earring, Louise," Hortense spoke.

Bess jumped up from the sofa and faced her grandmother.

MURDER AT CASTLE MORSE

"What earring?"

It was something they had learned via the servants.

"You know the pub in Chipping Woodbury is owned by Jones, our housekeeper's brother?" Louise asked.

Bess rolled her eyes. She was well acquainted with the place.

Apparently, the three constables from the villages of Buxley, Ridley and Morse met there for a pint. The conversation had naturally turned to the unsolved murder of Joe Cooper. Constable Yates of Ridley village had a keen interest in the matter since Joe was his nephew. He had prevailed upon Bright, the man from Morse, to provide some details of the investigation.

"The police found an earring in the stall where Joe Cooper died," Louise stated.

"And you are telling us about this now?" Bess cried. "Eileen is the only woman we suspect so this ornament must belong to her."

The aunts advised caution.

"The constables might be simple minded but that Inspector from Scotland Yard knows a thing or two."

Bess was fuming with indignation.

"Why has he not arrested Eileen until now? He is just enjoying making Richie stew. Lord Morse will not be happy about this."

Louise told her to stop jumping to conclusions. The Inspector would have a valid reason for keeping the case open. Maybe he was gathering more evidence.

Bess thought they had their killer. Eileen openly hated Joe Cooper. She had the strength of a giant and could easily have swatted him like a fly. And she was on Morse land that morning, near the stables.

Vicky felt sorry for Eileen.

"I don't think she planned it, if she is guilty. She must have come across Joe by chance. Maybe he even insulted her."

"Provoked." Hortense agreed.

Bess had walked over to the window and was gazing across the parkland at the setting sun. She had a clear view of the formal gardens near the manor, studded with enormous topiaries. Her eyes bulged as a couple came into view, strolling down a path lined by boxwood hedges on either side. The man turned toward his companion and said something, making her look away.

"I say!" Bess waved at the window.

Vicky joined her, wondering what could possibly cause her twin to become tongue tied. She recognized the couple and beamed, going closer to get a good look.

"Care to enlighten us, girls?" Louise drawled. "Don't tell me there is an elephant on the lawns."

"Even better." Vicky turned around, her eyes crinkled in a smile. "Mom and Pops are taking a walk in the garden."

Chapter 20

Bess and Vicky stayed another day at Buxley at Nigel's urging.

"Your mother wants to spend more time with you, Bessie. It's time you got to know her."

It was exactly why Bess was not keen on sticking around at Buxley Manor. Was Annie going to drive her away from her own home now? Vicky said nothing but could not hide her dismay.

The Ridleys came to dinner on both nights, bringing their esteemed guest along with them. His eyes turned wary when he spotted Bess and she was glad he didn't say much to her. The German Shepherd followed him around and took a shine to the twins, giving a joyful bark every time he saw them.

The third day saw them on the road back to Castle Morse. True to his word, Nigel insisted they let the chauffer drive them in the Rolls. He would stay at Morse and come back to Buxley when summoned.

Pudding was pacing around the room, her face red, when Norton led them to the parlour. She rushed toward Bess and wrapped her in an embrace, her breath ripe with onions.

"I thought you weren't coming back."

Bess saw the sheepish grin on her friend's face and felt a ray of hope.

"Don't be silly, old bean. Have I ever left you in a pickle?"

"Sir Lawrence can be a bit pompous but he's a nice chap. He taught me a new trick to eat an onion."

Vicky bit her lip and gave a subtle shake of her head, silently warning Bess to say nothing. So Pudding's infatuation had not waned, nor had her determination to participate in the onion festival.

Bess told her they had been blessed with his presence.

"Twice in the last two days." Pudding gave a dramatic sigh. "How I envy you. Did he mention me at all, Bess?"

Lady Morse breezed in, saving her from a reply. Tea was ordered, with coffee for Vicky. After fortifying herself with a good amount of Empire fruit cake, Bess broached the subject of Joe Cooper's murder.

"Anything new happen here?"

The work for the memorial had begun and spirits were high in the village. The story of Joe Cooper's cowardice had slipped out and Richie was finally getting his due. Bess wondered if Nash was responsible for it. He was determined Joe Cooper would not receive an ounce of gratitude even in death.

Lady Morse reminded Pudding she had promised to visit a sick tenant. They all decided to accompany her. The weather was mild and the cool breeze provided some relief from the warm sun.

"How well do you know Constable Bright?" Bess asked Pudding. "I hope you are not in his bad books?"

Vicky told her about the earring and the plan they had devised to have a look at it. Pudding brightened when she learned about this piece of evidence.

"I can imagine Eileen doing it." She bobbed her head. "And Constable Bright dotes on me. He will never question anything I say."

Bess hoped the constable at Morse was as gullible as the one at Buxley. Vicky had her doubts. They could not pull the same stunt again and get away with it.

MURDER AT CASTLE MORSE

"Do we have to mention the Inspector?" she groaned. "He won't be pleased, Bess."

They went back to the castle and headed to the telephone in the hall. Bess and Vicky stood at either end of the passage to make sure they would not be interrupted. Pudding called the local police station and spoke to the constable, crossing her fingers behind her back.

"He's on his way," she beamed after she placed the receiver back in its cradle. "I would never have thought about this, Bess."

Lady Morse had been invited to lunch at Ridley Hall so she was conveniently out of the way. Annie would be there too so it promised to be a long visit.

They sat in the parlour, Bess glad Pudding stood at the window.

"He's here." Pudding picked up a magazine and began flipping it.

Norton announced the visitor and left them, his curiosity written plainly on his face. Constable Bright had a sheen of perspiration on his brow and clutched a small box to his side.

"I cycled as fast as I could, Miss Winifred." He looked around the room. "Is the Inspector not here yet?"

"DI Gardener just telephoned," Pudding replied. "He had some problem with his motor and will be a bit late."

Bess invited the constable to sit. He hesitated, perching on the edge of a chair with the box still balanced on his knees.

"I say, you must be parched."

Pudding rang for the maid. Norton arrived almost instantly, proving he had been loitering outside.

"Can we have some tea while we wait for the Inspector?"

Norton took in the dusty, sweaty form of the constable and grimaced, his revulsion clear.

"Right away, Miss. Constable Bright can have a cuppa in the kitchen."

Already conscious of his surroundings, the poor constable sprang up and dropped the box. Bess wasted no time in picking it up.

"I say, is this the evidence DI Gardener was talking about? We will take good care of it."

Constable Bright hesitated, then followed Norton out of the room, looking bemused.

"Quick!" Vicky cried as soon as the door closed. "Open it, Bess."

Pudding handed her a Swiss army knife she had purloined from her father's office in case they needed to pick the lock. But the box was open, providing them no little relief.

"Whew!" Pudding breathed, making Bess shrink back.

"Keep your mouth closed, old girl. You do realize how foul your breath is?"

Vicky rummaged through the box, crying out with triumph when something glittered in the light.

"Found it!" she held up an ornament three quarters of an inch in length. "Looks like gold."

Shaped like a leaf, embedded with a tiny pearl and rubies, the dangling earring was a beautiful piece of workmanship. Vicky pulled out her notebook and set about sketching it.

"Must be an heirloom."

Pudding thought it looked expensive.

"Not something Eileen might own."

MURDER AT CASTLE MORSE

The telephone in the hall rang, spurring them into action. Bess volunteered to answer it since Norton was below stairs.

"Castle Morse," she spoke into the receiver.

"Lady Bess?" a rich baritone that was all too familiar queried. "Are you up to your old tricks?"

Bess felt a thudding in her chest.

"Why Inspector. Good day to you too."

DI Gardener warned her to stay out of police business. "You better not be tampering with evidence. Scotland Yard takes this kind of thing very seriously, my lady."

Bess asked him about his investigation.

"Are you close to making an arrest yet?"

DI Gardener evaded the question and ordered her to release the poor constable. Bess replaced the receiver and rushed into the parlour.

"Game's up, girls. Let's put everything back like we found it."

Norton arrived with Constable Bright in tow.

"There has been a change," Pudding informed him. "The Inspector called. He won't be coming here after all. He has requested you go back to the police station."

Left to their own devices for lunch, the girls requested a picnic from Chef Henri. Two footmen lugged a basket between them and followed them to a copse by the river. Pudding directed them as they spread a blanket on the ground and set out the food.

"Eileen lives behind the butcher shop, doesn't she?" she asked the footmen.

One of them shrugged while the other looked almost fearful.

"That's where her brother lives with his family, Miss. Herself has a cottage yonder, on the hill behind the church."

Chef Henri had provided a roast chicken and crispy potatoes along with tasty salads and petit fours. The girls ate every bite with a fine French wine and dozed off, unable to keep their eyes open.

Vicky stirred a while later and shook the other two awake.

"What now?" she asked. "Are we going to confront Eileen?"

Bess thought she was daft.

"As if she will be honest with us! No, my dears, we have to visit her cottage and take a look for ourselves." She paused. "In her absence, of course."

Pudding balked at the idea.

"What if we are caught, Bess? Eileen is unpredictable enough on a good day. I dare not think what she will do."

Vicky brought up the Inspector.

"DI Gardener will probably arrest us."

While going back and forth over their course of action, Pudding mentioned she needed to attend a meeting for the onion festival.

"Won't Eileen be there too?" Bess pounced. "This is a golden opportunity, old girl. You go there and keep her busy. Vicky and I will go and look around her cottage."

The festival committee was meeting at the vicarage at 4 PM sharp. Not a single soul had ever dared to be late for it. Pudding assured them Eileen would be there on time.

"Miss Hastings will give us tea so you will have thirty minutes at the very least."

MURDER AT CASTLE MORSE

Finding Eileen's cottage did not prove difficult. It was clearly visible from the vicarage, sitting alone on top of a hillock dotted with sheep. Pudding wished them luck and went in while Bess and Vicky took a circuitous route up the hill, pretending to be interested in the foliage.

"If anyone asks, we are here for the view," Bess reminded Vicky.

Even up close, the cottage could hardly be called sprawling. The thatched roof was in good condition but the yellow stone walls had the patina of time. A wisteria grew over the door and a small vegetable patch was visible at the side.

The door was slightly ajar, making them wonder if Eileen was still inside. An aged terrier sat on the steps, soaking in the sun. He gave a tiny yelp when Bess stepped over him but did not stir. Vicky stopped to pet him, giving him a good rub behind the ears.

They entered a cozy room with a fireplace and ancient sofa. There was a kitchen with a small table and chair. A set of stone steps led to another room under the eaves. Bess headed to a chest of drawers and began pulling them open.

"This doesn't feel right." Vicky looked around. "We are violating her privacy, Bess."

"I say!" Bess brandished a tiny jewellery box and snapped it open. "Look, Vicky."

A single earring rested on a bed of velvet, along with a faded miniature and a folded paper. Vicky held it aloft and noted the design. It matched the one Constable Bright had in his possession.

Bess put everything back the way she had found it and they hurried out of the cottage, climbing down the hill at a different spot and taking the long way back to Castle Morse.

Norton had just served tea when Pudding arrived, bursting with curiosity and redolent of more onions.

"So? I made Eileen watch me eat an onion. She thinks the trick Sir Lawrence taught me has great promise. I might just win the contest."

Bess nudged her toward the farthest chair and asked her to focus.

"Oh Bessie, you are the cat's pyjamas!" she cried after she heard what they had found. "Now what?"

"Simple," Vicky grinned. "We inform the police."

It was not, Pudding argued. They could not say they had searched Eileen's cottage. Evening came with no solution. Bess went off to take a bath before dinner. Vicky was heading toward the library when she heard raised voices.

"You can ask me these bally questions a hundred times, Inspector." Richie sounded peeved. "But my answers will not change."

A door slammed and DI Gardener came out, furious. He was not pleased to see Vicky.

"And you! Stop interfering in police business. I am warning you, Bess."

Vicky gave a nod but did not correct him.

"Have you questioned Eileen Harris?" she folded her arms. "Earrings always come in pairs, Detective Inspector."

Chapter 21

The next two days were a trial of wits. As the onion festival approached, Pudding worked herself into a frenzy, eating as many as nine onions in a single day until she had blisters in her mouth and nobody could bear to be in the same room with her. Lady Morse sent her to bed and called the doctor.

"There's nothing wrong with me, Mama," she insisted.

Bess and Vicky were stoic, waiting on tenterhooks for an update from DI Gardener. They had almost made up their minds to confront him when he telephoned the night before the onion festival. Norton had just announced dinner. Bess excused herself and almost ran into the hall, tugging Vicky along with her. They were in for a disappointment.

"You are barking up the wrong tree, Lady Bess." He sounded disheartened. "The police went through Eileen's cottage and found nothing incriminating." He cleared his throat. "We did find a pair of earrings in a box."

"A pair, did you say?" Bess cried. "But that is impossible."

The Inspector warned her to consider what she said next.

"You are a loyal friend, my lady. Richard Morse is fortunate to have you in his corner."

Somehow, Eileen had managed to have a duplicate made before the police searched her cottage. Bess chewed her lip, trying to control her anger as they entered the dining room and took their seats. She would not let Eileen outwit her much longer.

Breakfast was rushed next morning, the entire family eager to go to the village green for the festival. The servants had the afternoon off. Like every year, Lord Morse inaugurated the onion festival amidst a lot of pomp.

The Ridleys arrived with Sir Lawrence. Pudding squealed in a most unladylike manner and rushed to greet him.

"You came!" She shook hands with him and 303. "I fear you may be in for a disappointment though."

"Never." Sir Lawrence was fervent. "Takes guts to do something new, my dear."

Lady Morse accompanied the Ridleys who were busy looking down their noses, disparaging everything. Bess guessed they had come just to appease their guest.

Lord Morse gave out prizes for everything from the biggest marrow to the best pie. Finally, it was time for the onion eating contest.

Pudding took her place with the rest of the contestants, regal as a queen. Vicky admired her grit. Every contestant was handed a raw onion weighing a quarter of a pound. Someone fired a pistol and they set off, biting and chewing while the crowd cheered. Eileen finished first, breaking her own previous record. Pudding came in last.

"Bravo! Good show!" The group from the castle cheered and patted her on the back.

"You do know I lost, Papa!" she moaned. "Maybe if I practice more, I can win next year."

Lord Morse shuddered as he held her close.

"My dear, not a single Morse has dared to compete in that contest until now. But I beg of you, no more."

Pudding joined in the laughter that followed, admitting she never wanted to eat onions again.

Eileen was strutting around with her little trophy, reminding everyone she had won again. Vicky thought she looked pretty and vulnerable and found it hard to believe she was a killer. The earrings she wore glittered and it was clear she was wearing two of them.

"I have an idea, Bess. Do you know of any jewellers in the area?"

"Where one can commission a piece of jewellery." She thumped Vicky on the back. "You are the bee's knees."

Newman's in Chipping Woodbury was known for their unique designs and filigree work. It had been around for three centuries and the artisans they employed had been with them for generations. Bess proposed they leave immediately. Pudding declined. She was going for a drive with Sir Lawrence.

"It's just us." Vicky sighed with relief.

The weather was fair and the drive to the town pleasant. The chauffer stopped at the mouth of a narrow lane, saying he could not go further. Bess told him to park the car somewhere and have a pint.

A stunning array of jewels was displayed in the shop's window, made up of a variety of gemstones. Bess looked at Vicky.

"We should have matching pendants made," she smiled.

They walked into the shop and asked to look at some designs. The clerk recognized Bess and bowed.

"Mr. Newman will be with you in a minute."

A short, plump man with a full head of white hair was busy talking to another customer. He was equally short, dressed in riding clothes, possessed of a set of broad shoulders.

"What ho, Richie!" Bess slapped him on the back. "Fancy meeting you here."

He turned around, looking gobsmacked.

"I say, Bess, err ... what, what? What are you doing here?"

Vicky told him they wanted to buy some new jewellery.

"Of course!" Richie stood up straighter. "That is exactly why I am here. Mama's birthday is coming up, you know."

He gave Mr. Newman a nod. "Thank you, Mr. Newman. I will be in touch." He gave Bess a playful tug on her sleeve. "See you at home then."

The door closed behind him and opened again.

"Oh, by the way, Bess. Do you remember those flowers I smelt by the stables? Someone must have brought them to the festival. Lilies, I dare say."

Mr. Newman greeted them and asked how he might be of service.

"This is my twin, Mr. Newman." Bess introduced him to Vicky. "Perhaps some matching pendants?"

The old man welcomed Vicky with a twinkle in his eye and told them about two gold chains the Dowager had commissioned at their birth.

"How is your grandmother?" he asked. "Indomitable as ever, I dare say."

Bess told him he was right. They discussed the merits of pearls over diamonds and emeralds over rubies and perused a catalogue of designs. They did not have trouble choosing one and placed an order immediately. Bess broached the matter of the earring.

"We came across a peculiar pattern in an earring, Mr. Newman. I wonder if it was made by you."

MURDER AT CASTLE MORSE

Vicky described it, pulling out her notebook at the last moment to show him the sketch. Mr. Newman did not disappoint.

"It is one of our designs, my lady. Almost a hundred years old, actually. I remember because we recently received an order for only one of these."

A young lady found a single earring in her dead mother's things. She had wanted the complete pair. Mr. Newman pointed out the nuances of the design, bragging about the fine etching in the gold.

"You are sure this is not available anywhere else?" Bess poked.

A duplicate could be attempted, Mr. Newman agreed, but it would be impossible to have an exact match. The technique used in the etching was the trademark of a certain family of artisans. Newman's employed him.

Bess thanked him and fixed a time to come back for the pendant.

"Please don't trouble yourself, my lady. I will send them to the manor once they are ready."

Bess felt they had finally made some progress.

"Good work," Vicky nodded. "Shall we get a bite to eat? We can go to the Laughing Dog."

"Laughing Mongrel, you mean." Bess placed a hand on her stomach. "Let's go, old girl."

They walked to the pub and were greeted by the proprietor who was the younger brother of their housekeeper Mrs. Jones.

"Lady Bess!" he cried. "You are a sight for sore eyes. That fancy Frenchie has you in his clutches."

Bess and Vicky laughed, not surprised by his claim.

"Not quite, my man. I have been dreaming of a good sausage. But please, no onion gravy today."

They bagged a table and looked around. A couple huddled at a window, engrossed in an intense discussion. Their voices reached Bess.

"Is that Ballard?" she peered into the dim light. "Yes. And that vulgar woman he brought to dinner with him."

Vicky surmised it must be the assistant. She thought of what Ballard's students had suggested.

"They really are an item, Bess," she murmured.

"As long as they stay in their corner. I do not have the capacity for any more small talk."

The sausages arrived, slightly burnt at the edges, resting on a mound of creamy potatoes, smelling delicious. Jones set a pot of rich gravy before them, promising them it did not contain any onions.

Vicky poured it over her food and tasted it.

"I think this trumps the onion gravy, Bess."

Neither spoke until they had made a significant dent in the food. A shadow fell over the table, prompting Bess to look up. She could not hide her shock.

"I say! What are you doing here, Eileen?"

The fine hair on her arm stood up as she realized she might be facing a murderer.

Eileen waved her hand at a large group seated a few tables over, comprising of half a dozen rambunctious children. Their facial features clearly indicated they were part of the Harris clan.

"We are having a celebration." Eileen grew more imposing before their eyes. "I won the onion festival for the 15th year in a row. And a new record!" She roared with laughter. "Poor Miss Morse. She tried hard. I will give her that."

Vicky congratulated her. "We never thought she would beat the reigning champion." She pointed at Eileen's ear. "You look pretty wearing these."

"Belonged to my Ma," Eileen sighed. "And her Ma before that. I wear them on special occasions."

They resumed eating while Eileen invited herself to sit and gave them a minute by minute account of the onion eating contest.

"We know, old girl." Bess sat back in her chair. "We were there."

One of the Harrises hailed Eileen and she finally stood up to leave, turning around and slamming into Stephen Ballard.

"Here now." He lashed out. "Are you blind?"

Eileen flexed her shoulders and opened her mouth. Bess braced herself to witness a brawl. But Eileen smoothed her features, flashed a smile and left without a word.

"Insufferable woman," Ballard muttered under his breath, going back to his table.

"Did he not see us?" Vicky frowned. "That man is so crude."

Bess agreed. Maybe it wasn't a good idea inviting him to dig at Buxley.

They said goodbye to Jones and his family and dragged their feet to the car, dozing on the way back to the castle. The Morses were assembled in the parlour and Sir Lawrence could be heard narrating yet another escapade.

Bess felt a rumble in her stomach.

"I say," she whispered. "We better go up."

Vicky admitted she was a bit queasy.

They sneaked past the parlour and ran up the steps, reaching the bathroom just in time. Half an hour later, they lay on the bed, exhausted. Both had been sick multiple times.

"You think we ate too much?" Bess groaned.

Vicky rang for the maid and asked for lemonade with plenty of sugar and salt. Pudding came in, bursting with news, shocked to see their pale faces.

"I say! What's wrong? You are white as a sheet, Bess."

She rushed out to report to Lady Morse who in turn called the doctor. Worried about her friend, Pudding hurried back to her room.

"Don't fuss," Bess groaned. "It's nothing."

Vicky was quiet. The doctor confirmed her suspicion after he examined them.

"I believe you have suffered from food poisoning, my lady." He pinned a thoughtful gaze on them. "Something you ate at the onion festival, perhaps? I must prepare myself for more patients, if that is the case."

Bess shook her head.

"But I have eaten at The Laughing Mongrel for yonks. Jones would never serve food that has gone bad."

The doctor, himself a patron of the famous pub, agreed with her.

"Maybe an errant mushroom? I will be frank, my dear. You have had a close call. I am ordering complete bed rest for the next three days. Plenty of broth and rest."

Beth protested in vain. Vicky assured the doctor they would comply.

"Say what you will," Bess argued after he left. "I refuse to believe Jones served bad food."

Pudding had been watching everything from her seat in the window. She jumped down, looking stricken.

"Good Lord, Bess. Do you mean someone just tried to kill you?"

Chapter 22

Bess and Vicky didn't have the energy to leave their bed. The doctor came to check on them twice a day. Lady Morse felt it was her duty to call Buxley Manor and apprise Clementine about the twins' ill health. A gaggle of women descended on Castle Morse the next morning, comprising of Clementine, Momo, Bubbles and Annie. Nigel had given them strict orders to bring the girls home.

"Mama sends her love," Clementine told Bess and Vicky. "And this note."

Vicky smiled as she skimmed through the note. The Nightingales wanted them to stay hot on the trail of the killer. It was obvious they were close to cracking the case.

"I hope Mama advises caution?" Clementine pursed her mouth.

"Something like that, Aunt Clem," Vicky agreed. "Why are you all here, Mom?" she turned toward Annie. "Why all the fuss?"

Lady Morse was apologetic.

"Clive and I feel responsible. He is talking to that Scotland Yard man right now, giving him a talking to."

"DI Gardener is here?" Bess croaked. "But why?"

Pudding had been less than discreet. She told her parents everything, spurring them into action.

"My dear, you have done enough. Now the police need to try harder to catch this culprit."

Annie was of the same opinion.

MURDER AT CASTLE MORSE

"You are coming home with us now, girls. Nigel is terrified. He told me about your accident, Vicky." She was stern. "The same one you told me nothing about."

There was a knock on the door. Lord Morse came in, accompanied by DI Gardener.

"Shall we go down and have some tea, ladies? The Inspector would like to speak with these two."

Clementine bristled with indignation. "That is highly improper. I cannot leave them unchaperoned with a single man."

The Inspector turned on his charm.

"I promise I will curb all my baser instincts, my lady."

His demeanour changed after the room emptied. Bess watched him shut the door and pace the floor, hands clasped behind his back. She folded her arms, prepared for an onslaught.

"What on earth were you thinking?" He came to a stop before her. "And you?" he whirled and faced Vicky. "I thought you had more sense but I was obviously mistaken."

Bess was not going to take these insults lying down.

"I say! What have we done wrong, exactly? Just had a meal in a pub I have eaten in dozens of times."

"It's what you did before you went there."

Vicky sided with Bess.

"You are being unfair, Inspector. Would you rather not go and arrest Eileen Harris?"

"Is this the same Eileen Harris whose cottage was searched based on your insistence?" He clucked. "She is already claiming police harassment."

Bess outlined her theory about Eileen and her motive. Plus she had sat at their table at the Laughing Mongrel and could easily have slipped something in their food. Vicky told him about their visit to Newman's.

"Have you made inquiries there, Inspector?" she asked. "We believe Eileen lost her earring in the stables when she killed Joe Cooper. She had a second one made after that, just so she could claim she has the pair."

James Gardener held up his hand, his face dark.

"Stop right there. Do you think Scotland Yard is at your beck and call? I warned you to stop meddling in my case. What if you had succumbed to this poison? Sir Edward would have my head on a platter."

"So you do agree this was an attack?" Bess pounced. "That means we are getting close."

James seethed in frustration.

"Don't you value your life at all?"

Bess told him she believed in Richie's innocence.

"I have given my word to Pudding. You might be used to having several cases unsolved but this is a man's future we are talking about. My family knows what it is like, living with a sword hanging over your head. Why, Papa still can't hold his head high in the village even though he never harmed Philip."

James uttered a string of curses under his breath.

"Will you promise to stay put if the police go and question Eileen Harris?" He wrung a hand through his hair. "I hope I don't regret this, Bess."

There was a stunned silence after he slammed the door behind him.

"That was harsh," Vicky giggled and burst out laughing.

Bess joined in.

"He's a good sport. But he's right, old girl. We are terrible."

Pudding bounced in, bearing more news. The doctor had arrived and met the contingent from Buxley Manor.

"You are to stay here one more day, after which Papa will personally escort you back to Buxley. He is raving mad, by the way."

Bess was hungry. She cajoled Pudding into going to the kitchen and filching something for them.

"Real, solid food, okay?" Vicky urged. "I can't bear to look at broth or gruel."

Pudding obliged them by being a loyal friend and they spent a few hours playing cards, munching on the assorted titbits she had managed to steal from the larder. Finally, Vicky's eyelids began to droop and Pudding announced she had to leave.

"Will you come down to dinner?"

Bess did not think so. She guessed what Pudding was up to but refrained from asking anything.

The nap refreshed them, making them long for more food. Lady Morse sent dry toast with tea.

"We are falling behind in our other mission," Bess reminded Vicky. "All we have learned is Philip hated French food, which sounds irrelevant since he met his death falling off a horse."

"Sir Lawrence seemed to be really close to him," Vicky mused. "I wonder ... do you think Philip might have gone to Africa to hunt big game?"

Bess thought he would be the worst kind of cad if he did that.

"Momo was expecting their child. Considering how much the villagers idolized him, Philip would not leave his wife in a delicate condition and go haring off to another continent."

Vicky sat up. "What if Sir Lawrence felt betrayed?"

Bess ridiculed the idea. One Eye Watkins might have killed a thousand lions but he was not the violent sort.

"He was here for the hunt, wasn't he?" Vicky challenged. "Who was he riding with? Where was he when Philip died?"

Bess got caught up in her excitement.

"We should talk to Papa about this."

The dressing bell rang. Bess pondered joining others in the dining room.

"They will not send us back, will they?" she sighed. "Oh well, let's hope Chef Henri takes pity on us."

A maid arrived a few minutes later with their dinner.

"Not bad." Bess eyed the boiled chicken, mashed carrots and rice pudding and picked up her fork.

A loud banging began downstairs. A whistle blew and several boots could be heard thundering through the hall below.

"I say!" Bess flung her napkin and ran out on the landing, forgetting she was wearing her nightgown.

Vicky pulled her back but they stood still, amazed at the drama unfolding below.

DI Gardener led a group of policemen who held a squirming Richie. They handcuffed him and began leading him out.

"What in blazes is the meaning of this?" Lord Morse thundered. "You are about to lose your job, Inspector."

MURDER AT CASTLE MORSE

James glanced up at the spot where Bess had been. She could see he was distressed.

"I beg your pardon, Lord Morse. But there is overwhelming evidence against your son. I have to arrest him for the murders of Joe Cooper and Eileen Harris."

Bess and Vicky sucked in a collective breath, shocked to hear Eileen was dead.

The police left with Richie, leaving Lord Morse staring at their backs. Chaos ensued after that. Bess and Vicky ran down without caring about their attire. Lady Morse had swooned and Pudding was fanning her face while Norton fetched some smelling salts.

Dinner was put off and tea was ordered. The telephone rang. DI Gardener wanted to talk to Bess. She came back, looking puzzled.

"Richie paid for the earring," she mumbled. "We did see him at Newman's."

Lord and Lady Morse grew quiet when Vicky explained what Bess was talking about.

"Don't you see?" Pudding cried. "Richie was just being nice. He probably took pity on Eileen and paid for the new earring."

Bess shook her head.

"The police think Richie and Eileen colluded to kill Joe Cooper. Eileen got cold feet when the police searched her cottage and was planning to squeal. So Richie silenced her."

That was the prevailing theory, at least.

"My poor boy!" Lady Morse wailed. "He is a war hero, you know."

Neville surprised them by getting up and leaving the room. Lord Morse thought they should all go to bed. Nothing more could be achieved that night.

Morning arrived with a telephone call from Buxley. Nigel was on his way to pick up his girls.

"You won't give up on Richie?" Pudding was teary eyed as she said goodbye.

"As long as he is innocent," Vicky promised.

Lady Morse invited Nigel to come in and have breakfast but he declined.

"Time I took them home." He was polite but firm. "They have imposed on you long enough."

The drive home was conducted in silence. None of them wanted to get into a heated discussion in front of the chauffer. Bess leaned against Nigel's shoulder and fell asleep.

"I'm glad you came, Papa," she whispered.

Annie stood on the top step at Buxley Manor, next to Barnes. Her shoulders slumped in relief when Vicky stepped out of the car and ran up to embrace her.

Bess felt a flutter in her heart but stayed put.

Breakfast was in full swing and Clementine welcomed them home, insisting on filling their plates from the buffet. She handed Bess one loaded with kedgeree and asked Norton for a fresh pot of Darjeeling.

"Railway Mutton Curry for lunch," she assured her. "And bread and butter pudding with blackberry jam. You must have missed Mrs. Bird's cooking."

Bess felt her eyes grow moist, realizing she had missed her oddball family. She scarfed down the kedgeree, letting Bubbles regale her with the latest gossip, feeding bits of bacon to Polo under the table. All the eyes in the room gazed at them with varying expressions.

"Papa, we are fine!" she exclaimed. "Momo, Bubbles, Aunt Clem, Annie!"

"Nothing happened," Vicky nodded. "We are both fit as a fiddle."

Louise and the aunts had summoned them. After several more assurances to the members around the table, Bess and Vicky headed to the west wing.

"What ho, Grandmother!" Bess hailed. "Aunt Hortense. Aunt Perpetua. We are back."

"And not a moment too soon." Louise sounded hoarse. "We are ill equipped to handle shocks at our age."

Bess remembered what her note had said and smiled.

"We love you too, Grandma!" Vicky laughed. "And we missed all of you."

"American." Hortense gave a snort.

"Are you done acting like cry babies?" Perpetua demanded, rubbing her mole. "Tell us about the case."

Vicky and Bess took turns, giving them a first hand account of what had befallen them. Louise and the aunts shared a knowing glance.

"Do you still believe Richard Morse is innocent?" Hortense asked.

Vicky thought Nash was a viable suspect. Eileen had seen him near the stables on the day Joe died. She might have mentioned that to someone in the village. Nash found out and decided to silence her.

"Let's not forget the earring." Bess was quiet. "Eileen did get a new one made, proving she dropped one in the stables."

Louise was thoughtful.

"All that means is Eileen went to the stables for some reason, presumably to meet Joe Cooper. But he might have been alive when she left."

Vicky felt a weight settle on her chest. She felt Bess move closer to her and realized she was thinking the same.

"Are we responsible for Eileen's death?"

Chapter 23

Nigel put his foot down. His girls needed to spend a few days at home before rushing off to Castle Morse again. Bess guessed he was trying to create situations where she would have to talk to Annie. But she wasn't ready for that yet.

Bess and Vicky sat in the Buxley Arms one afternoon, at a loose end. The Nightingales had gone over everything several times, not very excited about the options. Nothing more could be done unless they went back to the castle.

"I am bored." Bess stifled a yawn. "Do you fancy a ride, old bean?"

Vicky shook her head. She was listless, thinking about her future as a doctor. The road ahead would not be easy.

"You are strong enough, Vicky. This is not the time to doubt yourself."

The autumn sun was hugging the horizon and a steady stream of farm workers began, eager to get off their feet and indulge in their daily pint. Bess did not notice the buzz around them until it grew in magnitude and turned into an uproar. Mrs. Harvey, the proprietor's wife, came to check on them.

"You sure you don't want anything more, ladies?"

"What's all this fuss?" Vicky asked, causing her to press her lips together and shake her head.

Bess asked for a pot of tea. The Buxley Arms did not serve coffee so Vicky would have to go without.

Harvey himself arrived some time later, looking apologetic.

"Don't mind them, my lady. A bunch of fools they are. Don't know which side their bread is buttered."

Bess had finally picked up some snatches of conversation and knew they were talking about Philip's death.

"Not that same palaver again!" she sighed and stood up.

A sudden hush fell as Bess put two fingers in her mouth and gave a piercing whistle.

"Listen up. My Papa had nothing to do with Philip's death and I am going to prove it. Anyone who does not believe in Lord Buxley's innocence can start looking for another place to live."

The crowd was silent for a minute or two, then everyone began talking again. Harvey stood by their table, a frown on his face.

"It's that hunter from Africa, my lady," he muttered. "He done riled everyone up."

One Eye Watkins had always cut a dashing figure wherever he went. Some of the older men remembered him well and asked why he had not visited for so many years. He told them Buxley held no appeal for him once Philip was gone.

"He's asking questions about that day," Harvey explained. "Wants to know if anyone saw Lord Philip, who he was with and what not. Set tongues wagging."

Bess could feel her ears turn warm. Her lip quivered as Sir Lawrence's face swam before her eyes. Vicky placed a hand on hers, silently urging her to calm down.

Harvey was not done. His voice dropped as he leaned toward them.

"Wants to know where Lord Buxley, I mean, your father was. Men in the village are going around asking if anyone remembers seeing him."

"And do they?" Vicky was hopeful.

Maybe they would unearth some vital information from all this. But Harvey shook his head. Not a single person in the village had come across Nigel that day.

Bess thanked him and stood up to leave. Many of the men doffed their hats out of habit. Others glared at them through hooded eyes.

Vicky clutched the car door as Bess pressed her foot down on the accelerator and headed to Buxley Manor. Barnes greeted them at the door and merely raised an eyebrow when Bess stalked past him without a word.

Vicky muttered a quick apology and ran after her. They traversed the passage and headed to Nigel's study, Bess coming to a stop all of a sudden, causing Vicky to slam into her. They stared in unison at the short, stocky figure coming out of the door, dressed in a safari suit. Vicky grabbed Bess's arm, urging her to be quiet.

"Hello, my dears." Sir Lawrence nodded at them and walked away.

Bess barged into the study and looked around for Nigel. He stood with his back to them, staring out of the window. Polo was running circles around him, barking madly.

"Papa!" Bess cried and rushed toward him. "What was that buffoon doing here?"

"What did he say?" Vicky added, giving in to the tension in the room.

Nigel's dismay was evident. He let Bess lead him to a chair by the fire, startled to see Annie on the sofa, her expression stony.

"Mom?" Vicky cried, noting her cold eyes. "Tell us what that vile man said."

Nigel cleared his throat, trying to get a grip.

"Sir Lawrence deserves some respect, my dear."

"He bally well doesn't!" Bess roared. "Do you have any idea what he has been up to, Papa?"

Nigel gave her a helpless look.

"He wants me to confess, girls. Appealed to my sense of honour as an earl. Asked me to do the right thing."

Annie began pacing the room. Nigel's eyes followed her, growing more desperate by the second.

Vicky took her mother's arm and forced her to sit.

"You will do no such thing, Papa." Bess swore under her breath. "I hope you won't let that scoundrel influence you."

Vicky urged her to be quiet.

"Relax, everyone," she soothed. "He's just shaking the tree, hoping something will fall out."

Nigel apologized to Annie. Nothing had changed in twenty years. He wouldn't blame her if she wanted to turn tail and go back to America.

There was a knock on the door. Clementine breezed in, a vapid smile on her face.

"That Sir Lawrence! He is a force to reckon with, even with one eye."

Bess glared at her. "Stop consorting with the enemy, Aunt Clem."

Nigel gave his sister a brief account of what had transpired.

"I think someone has it in for you, Nigel. That's why they keep stirring up this old business."

Dinner was morose, with everyone picking at their food. There were no guests for a change, saving them the need to make small talk.

MURDER AT CASTLE MORSE

Bess woke early the next morning and went for an early ride. The leaves were beginning to turn and the air was cool, a welcome change after the long summer. She emptied her mind of all thought and focused on galloping across the verdant acres. Breakfast brought kedgeree, managing to cheer her a bit. Bubbles proposed taking the midmorning train to London to have lunch at the Savoy.

"Why don't you come too, Annie?" Her smile held mischief. "Just like old times."

Barnes arrived with a message for Bess.

"You are wanted on the telephone, my lady."

It was Pudding and she was bursting with new information.

"I say, Bess!" she cried. "When are you coming back?"

"We are all going up to London. Why don't you come too?"

Pudding told her London could wait. Something remarkable had happened.

"You know how Papa likes to invite people for dinner?" She didn't wait for a response. "Well, the vicar was here again last night, with his sister. And so were Ballard and that sour puss partner of his." She giggled. "Sir Lawrence was here too."

Bess told her to move on.

"Are you telling the story or I am? I will not be rushed, Bessie." She muttered a few more things before going ahead. "Well, Nash had been working late with Papa so he also stayed. Miss Hastings, the vicar's sister, told him she saw him going up the hill behind the vicarage."

"Isn't that where Eileen lives?" Bess caught on right away. "Why was he going there?"

That is exactly what Miss Hastings had wanted to know but he was not going to be gossip fodder. He denied being anywhere in the area, assuming she had mistaken him for someone else.

"She pointed at his arm," Pudding gushed. "Actually pointed at the missing arm and said there was no way she would not recognize him."

Alfred Nash had stuck to his guns, turning the whole meal into an awkward affair.

"Mama was not pleased, I tell you," Pudding spat.

Bess let her prattle on, scarcely hearing a word more. Eileen's cottage was situated on the hill behind the vicarage. Of course, Nash could just have been taking a walk. She realized the line was dead and went back to the parlour.

"Change of plan, Bubbles. Vicky and I have to go to Morse."

"You are such a bore, Bess." Bubbles gave a pout. "Just when Momo finally agreed to take a look at my flat."

Vicky told her they could still go ahead with their plans. The group broke up, heading in opposite directions.

Bess brought Vicky up to speed on the drive to Buxley.

"Let's corner him right away."

Lunch was in progress when they reached Castle Morse.

"Oh, you are here." Pudding greeted them.

Lady Morse insisted they eat first.

"You might have let me know, my dear," she rebuked her daughter. "At least it's just us girls."

Richie and Lord Morse were meeting some people on the estate. The police had let him go after DI Gardener admitted the evidence they had against him was flimsy at best.

MURDER AT CASTLE MORSE

Famished after their journey, Bess and Vicky enjoyed the delicious meal. Pudding declared she was going on a drive.

"I have been cooped up here for days, Bess. Some fresh air is what I need."

Vicky and Bess went in search of Nash. He was in the tiny room that served as his office, staring in space. A plate of food sat before him, untouched.

"What ho, Mr. Nash." Bess invited herself in.

"Lady Bess, Lady Vicky." He looked dazed. "How can I help you?"

Bess got straight to the point and asked him why he was at Eileen's cottage. He was so shocked he didn't deny it.

"We know you hated Joe Cooper," Vicky began gently. "What he did to you was unforgivable. Seeing him every day must have been brutal."

"I don't blame you for losing your temper and doing away with him," Bess added. "But Eileen? She was an innocent."

Nash had turned white as he listened to them.

"What are you saying, my lady? I told you I did not hurt Joe Cooper."

Vicky told him he could stop hiding. Eileen had seen him near the stables that day, putting him right at the scene of the crime.

"Is that why you killed her?"

To their consternation, Alfred Nash burst into tears.

"Why would I kill her? I was in love with her."

Bess and Vicky stared at each other, their mouths hanging open.

"I say ... did Eileen know?"

Nash was several years older than Eileen and had not spared her a look when he went off to war. But he had come to know her through the letters she wrote her brother. Then the Morse 13 came back and everyone expected Joe and Eileen to get married. He had seen how devastated she was when Joe declined.

"She ran the butcher shop on her own." His admiration for her shone through. "Took care of the family through the war years. I began to like her, Lady Bess."

He had been working up his courage, wondering if she would even entertain him.

"She is everything I am not." He glanced at his missing arm. "Was, I mean."

Bess asked what he was doing on the hill. He replied he was hoping to run into her and strike up a conversation. But he had lost his nerve before he reached there and turned back.

"Did anyone in the village hold a grudge against her?" Vicky asked.

Alfred didn't think so. She was a bit rough around the edges but had a kind heart. Many a struggling family in the village were grateful for the odd ham bone she set aside for them.

"What was she doing by the stables?" he wondered. "If she saw me, she might have come across Joe's killer."

Chapter 24

Bess stood at Sindbad's stall in the stables at Castle Morse. It had a battered leather sofa at one end. Richie would often be found there, chatting with his prized horse. Sometimes he even spent the night. What had Joe Cooper been doing there? Sindbad was already dead and the stall had been left empty on Richie's orders.

"He wasn't the emotional type," she mused. "Why do you think he came here that morning, Vicky?"

They took a circuitous route back to the castle, looking forward to tea. Bess was longing for the macarons Chef Henri baked fresh every day. Lord Morse and Richie were back but Pudding was nowhere in sight.

"Isn't she with you, Bess?" Lady Morse asked.

The butler ushered in a maid carrying platters of cucumber sandwiches and fruit cake. Lord Morse rubbed his hands and accepted the plate his wife handed him.

They were half way through tea when Pudding arrived, looking flushed.

"Where have you been, young lady?" Lady Morse wrinkled her nose in disapproval. "It's not like you to be late for tea."

Bess was familiar with the dreamy expression in her friend's eyes. She gave Vicky a nudge and sat back for the explosion.

"Will you visit me in Africa, Mama?" Pudding took a sip of tea. "They say it's just glorious, warm all the year round."

Lord Morse sported a bemused expression. "What on earth do you mean, my dear? Are you planning to run away?"

Pudding lowered her eyes and giggled. She told them she was getting married.

"We might come to England every few years but I think we will make our home in Africa. In the Happy Valley, perhaps. I am not really sure where."

Bess noted the alarm on Lady Morse's face and finally stepped in.

"I say, Pudding, old thing. What are you going on about?"

"My life after marriage, of course." Pudding was surprised. "I will be Lady Watkins. Doesn't that sound grand? Of course, we will travel around Africa, depending on the commissions he gets."

"Lady what …" Lord Morse sputtered and turned to Bess. "What kind of horseplay is this?"

Bess assured him she was not involved. Lord Morse wasn't convinced.

"You are too old for silly pranks, my dears. When will you get serious about your future?"

Pudding told him that's exactly what she was talking about.

"I suspect Sir Lawrence will ask for your blessing soon, Papa."

Lady Morse started laughing. Everyone joined in. Pudding stomped out of the room in high dudgeon.

"Did you put her up to this, Bess?" Richie asked, reaching for a slice of cake.

Bess told them Pudding was serious.

"She believes she is in love with Sir Lawrence. We need to keep an eye on her."

The evening stretched before them. Vicky suggested going up to Eileen's cottage to have a look around.

MURDER AT CASTLE MORSE

"Why didn't I think of that?" Bess agreed readily.

Pudding was nowhere to be found so the twins set off on their own. They ran into Miss Hastings outside the church and had to stay and listen to her talk for a while. Vicky finally put a hand on her arm and said goodbye.

"Funny thing." Miss Hastings narrowed her eyes. "I saw Miss Winifred drive by some time ago. Isn't she looking after you, my dears?"

Bess told her Pudding was on a mission for her mother.

"Morse is my second home," she assured the woman. "We are meeting her for dinner later."

They finally extricated themselves from the woman's clutches and started climbing the hill. Halfway up the hill, Bess realized she did not have a key. They would have to be creative about getting in.

Vicky nodded and crossed her fingers, hoping the door would be open and they would not need to break it down. Neither of them expected the sentry at the door. He was dressed as a constable but was not familiar.

"Hello!" Bess called out. "Are you new here?"

He introduced himself. He was there from Chipping Woodbury on special duty. Bess talked about a scarf she had lent Eileen. Could they look around inside and take it back?

He was not as gullible as he seemed.

"DI Gardener warned me about you, my lady. I am not to let anyone in, on any account."

Bess fluttered her eyes.

"Oh please, Seargent. We are going to this party in London and I simply have to have that scarf. It's the only thing that goes with my new frock. Be a darling and let me get it, please."

Vicky folded her hands and joined in.

"She's in love with this Marquess. He is about to get engaged and this is her last chance to impress him."

"Have you ever been in love?" Bess gave a deep sigh. "You will be helping two lonely hearts unite."

The poor sentry was helpless against this onslaught of feminine wiles. He was about to back down when they heard the roar of an engine climbing up the hill. Bess gave a groan as a red Hispano Suiza came into view.

"Here is the Detective Inspector." The young sentry looked relieved. "You can ask him yourself, my lady."

James crooked a finger in their direction, summoning them. Vicky greeted him with a smile.

"Hello Detective. Do you have any new leads?"

He wished her a good evening and directed a stern glance at Bess.

"Are you done harassing the poor boy? What faradiddle have you supplied this time?"

Bess decided to be nice. What was the harm in letting them have a look around, she asked? Surely the police had already searched the tiny cottage from top to bottom.

"That's right." James was firm. "And we found nothing. So why don't you save yourself the trouble?"

Vicky agreed with him and pulled Bess along with her. They would be late for dinner if they didn't hurry.

"Listen to your sister, Lady Bess." James winked. "And think twice before you interfere in a police investigation."

Bess could barely hold her temper as they chose their steps down the hill.

"Why did you give in so easily?" she snapped at Vicky. "Whose side are you on?"

"No point getting his dander up. We can always go back."

Bess began to make plans. She hoped Pudding would be back and in a better mood. They needed someone to keep a watch while they rifled through the cottage. She saw a familiar car pull in just when they reached the castle. The Ridleys stepped out, accompanied by their esteemed guest.

"That insufferable brute!"

Vicky reminded her they were guests too and needed to behave in a decent manner. So asking for a tray in their room was not an option.

"Let's just hope we are seated far away from him," Bess muttered.

"Isn't this what they prepare you for in a finishing school?" Vicky asked.

Bess reminded her she had not even finished boarding school, running away to join the war at sixteen. But she had grown up under Aunt Clem's watchful eye.

"I can behave myself for one meal."

Pudding was coming out of the bath when they reached the second floor landing. She wore a red silk robe with a dragon painted on it and smelled of roses.

"I heard a car," she gushed. "Is he here already?" There was a note of panic in her voice.

Bess told her to relax. They had ample time to dress and primp before drinks were served. She told Pudding about the excursion planned for that night.

"Are you game, old bean? You wanted to liven things up a bit."

"Sure thing. You can count on me, Bess. Now hurry up and put on a nice frock. I am parched."

Richie was mixing cocktails when they went down to the parlour. He handed Bess a pink fizzy drink garnished with sprigs of rosemary. The men were huddled together at one end of the room, leaving Pudding no choice but to stick to the twins.

"I will knock on your door at midnight," Bess whispered.

Dinner passed without any incident. Richie played records on the gramophone and the group broke up after tea was served.

Bess opted to stay awake for the first hour. Vicky closed her eyes and fell fast asleep. She sat up at eleven and promised to alert Bess at midnight. They were dressed in dark clothes and ready to leave on time, carrying torches and wearing rubber soled boots.

"Let's get Pudding," Bess whispered.

A knock on her door yielded no response. They waited for a few minutes and gave up, thinking she must be fast asleep.

Bess did not dare to start her car for fear of waking someone up so they walked to the village. The moon provided just enough light and they did not encounter anyone, the pub having closed hours ago. By the time they climbed the hill to Eileen's cottage, they were both panting with the exertion.

"I say," Bess groaned. "Aren't you hungry?"

Vicky produced a bar of chocolate. She broke it in two and handed a part to Bess. They tiptoed into the cottage, whispering in the dark until Bess suddenly laughed out loud.

"We can talk. There's no one here, old girl."

MURDER AT CASTLE MORSE

Vicky lifted the lid of a battered chest and began pulling out some clothes. Eileen had few possessions. There was a box of keepsakes containing an old letter, a faded photograph and a dried flower. Vicky marvelled at how anyone could get by with so little.

Bess was busy opening pots in the makeshift kitchen. Neither heard the door open. A loose floorboard creaked, alerting them. Vicky flattened herself against the wall, hoping Bess was doing the same. It was pitch dark since they had not switched on their torches.

Someone was in the cottage, flinging things around. Clearly, this person was not exercising any caution. Vicky held her breath, feeling her pulse race. She knew the intruder could not hear the thudding of her heart but she could not help being afraid. There was a cry of pain and an exclamation followed by a big thud. Something landed inches from her feet. Vicky froze, unable to move. She almost cried out when a hand clutched her arm and pulled her. Then she recognized Bess and allowed her to drag her away. Two minutes later, they were out of the cottage and fleeing down the hill.

"What just happened?" Vicky stopped half way down to catch her breath. "Hold on, Bess. I have a stitch in my side."

"I tripped that bally prowler, of course. Do you think that was a thief we just encountered?"

Vicky shook her head. "Nothing worth stealing there."

"Yes, but he does not know that."

Vicky thought the person had come there with the same intention as them. He was looking for something. Bess hoped he had not come after them.

"Do you think it was Nash? He moves around quite freely in the castle. He might have heard us talking to Pudding."

Vicky gave a shrug. Maybe they should have stuck around to see who it was. Bess told her that would have been foolish.

"Mark my words, Vicky. That man was there for one reason only. To get rid of evidence."

They had almost come face to face with Eileen's killer. He could have been armed for all they knew.

"That was a narrow escape." Vicky moved closer to Bess as they entered the castle's grounds. "Let's just go back home."

Chapter 25

The sky grew lighter, ushering in a new dawn by the time they reached their room. Exhausted by their sojourn, both sisters fell into a deep sleep, not waking when the maid came in with their chocolate and croissants. Bright sunlight was streaming into the room when Pudding entered and began shaking Bess.

"Wake up! You missed breakfast."

Bess groaned and turned on her side but Vicky sat up in bed.

"What time is it?"

"Almost 10 AM." Pudding rolled her eyes. "You are not sick, are you? Mama is talking of calling the doctor again."

Vicky assured her they were fine. Just tired.

"You were supposed to come with us." Bess buried her head under a pillow. "What happened?"

Pudding evaded the question and asked if they were hungry. Breakfast had been cleared. She proposed going to the pub, finally prompting Bess to abandon the covers and get up.

"I could eat a horse." She stretched her arms above her head and gave a big yawn. "You let the side down, old bean. We needed you last night."

Pudding's eyebrows shot up when the twins gave her a brief account of their visit to Eileen's cottage.

"I say, will you forgive me, Bess?" Pudding was contrite. "Are you hurt?"

Vicky chortled with glee. "We are not, but he might be."

They dressed quickly and went down to assure Lady Morse they were fine.

"Shall I ask Chef to whip up an omelette for you?"

"Oh no!" Bess assured her. "We can eat at the pub. It will be a nice change."

The drive to the village was accomplished shortly and they entered the dim interiors of The Crown. Breakfast was ordered and they got ready to tuck into a hearty meal.

The proprietor set a pot of tea on the table along with two bowls of porridge and promised the rest would be there soon. A group of men in crumpled clothing came in, talking in loud voices, laughing. Bess looked up and was surprised to see Nash among them.

One of the men spotted Pudding and came to their table.

"Good morning, Miss." He beamed. "My Julie gave birth to a healthy boy at dawn."

"Congratulations, Mr. Martin." Pudding's face was wreathed in smiles. "That is splendid news."

She inquired after the well being of the mother and child.

"All well." The man looked relieved. "Had a rough time, poor thing." He nodded at the men who had come in with him. "I would have been a nervous wreck but the boys stayed up with me all night."

"Mr. Nash too?" Bess interrupted.

"We played cards and talked about how lucky we are."

The food arrived, eggs, bacon, sausages, potatoes, all fried to perfection, served with toast and butter as Bess preferred. Pudding regaled them with the man's history. He was one of the Morse 13 and very close to Alfred Nash. Martin worked with a solicitor's firm in town. His child was the first offspring of the Morse 13.

"So it could not have been Nash," Bess grumbled.

MURDER AT CASTLE MORSE

Vicky laid out the facts for Pudding. Assuming Richie had nothing to do with Eileen's death, they were left with only one suspect. Alfred Nash. But he could not have been the intruder in the cottage if he had been at the Martin house all night.

Bess popped a piece of generously buttered toast in her mouth, her eyes narrowed in speculation.

"What if it was Ron?"

They had overlooked him because he had a strong alibi for Joe Cooper's death. But he might have managed to slip out and come across Eileen.

"Not sweet Ron." Pudding shook her head. "He wouldn't hurt a fly."

"That would leave Richie." Vicky raised an eyebrow. "Would you rather he was guilty?"

Bess proposed visiting Ron in his store. Pudding could pretend to be looking for some lace for a new frock.

They stepped out in a sunny day and walked the short distance to the haberdashery. Ron gave them an effusive greeting. Bess thought he looked like a new person.

"You seem happy, Ron." Vicky couldn't help smiling. "As if the weight of the world has been lifted from your shoulders."

He bobbed his head in agreement.

"You are absolutely right, your ladyship. They are finally building the war memorial, did you hear? My brother will get the respect he deserves."

Bess mentioned it had happened at the cost of a man's life.

"I am not sorry Joe Cooper died." Ron winced. "He was being stubborn for no reason. I think he came to a fitting end." He gave a shrug. "I will never understand how he managed to get so many people on his side. But good riddance, I say."

Vicky asked if he felt the same about Eileen. Ron hung his head in shame.

"You must think I have no heart, my lady. The whole village mourns Eileen. She had a sharp tongue but she was a gentle soul."

Ron felt some of the villagers had taken advantage of her kindness. She had many layers, just like the onions she ate.

"Why would anyone want to kill her then?" Bess probed. "Do you have any idea who might have done it?"

Ron lifted his shoulders in a shrug. That's what the whole village had been talking about. None of them had an inkling. All he could tell them was that Richie was innocent.

"My brother Raymond worshipped him. We owe him a lot for bringing Ray back to us. Ma is thankful we got to say goodbye."

Pudding asked for lace, hoping to distract him before he grew more maudlin. Ron went into the back to look for it.

"Well?" Vicky shared a glance with Bess and gave a shrug.

They had made no headway. Chances of Ron being their man appeared slim.

A middle aged woman in a large hat festooned with fruit came in with a pink faced girl wearing thick spectacles. Two buck teeth protruded from her thin lips and mousy brown hair peeped out of a bonnet. As unfortunate as the girl seemed, Bess thought she could benefit from the attention of a skilled maid.

"Hello Mrs. Birdwhistle," Pudding hailed. "Hester." She nodded at the girl. "Shopping for a new dress?"

The older woman launched into a monologue, detailing the various fabrics she had acquired in order to buy her daughter some new frocks. There was also a special pale yellow silk for the upcoming ball season. Ron came out with a box while she was still speaking and began setting out its contents.

"That's the one." She cried suddenly, placing a chubby finger on some beautiful handmade lace. "Ring this up for me, Ronald."

"But this is for Miss Morse," he objected. "She asked for it first."

Mrs. Birdwhistle graced Pudding with an unctuous smile.

"You can find something better in London, I am sure. My poor Hester will be twenty five this year. She needs all the help she can get."

Ron boasted they could not find that lace in London. It was made by nuns in a convent in Northumberland and was in high demand.

Pudding took pity on Hester.

"I say, Ron. Let Hester have this one. You can order more for me."

"Jolly good, jolly good." Mrs. Birdwhistle beamed. "You are too kind, my dear. Tell your mother we are looking forward to the hunt ball."

She paid for the lace, frowning at Ron.

"And why were you loitering near the vicarage at dawn, young fellow? Up to no good, I bet."

Ron appeared dumbstruck.

"My sister left on the milk train," Mrs. Birdwhistle continued speaking. "I saw her off and what do I see on my way back home? You limping across the street near the church."

"I was visiting Raymond." Ron finally found his voice. "It is his birthday today."

Everyone rushed to say something appropriate and the group broke up. Bess was thoughtful as she climbed behind the wheel of her car.

"The vicarage is awfully close to Eileen's cottage. Do you think he might have been coming from there?"

Pudding thought Ron would never lie and Vicky also seemed sympathetic.

"We have nothing, Bess. I think we should go back home."

Pudding gave her a ghastly look. Bess assured her they would not give up that easily.

"Say, how sweet is One Eye Watkins on you, really? Will he do anything for you?"

"Are you being horrible again?" Pudding cried. "He is the kindest, sweetest man I know."

Vicky stifled a yawn.

"Will he lend you his dog?"

Bess and Vicky smiled at each other. They had both had the same thought.

"We don't want to repeat last night's mistake," Bess explained. "A word of warning will be nice. 303 can do that for us."

Pudding claimed she could do the same.

"Like last night?" Bess winked. "No, darling. You can help us search the cottage if you want."

Reluctant to lose face, Pudding agreed to procure the dog for them.

Vicky had another thought. What if someone could keep a watch on Ron while they were up on the hill? Bess thought it was a good idea.

MURDER AT CASTLE MORSE

"Richie will do it. He can take Ron to the pub and buy him a pint. Wait a minute, isn't it Raymond's birthday? Well then, maybe all the Morse 13 can be there. Or what's left of them."

Vicky had another stipulation. They would not wait until midnight. Just after dark was good enough. Bess agreed. She drove straight to the stables once they reached the castle, hoping to find Richie there.

"Hey sleepyheads." He greeted them, coming out of the stable with his arms full of fresh hay. "This looks like an ambush."

They quickly outlined the plan and warned him he did not have a choice.

"It's this or a prison cell," Bess warned. "You better buck up, old boy."

Richie told them he had no objection to treating his men to a pint or two at The Crown.

"Martin just became a father. The men will be there and so will Ron. You are a brick, Bess. You too, Vicky."

Lady Morse was astonished when they announced they were going to Ridley Hall for lunch.

"Bubbles could use the company," Bess lied. "You know how antsy she gets at Ridley."

They piled into the car again and Bess drove at break neck speed, enjoying the wind in her hair. Lunch was in progress when they reached Ridley Hall. The butler ushered them into the parlour and asked them to wait.

Pudding paced the room, looking more and more distressed.

"Don't you get cold feet now," Bess warned.

"What if he says no?"

"He won't," Vicky assured her. "Don't give him the chance."

Unlike his host, Sir Lawrence was happy to see them.

"Winifred, my dear!" he exclaimed. "This is a nice surprise."

Pudding blushed furiously.

"It's a ggglorious day, isn't it, Sir Lawrence?" she faltered. "I thought we might go for a walk."

The poor man looked bewildered. Lady Ridley took pity on him and offered to accompany them for a stroll in the rose garden. Bess claimed she was tired and opted to stay in the parlour with Vicky.

Half an hour later, they were speeding back to Castle Morse, 303 ensconced in the back seat with Pudding.

"I told him it was just for a few hours, since he is coming to dinner anyway."

Bess turned around and stared 303 in the eye. "Are you ready to sing for your supper, old man?"

Chapter 26

The girls were starving by the time they reached Castle Morse. Lady Morse had just ordered tea. They fell upon the cucumber sandwiches and cake, going through everything on the table at a rapid pace.

"One might think you did not have lunch," Lord Morse chuckled and asked the butler to get more food.

303 sat at Pudding's feet, looking like he belonged there. Bess asked Norton to take him to the kitchen and make sure he was fed well. Lady Morse reminded them they had company for dinner.

"When do we not, Mama?" Pudding smirked. "I hope Chef Henri is making something nice."

The girls went up and changed into dark outfits, Bess and Vicky choosing trousers. They crept down the back stairs and took an isolated path down to the village. 303 wagged his tail, happy to go on a long walk.

"I hope Richie keeps his word." Vicky was tense.

The sun set in a riot of colour and the sky had grown dark by the time they trudged up the hill to the cottage. Bess had a moment of doubt when they reached the door. What if the intruder had locked it? But it opened with a slight push and they were in.

Pudding looked around for a light switch.

"I don't think Eileen had electricity."

Bess hushed her and asked her to keep an eye on 303. Pudding told her she had already put him on guard. He would let them know if any unexpected visitors decided to crash their party.

They tried to be more methodical this time. Every pot and pan was turned over, clothing was shaken loose and refolded and walls and drawers were tapped to look for hidden compartments. Bess got down on her knees and peered under the bed.

"I say, I can't see a thing. Can you shine the torch here, Vicky?"

"Nothing, apart from a few cobwebs, Bess." Pudding laughed.

She had joined Bess on the floor.

"Wait a minute." Vicky pointed at a spot in the middle of the floor. "That looks different, as if it's been dug recently."

They gritted their teeth and managed to move the bed so Bess could slide closer to the spot and examine it. There was a slight wobble in the stone.

"Help me move this," she grunted, and began digging the soil around it with her fingers.

They managed to dislodge the stone with considerable effort. Bess plunged her hand in the space where it had been and pulled out a small cloth sack. She shook it, afraid someone might be playing a prank on them. There was a distinct clink.

"Open it, open it," Pudding cried.

Bess was ahead of her. She untied the string and peeped in, her eyes growing wide when she saw what was inside.

"Gold." She grabbed a fistful and showed them. "Coins, jewels ... this is a fortune. How did Eileen get this?"

Vicky thought she might have been saving for her future.

MURDER AT CASTLE MORSE

"Are you daft?" Pudding did not hide her scorn. "Look around you. She was poor as a church mouse."

Bess agreed with her.

"Let's get out of here before anyone catches us."

"But what about that?" Vicky pointed at the sack.

303 greeted them with a woof and led the way down the hill. They reached the castle minutes before the dressing bell rang.

"I don't know about you," Bess declared, putting on her favourite black frock. "But I plan to enjoy my dinner. Enough of this malarkey, I say."

Drinks were in progress when they went down. Richie was back from the pub, pleasantly inebriated. Sir Lawrence sipped his whiskey and soda, patting 303 with his other hand.

"He is back in your care, safe and sound, Sir Lawrence," Pudding teased. "I am a responsible young woman, you know."

Bess planted an elbow in her side.

"Laying it on a bit thick, old girl."

The butler announced dinner and they went in, ready to enjoy another gourmet meal. Bess found herself seated next to her nemesis, One Eye Watkins. She gave him the cold shoulder for the entire meal, sitting at a slight angle away from him. Richie had whispered in her ear before they went in.

"Ron never left The Crown, my dear."

Lady Ridley cornered the twins after dinner.

"Have you visited this flat Bubbles has? Is it as bad as Sir Dorian says?"

Bess had to be honest. "It is a bit avant garde, I suppose."

"What does that mean?" Lady Ridley was mystified. "Does it look like a courtesan's chamber? Are you telling me she intends to behave as one?"

"Why don't you ask Bubbles?" Bess countered. "Better yet, go and see the place yourself."

The guests did not linger and every one decided to have an early night. Bess and Vicky fell asleep as soon as their heads hit the pillow, waking up refreshed when the maid came in with their hot chocolate.

"I say, do you think Ron gave her that gold?" She tore off a piece of her croissant and dipped it in the chocolate.

Vicky told her to take a step back. How did Eileen come in possession of that gold? Were they going to assume it was payment in order to keep her quiet?

"What else?" Bess argued. "Obviously, she did not inherit it or earn it."

Pudding barged in, dressed to go out.

"Where are you off to?" Vicky asked.

Pudding told them she was bored and was going to London.

"Give us thirty minutes," Bess swung her feet off the bed. "That sounds like a marvellous idea."

Pudding checked herself in the cheval mirror placed near a wall and shook her head.

"Can you promise you won't mention the murders? They give me a terrible headache."

Vicky reminded her why they were at Castle Morse. Richie was still under suspicion and the police could take him away any moment.

"I feel so stifled." Pudding yawned. "A day in the city will cheer me up. I might do some shopping and take in a show at the Strand."

Bess and Vicky wished her a good day.

"You won't mind if we go home then, old bean?" Bess sounded calm but her eyes flashed with annoyance.

Pudding swept out of the room, waving a hand in the air.

"She's in love, Bess." Vicky laughed. "Everything else must fade in comparison."

They went down but did not dawdle over breakfast. Lady Morse was surprised they had not left with Pudding. Bess made some excuse about being wanted at Buxley.

"Papa gets fidgety if Vicky stays away too long."

She telephoned Buxley Manor to let Clementine know they would be there by lunch. The weather was cool and the sunny day lifted their spirits. Barnes was standing on the front steps to greet them.

"Lord Buxley has requested your presence in the study," he warned. "Right away."

Bess rolled her eyes.

"Is Annie there too?" she fumed.

Barnes assured her she was not. Lord Buxley was a bit vexed though.

Clementine saw them stalk down the hall and called out.

"Do you want a pot of tea, Bess? Lunch will be served in thirty minutes."

"I'm fine, Aunt Clem."

Vicky reached the study first and gave a loud rap before pushing the door open. Nigel was pacing before the fireplace, his hands clasped behind his back. Polo followed him around.

He gave a yelp as soon as he saw the twins and ran to welcome them. Bess picked him up.

"What ho, Papa! You wanted to see us?"

"Bess, Vicky, high time you came back home."

Vicky told him he just had to telephone whenever he wanted to see them.

"All that is fine, girls, but this is your home, not Castle Morse. You are needed here."

Bess had an idea where he was heading. She sat on the sofa, stroking Polo's back, her eyebrows scrunched together.

"Do you know what's for lunch, Papa?"

Nigel ignored the question, recognizing it as the stalling tactic it was.

"When are you going to talk to her, Bessie?"

Vicky was quiet. She believed their mother had wronged both of them by choosing to flee. Bess was a victim of Annie's actions.

"Dear Papa," she began. "Please don't rush Bess. She will talk to Mom when she is ready."

Bess got off the sofa and smoothed her skirt.

"Never mind, Vicky. I will go see her now."

Barnes was standing outside and Bess was sure he had heard everything. He gave her an approving nod. She stalked out of the manor through a side door and went in search of her mother. Although nobody had mentioned her whereabouts, Bess had a good idea where she would find Annie.

Her temper cooled by the time she walked across a well maintained gravel path, surrounded by boxwood hedges. Eden, the wild garden Annie loved, was tucked away in a remote corner near the stables and was the best kept secret at Buxley.

MURDER AT CASTLE MORSE

Bess stormed inside and looked around, trying to spot her mother.

Annie sat on a bench by the pond, staring at the swans.

"Your father named them." Her face lit up when she saw Bess. "He had a great sense of humour."

"Not anymore," Bess shot back. "All the humour vanished from his life when he was accused of murder."

Annie was quiet for a minute.

"I don't think anyone actually accused him. Not even Philip's mother Beatrice. But she dropped plenty of hints."

Bess folded her arms and leaned against the bench.

"She has never stopped doing that, according to Grandmother. She must hate Papa a lot."

Annie shook her head. Beatrice was a grieving mother and was just lashing out.

"Where was all this wisdom twenty years ago?" Bess tugged at a blade of grass, observing the emotions flitting across Annie's face. "What kind of mother are you, Annie? You left me to rot here and didn't even look back."

Annie's eyes filled up.

"You had a houseful of people to look after you, sweetie. And your father. I was sure you would be okay."

Bess told her she had lacked for nothing. There was a nurse and a governess to take care of her education. The older ladies indulged her every whim. Momo and Bubbles laughed at her pranks and spoilt her with gifts she did not need. Aunt Clem made her mind her Ps and Qs.

"Why did I still yearn for a mother?" Bess tossed a pebble in the pond, startling the swans. "Papa was like a shadow of himself. I wracked my brains to figure out why he never seemed happy." She took a deep breath. "Now I know. You broke his heart, Annie."

Mother and daughter said nothing for a while, choked with emotion.

"I know I made a lot of mistakes, Bess. But I'm here now. And I am ready to do whatever you want to make things right between us. The only thing I cannot do is turn back time."

Bess was grave when she finally stared into Annie's eyes.

"You expect me to trust you but can you do the same?" She wiped away a lone tear that was flowing down her cheek. "Are you finally ready to trust Papa?"

Annie hesitated. Bess grew more incensed.

"Do you believe he is innocent of all these silly allegations? Or do you think he murdered Philip?"

"I love him."

"You are a horrible woman, Annie. Why did you have to come back here?"

Bess stood up and walked away, unable to stem the tears rolling down her cheeks.

Chapter 27

Bess was quiet through lunch. Even her favourite spicy food did not improve her mood. Bubbles asked if anything interesting had happened at Morse.

"Lady Ridley was asking about your flat," Bess told her. "Why don't you take her up to London, Bubbles? She is longing to have a look at what you have done."

Momo thought it was a good idea.

"Let's do it, Bubbles. You, me and Mama. We have not had fun together in yonks."

Annie had not joined them, inviting comment. Nigel darted questioning glances at Bess but she did not say anything.

"Are you done rushing around, young lady?" Louise asked. "I have a task for you."

Bess and Vicky took the hint and followed their grandmother and great aunts to the west wing. They assumed their favourite seats, leaning forward in anticipation.

"Well?" Louise barked. "Any new developments?"

Vicky opened her capacious bag and took out the gunny sack they had found in Eileen's cottage and handed it to her grandmother.

"Open it." Perpetua and Hortense spoke at once.

Louise untied the string and peeped in, her face spreading into a big smile.

"Golly!"

She pulled out a handful of the gold coins and faced Bess and Vicky.

"Are you going to say something?"

Bess told them where they had found it. Everyone agreed it was a veritable treasure for someone as poor as Eileen.

"I think it is safe to say this is the cause of the girl's death," Hortense declared, crumpling her handkerchief. "But she cannot have procured these via honest means."

Bess thought they needed to know more.

"We have no idea when Eileen died or how. If only that Inspector was more forthcoming."

Louise had a twinkle in her eye when she spoke to them.

"Tea can loosen tongues, my dear."

Bess told her to stop talking in riddles. Vicky caught her meaning and laughed.

"How did you manage to make him accept?"

"There are some perks of being old and wrinkled," Louise replied. "That boy could not refuse us."

There was a knock on the door and Barnes came in.

"It is fifteen minutes to four, my lady."

"Time for tea!" Perpetua chortled. "Thank you, Barnes. We shall be down momentarily."

When the weather was pleasant, tea at Buxley Manor was served on the lawn, under a giant oak. Clementine was keeping DI Gardener company when the Nightingales reached them.

"Good to see you are punctual for a change, Bess," she remarked.

"Hello Inspector." Bess ignored her aunt, deciding she had bigger fish to fry. "This is a surprise."

He thanked Louise for inviting him.

Barnes led a procession of footmen from the house, carrying trays loaded with pots of tea and platters of food.

MURDER AT CASTLE MORSE

Bess filled a plate with cucumber sandwiches, biscuits and Mrs. Bird's sponge cake and handed it to James.

He expressed surprise at seeing them at home.

"Would you not have come if you knew?" Bess fluttered her eyes.

Vicky asked if they had made any progress in Eileen's case. Clementine reprimanded her immediately.

"No morbid talk at my table, Vicky."

Nigel arrived and soon all the other inhabitants trickled in. The Inspector was completely at ease, chatting with each one of them on a variety of topics. Bess wondered about his background. Finally, the meal wound up and James stood up to take his leave.

"Have you seen the rose garden, Inspector?" Vicky quipped. "It's worth a look."

He offered her his arm and they set off. Bess hastened to follow them but Louise held her back.

"Every battle need not be won, my dear."

Her advice proved valuable. Vicky returned to the west wing half an hour later, wreathed in smiles.

"Spill the beans," Perpetua boomed.

Vicky climbed up into a window seat and tucked her legs beneath her.

"Eileen probably died in her sleep. She was bashed to death, poor thing. The post mortem report places her time of death between six and eight in the morning. The doctor believes it was before seven. Any later than that and the hustle and bustle of the day would have begun."

Bess asked how she had managed to squeeze so much out of the Inspector.

"Never mind that," Louise interrupted. "Did he say why the police suspect Richie?"

Vicky told them he hadn't been that open.

"My guess is they zeroed in on him because he paid for that earring. But they do not have any other definite proof against him."

Richie might have paid for the earring for any number of reasons. The Inspector was smart enough to know that.

Bess hoped Vicky had not mentioned the gold.

"Of course not, Bess." She looked hurt. "Give me some credit."

Louise thought the gold changed everything. Eileen had become a target, just by being in possession of so much wealth.

"She told someone," Hortense spat.

"We don't know that," Perpetua argued.

Bess figured out what they were trying to say.

"You mean Eileen bragged about the gold in the village. Surely not? She was a tough nut."

Vicky told them Eileen had been a simple village girl, all said and done. Although she put on a brave front, she had no guile.

"It would be hard to keep such a big thing to yourself."

Louise agreed with her.

"My dear Bess, this gold must have been the highlight of her life. Surely she told her family, at least? Or a close friend or two?"

They knew Eileen's brother was one of the Morse 13. But she had been on her own whenever they came across her.

MURDER AT CASTLE MORSE

"This is getting us nowhere, Grandmother. For the sake of this argument, let us assume that Eileen's death is connected to Joe Cooper."

The gold was to keep her mouth shut. Eileen had known something incriminating about Joe's killer. He paid her off to appease her but had second thoughts.

"So what? This scoundrel decided to shut her up forever?" Louise mused. "We know this person has no scruples taking a life."

They decided to revisit all the suspects, beginning with Richie.

"Pudding says he was just being kind." Bess lay down on the chaise and stared at the ceiling. "How did he know Eileen was missing an earring?"

Vicky reminded her what the jeweller had told them. Eileen had come to his shop on her own. Richie must have run into her over there.

Richard Morse was flush in the pocket and had a kind heart. But Eileen did not belong to his class. Was he not afraid she would misunderstand?

"By Jove!" Bess sat up with a jerk. "You don't think Richie was sweet on Eileen? That's bonkers."

Louise thought it was as fantastic as believing he killed a man over a horse, then murdered a woman to cover it up.

Hortense gave a wide yawn and called them to order.

"Move on."

Vicky picked Alfred Nash. He had a strong motive to kill Joe Cooper. Eileen had seen him near the stables, incriminating him. And they had seen him going up the hill to Eileen's cottage. So he definitely knew where she lived.

Bess held up a hand. "Hold on, old bean. Nash was sweet on her."

"That's what he told us," Vicky argued. "How do we know he was telling the truth?"

Louise and the aunts were quiet as they considered this new scenario.

"Do you mean he just pretended to like that poor girl so he could get close to her?"

The money did not add up in that case, Bess told them. And where was Nash going to have that kind of money?

Louise told them Alfred Nash had been working for Lord Morse for several years. If he was frugal by nature, he could easily have a nest egg put by.

"So he gave this gold to Eileen to buy time," Vicky muttered. "And all the while, he was just waiting for a chance to murder her?" She gave a slight shiver. "That is cold blooded."

Bess was not on board with them. Alfred Nash was a soldier. He might have killed Joe Cooper for revenge but he would never hurt an innocent. And she had seen his eyes when he spoke of Eileen.

"I believe he had some feelings for her, Grandmother."

The sun had set while they were engrossed in solving their conundrum. Twilight lingered over the ash trees, ready to usher in the night.

Clementine came in, startling them.

"Just as I thought. Are you staying back for dinner, Mama? You might have informed me earlier."

"Now you know." Louise ignored her daughter. "Leave us alone for now, dear."

Bess glanced at a clock on the wall and realized the dressing bell would ring soon.

"We might skip the drinks, Aunt Clem."

"We are having oysters," Clementine sighed. "And Mrs. Bird has roasted a duck in your honour. Please don't be late for dinner."

Vicky thanked her aunt for going to so much trouble.

"It's all I am good for, dear girl." Clementine squared her shoulders and left the room.

Louise asked them to move on.

"What about that young boy at the haberdashery?"

"Ron." Bess narrowed her eyes. "Well, he was in the shop all day when Joe Cooper was murdered."

Vicky wondered if they had missed anything. Ron did have a motive. And he had gained the most from Joe's death since the war memorial was finally going to be built. But she did not think he had a violent bone in his body.

Bess thought people did strange things for their family.

Louise told them it was time to wind up for the day.

"All three men had a motive to murder Joe. We need to find out what they were doing when the girl died."

The group broke up to dress for dinner. For a change, they were not expecting guests although the vicar and his mother were coming.

"How did you make the Inspector talk?" Bess had finished changing into a new sleeveless frock and was applying lipstick in the mirror.

Vicky sensed her sister was jealous.

"The police don't have much. I suppose he can use any help he gets, although he will never admit it."

Bess wondered if he took Vicky more seriously because she was a trained nurse.

"I am surprised he didn't ask you to mind your own business."

"He did warn me." Vicky sighed. "He was very grave, to be honest. A ruthless killer is roaming free and will not hesitate to strike again if needed."

Bess sprayed the new French perfume she had bought from the designer Chanel.

"Not one, Vicky. Two. Don't forget the man who killed Philip."

Chapter 28

Bubbles took it upon herself to take her mother to London. Momo could not turn her down this time. The sisters left for Ridley Hall the next morning, planning to spend a day there before going to London with their mother.

"You mean they already left?" Bess asked Clementine as she loaded her plate with kedgeree the next morning. "Finally, a proper breakfast. I can't tell you how much I have missed this, Aunt Clem."

Vicky sipped her coffee and ate a soft boiled egg. She did not think she could ever stomach fish for breakfast.

"Mrs. Bird is planning your favourite meals," Clementine told them. "I do hope you will stick around for a few days this time."

A footman arrived, bearing a platter of flapjacks and set it on the table. Vicky and Annie both exclaimed in delight. Barnes offered to pour the blackberry syrup.

"Don't give them ideas, Clem," Nigel muttered.

Vicky headed to the library to catch up on some reading and Bess sat in the parlour, flipping through the latest fashion magazines. Clementine found her dozing in her chair an hour later.

"How could Bubbles leave without meeting me, Aunt Clem?" she grumbled. "And Momo too. I am bored."

Clementine suggested meeting some friends.

"Why don't you go to Rosehill? Megan and Clara are feeling left out."

Bess thought it was a good idea. She rang for assistance and asked Barnes to have the motor brought around. Twenty minutes later, she sped through the grounds at Buxley Manor, wondering what Pudding was up to. Normally, she would have telephoned to talk about her trip to London. Bess had a sudden premonition but brushed it aside, slowing down as she reached the village. Lost in her thoughts, she failed to notice a muddy patch until she felt herself thrown forward and the car came to a stop.

"I say! What in blazes …"

A tall, imposing man with coppery brown hair stepped out of the pub and stopped in his tracks, surprised to see her.

"Well, well, well …"

"What ho, Inspector!" Bess glared.

"Detective Inspector," he corrected her. "You should try being nice to me if you want my help."

Children from the village surrounded the car, roving their hands over it, laughing. Bess did not mind. She jumped out and summoned the oldest, handing him a penny.

"Can you take a message to the manor?"

She headed to the Buxley Arms to wait until help arrived. James followed her in, choosing to sit at her table.

"Have you checked their alibis, Inspector?"

He assured her it was the first thing they had done. All the suspects had been in bed when Eileen died.

"You are welcome to enlighten me if you know different."

Bess gave a shrug. There was no harm in asking around.

"People are prone to keep things from the police. Most of the time, they are lying for silly reasons."

MURDER AT CASTLE MORSE

"All this for a rich, entitled young man with an obsession for horses."

Bess was seething inside. She thought he was a dog with a bone when it came to Richie. No wonder the press had labelled him 'Bulldog'.

"Are you envious?" she laughed. "Let me remind you that Richie is a decorated war hero who staked his own life to save his men."

Unlike him. James knew what she was leaving unsaid. He could not deny Bess had flaunted convention and done her bit for the war effort. She had earned his respect because of that.

"War heroes are governed by the same laws as the rest of us, Lady Bess."

Harvey arrived with two pints of ale and greeted Bess.

"He was here last night, my lady. Mrs. Harvey told him he was not welcome."

Bess guessed who he was talking about. One Eye Watkins had finally met his match. The Harveys could be more ferocious than a hundred lions when it came to protecting Lord Buxley. She peeped into the kitchen to thank the woman.

Barnes sent the chauffer to pick her up in the Rolls. She wished James a good day, ready to head out.

"Watch your back, Bess." He was grave.

"Pip pip."

Why was the Bulldog behaving like a fussy hen, she wondered on the drive back to the manor. And what was he doing in the village?

She cheered up after a sumptuous lunch, deciding to rest in her room. Barnes gave her the bad news at tea. The footmen had managed to push her car out of the mud but it would not start.

"I think it is safe to say there is a breakdown, my lady. The motor garage in Chipping Woodbury will send a man down to take a look."

Bess was listless the next day. She set off on a long walk, planning to spend the day at the folly. The cook packed some sandwiches for her, in case she did not return for lunch. Tea was being served when she finally made her way back to the manor.

"What ho, Papa! What ho, Vicky! What ho, Grandmother!" she greeted, pointedly ignoring Annie. "I say, we will have to take the train tomorrow."

Bess was determined to have breakfast at Buxley so they took a later train the next morning.

"I wonder why Papa did not offer the Rolls," she said suddenly.

Vicky told her he was taking Annie to visit some neighbours. Baron Shelby had invited them for lunch at Oakview.

"She's enjoying her holiday." Bess watched the countryside hurtling past out of the window.

Autumn had arrived and the countryside was a palette of yellows and browns interspersed with red. The hunt ball was approaching and Bess realized she and Vicky needed new gowns.

"Who do we tackle first?" Vicky nudged her with a toe. "Do you have a thing for Richie?"

"No." Bess frowned. "Do you?"

Each wondered if the other was lying but said nothing.

MURDER AT CASTLE MORSE

A car was waiting for them outside the station. Bess was not surprised, used to being waited on hand and foot. Pudding sat inside.

"I say!"

The two friends patted each other on the arm, Bess making it clear she was cross.

"Are you done being ghastly? You might have telephoned."

Pudding apologized and all was right between them once again.

Lord and Lady Morse were happy to see them. Richie ruffled Vicky's hair, thinking she was Bess.

"You were missed, imp."

There was grilled trout in a delicate butter and white wine sauce for lunch, along with roasted pumpkins and aubergines. Bess held off on mentioning anything unpleasant and was relieved when Richie broached the subject himself.

"Any news from the police, Bess? Have they found the scoundrel who killed Eileen?"

She shook her head.

"It's the time she died, you see, in the early hours of the morning. It's hard to find a witness who was up and about at that time."

Vicky took the cue.

"They must have been asleep, like you. Do you sleep in, Richie? Most of the young men I met here don't get up until noon."

Lord Morse told them Richie was not like that. Any man would be proud to have him for a son.

"He knows everything about the business. If anything were to happen to me, Morse Industries will not suffer."

Lady Morse chided him for being ridiculous.

"No more talk like that at my table."

"So you were at home that morning?" Vicky pressed. "What a pity!"

"Yes, Yes." Lady Morse was on the verge of losing her temper. "He was right here in the castle, fast asleep in his bed."

Vicky wondered if the servants would notice if Richie slipped out of the castle at night. Then she remembered their own sojourn. None of the inhabitants seemed to be aware of it.

Lady Morse was redecorating the ballroom and she wanted Pudding to help her after lunch. Bess thought it was a good opportunity to tackle Nash.

He was in his office as usual, having a solitary lunch.

"Lady Bess, Lady Vicky!" He closed the heavy ledger he was reading with ease. "How can I help you?"

Bess was reluctant to offend him so she tried to frame her question in an indirect manner.

"Are you an early bird, Mr. Nash? Do you wake up with the servants?"

"Good Lord, no." He was puzzled. "I like to give them an hour to clean up and get the fires going. But I do swear by the morning constitutional. An hour in the woods at the very least. Gives me an appetite for breakfast."

Vicky asked if there were any good spots where she could watch the sun rise.

"I grew up on the east coast of America," she explained. "Watching the sun come up over the ocean is the best way to start the day."

MURDER AT CASTLE MORSE

Nash agreed with her wholeheartedly, although he had been waking later since the weather cooled. Bess finally brought up the day Eileen was found dead.

"The police will try to establish where Richie was. You did not see him out and about that morning, did you?"

Nash took some time to think back to the day in question.

"Unfortunately, I did not go out for a walk that day, my lady."

He had a bout of indigestion and had been up for a large part of the night, falling asleep after three. The family had been at breakfast when he went down.

"Cold milk helps," he told them. "I went down to the kitchen to get a glass. Neville was already there."

"What?" Bess exclaimed.

Nash gave a shrug. He supposed Neville could not sleep either. They had a one sided conversation for a few minutes and he returned to his room. He had not encountered Richie but assumed he was asleep in his room.

"Do you have reason to think otherwise?" he asked.

Bess told him it was alright. It would just have strengthened Richie's case.

They thanked him and headed to the ballroom where a set of artisans were painting some frescoes on the ceiling. Lady Morse was busy directing them. Pudding stood by a window, lost in thought.

"Fancy a walk to the village?" Bess nudged her. "We need to talk to Ron."

Pudding agreed readily. She hoped Ron had acquired the special lace she needed. Vicky pleaded a headache and Bess and

Pudding set off on their own. The air was balmy, the kind that prompted one to make plans and talk about the future.

"We never went to that Swiss finishing school, Puds. I say, why don't we go there on a holiday once this nonsense clears up."

"Sure." Pudding's cheeks turned pink. "Or we can go to some exotic place like Africa."

"You are besotted." Bess rolled her eyes. "Want to see that lion slayer in action, I suppose."

They reached the store a few minutes later. Ron beckoned them with a smile.

"Your lace came in this morning, Miss. It is beautiful."

Pudding was effusive in her thanks, her face lit up by a wide smile as she examined it.

"Looks like the war memorial's almost done." Bess leaned on the counter. "You must be happy, Ron."

He admitted he was relieved. He no longer felt he had failed his brother.

"Do you visit him every day?" Bess tried to sound curious. "Must be quite inconvenient."

"Not at all, my lady." Ron was indignant. "I visit Raymond's grave before opening the shop every day, sometimes at the crack of dawn, when nobody's around."

Bess named the day of Eileen's death.

"Were you out there by any chance?" she asked. "Did you see anyone on the hill or around Eileen's cottage?"

Ron shook his head.

"Ma was poorly. She has this nasty cough that won't get better. I have been staying up with her for the past week. We read until she falls asleep."

MURDER AT CASTLE MORSE

They started back for the castle, Pudding clutching the packet of lace to her chest. Bess thought it was dashed odd but stayed quiet.

Tea was being served and Bess was glad to see Vicky seated next to Lady Morse, nibbling on a sandwich.

"What do you have there, Winifred?" Lady Morse missed nothing.

"Oh Mama," Pudding sighed. "It's that marvellous lace I told you about, the one I want on my wedding dress."

Lord Morse had just walked in with Richie.

"Why don't we find you a groom first, pet?"

"I say, Bess." Richie took a slice of the fruit cake. "One of the mares foaled last night." His eyes widened for a second, urging her to take the hint.

Vicky squealed in delight, begging him to let them have a look.

"Topping!" Bess nodded. "We can go after you finish stuffing yourself."

Richie crumbled the cake on his plate and drank some tea. "I'm ready."

Pudding had already been to see the foal and wanted a second cup of tea. Vicky and Bess followed Richie down a dark hall and stepped out into the fading sunlight in a deserted courtyard.

"What's the bally idea?" Bess pounced. "We are not in the stables."

Richie confessed he just wanted to get them alone.

"It's about the night Eileen died," he frowned. "I wasn't in my bed, Bess. What if the police find out?"

Ever since coming back from the war, Richie found it hard to fall asleep. He often went out in the woods at night, walking until exhaustion set in.

"The sky had lightened a bit when I came back. I haven't the foggiest what the time was but I saw Ballard by the river."

Bess asked if they had talked and was relieved when Richie shook his head.

"Maybe he did not see you."

Richie planned to go to the police and come clean.

"Am I signing my death warrant?"

"Of course not," Vicky soothed. "The police will appreciate your honesty and this might help them catch the real culprit."

Bess thought Vicky was over egging the pudding, getting his hopes up. But she saw the relief spreading across Richie's face and said nothing.

Chapter 29

Dinner was a crowded affair. Stephen Ballard arrived with his sister and the assistant who was doing double duty as his inamorata. Two neighbouring families had also been invited, among them the woman they had come across in Ron's shop. Bess managed to have a word with Ballard.

The twins excused themselves after dinner. Neither had the inclination to talk about the murder.

"This sleuthing business is not a walk in the park," Bess mused. "Good you have your life already mapped out, Vicky."

Morning brought a surprise. They were relishing mushroom omelettes prepared by Chef Henri when the telephone rang. The butler Norton came in to summon Bess. Her eyebrows shot up when she heard the person at the other end.

"All well, dear?" Lady Morse inquired.

"Grandmother put us to work. I am afraid we won't be here for lunch."

Vicky asked Pudding what her plans for the day were. Lady Morse was going to call on some neighbours and invited Pudding to accompany her.

"Sorry Mama. I have a terrible headache. I think I am going to lie down."

Vicky did not learn anything about the telephone call until they walked out of the house. She assumed they were taking a train back to Buxley.

"They are coming here," Bess grinned. "Grandmother and Aunt Hortense and Aunt Perpetua. We are to meet them at The Crown."

Vicky speculated about the reason. Had something happened at Buxley Manor?

They did not have to wait for long. Bess spotted the Rolls come to a stop outside. Louise was the first one out, refusing any help from the hapless chauffeur. Vicky went out to greet them.

"What ho, ladies!" Bess cried. "All well at the old pile?"

Louise gave her a withering look.

"Of course, my dear. You would be hotfooting it there otherwise."

Perpetua rapped the table. "Update."

Bess told them what they had managed to learn about their three suspects.

"None of them have alibis, really. Nash may have run into Neville Morse but Neville does not speak. Ron's mother could easily lie for him. And Richie is admitting he was outside."

Louise thought they should put the matter to rest. They had gone back and forth over the issue and come to the conclusion that Richie was their man after all.

"He is the only one who can afford to come up with all that gold," she stated.

"We know he was mad about that horse," Hortense began. "Eileen went to the stables for a reason we will not know. She saw Richie commit murder. That is when she panicked and did not realize she lost the earring."

"Richie tried to appease her," Perpetua continued. "First he paid for that trinket, then he gave her a bag of gold. Who can refuse that kind of money? But Eileen's conscience would not let her stay quiet. She must have declared her intention of going to the police."

"That's when Richie killed her," Louise finished. "Poor boy!" she sighed. "All that violence he saw on the battlefield must have addled his brain."

Bess did not believe that. The alternative was worse. Had Richie murdered two people in cold blood?

"Lord Morse would know if that much money went missing from the business."

They decided to beard the lion in his den. Bess ordered the chauffer to wait in the pub and got behind the wheel, arriving at the castle a short time later.

Norton was surprised to see the bevy of women bearing down on him when he opened the door.

"Lady Buxley." He bowed. "Please follow me."

The parlour was unoccupied. They chose their seats and let Louise take the lead.

"Ask Clive to come and see us immediately."

Norton fled without a word. Lord Morse arrived five minutes later, looking bemused.

"Lady Buxley, Miss Gaskins, Miss Hortense." He bowed. "To what do I owe the pleasure?"

"Tell him, Bess." Louise ordained.

Lord Morse listened, incredulous, while Bess outlined their theory. Vicky saw his jaw harden and his eyes grow cold.

"You believe Richie is capable of all this?"

Bess hoped she was mistaken.

"We are wondering if you can help us." She produced the bag of gold and set it before him. "Does this look familiar?"

Lord Morse permitted himself a small laugh, baffling the ladies.

"My dear, we are in the wrong century. All my money is tied up in the factories and mines. Most of what the estate produces goes back into maintaining it. Never in my life have I set my eyes on this amount of gold."

Bess was weak with relief. She began to apologize.

"I say. You must think I am the worst kind of bottom feeder but ..."

Lord Morse patted her arm. "My dear girl. Someone has to ask the difficult questions. But don't worry. There is no evidence against my boy because he is innocent."

Louise prayed he was right. They were back to square one.

"You must be tired after your journey, Lady Buxley. Norton has already notified the chef of your arrival. How about a glass of champagne?"

None of them wanted to say no to that. Bess asked if they were celebrating anything.

"The most wonderful thing has happened." Lord Morse beamed at them, all trace of his earlier distress nowhere in sight. "We heard back from the Royal Society. I mean, Ballard did. They have accepted him as a member and also declared that the mosaics we found were authentic."

Everyone rushed to congratulate him. He led them to the dining room and began handing out the flutes of champagne.

"Castle Morse has Roman ruins," he crowed. "We can cash in on this, you know. Build a small museum, maybe. Take children on a ride or an educational tour."

They wanted to know how it had happened.

"Ballard brought the news this morning. The man may be uptight but he came through for me."

Bess thought he was still holding back.

"I say, there is something more, isn't there?"

Lord Morse looked like the cat that swallowed the cream.

"Good Lord! Nothing gets by you, Bess. Actually, the mosaic was not the only item we sent for authentication."

A few slivers of gold had been discovered among the shards of pottery at the dig site. Ballard was confident they were Roman and he had turned out to be right.

"Golly!" The aunts spoke at once. "Does that mean there is treasure buried here?"

Lord Morse beamed with pride.

"Looks like it. I have just agreed to put up the funds required for a large scale operation."

Lunch was a fun affair. Lady Morse arrived just in time, happy to entertain her last minute guests.

"I say, where's Pudding?" Bess inquired when the footmen began serving the soup.

Norton told them she had taken a packet of sandwiches and gone for a long walk. She would not be back for tea.

"That's funny." Lady Morse caught Bess's eye. "I thought she had a headache."

The ladies from Buxley Manor praised the delicious food and spent the better part of the afternoon approving all the preparations Lady Morse was making for the hunt ball. They stayed for tea and finally said goodbye, thanking their hosts for the wonderful day.

Bess and Vicky went upstairs, longing to take a nap before dinner. The maid woke them at the stipulated time after which they each took a bath and dressed.

Bess was adjusting a long rope of pearls around her neck when the maid rushed in, her eyes wild with fear. She handed her a note and stood there, wringing her hands, begging to be forgiven. All Bess could figure out was that she had found it in Pudding's room, on her dressing table.

"What's this?" There was no name on the envelope so Bess tore it open and pulled out the note it contained. "By Jove!"

She sat on the bed with a thud and skimmed her eyes over the paper, unable to believe what it said.

"I say!" She stared at Vicky, stricken. "Pudding's gone!" She handed her the paper and put her hands around her head, trying to think straight.

Vicky told the maid to get Lord and Lady Morse.

"This says she eloped with the love of her life. We are to congratulate her."

"Wish her the best," Bess corrected automatically.

"No. This does say we should congratulate her. She thinks she caught a big fish."

Lord and Lady Morse burst into the room and looked around. Lady Morse was white as a sheet while her husband seemed about to burst.

"What is this new palaver, Bess?" he demanded. "Where is my daughter?"

The letter was handed over and the couple read it, their eyes wide in disbelief.

"Oh Clive!" Lady Morse cried. "Our daughter is ruined."

He told her to take it easy and turned to Bess. "Now, my dear. Who is this son of a gun she has been seeing? He better be ready to meet me at dawn."

There was another anguished cry from Lady Morse.

Bess advised them to calm down. She had been trying to think of the quickest way they could track Pudding down.

"We have to go to the police."

"Absolutely not!" Lord Morse boomed. "Once they get involved, her reputation will be in shreds."

Bess offered a different suggestion. Lord Morse slumped his shoulders in defeat.

"And you trust this man?"

Some instinct drove Bess to say she did. They went down to use the telephone. Bess called the police station at Buxley and spoke to the local constable. He hemmed and hawed but promised to pass on her message. Everyone jumped when the telephone rang fifteen minutes later.

"What have you done now, Bess?" the familiar voice crackled over the line, giving her a surge of confidence. She didn't waste any time in apprising DI Gardener of the situation. "He will be discreet," she told them after she placed the receiver back in the cradle.

Richie had arrived by then and was told about the situation. Everyone congregated in the parlour, throwing ideas back and forth, trying to think where Pudding might have gone.

"You are her closest friend," Lady Morse sobbed. "Hasn't she said anything to you, Bess?"

Suddenly, Bess had a nagging suspicion. She went back to the hall to place another call on the telephone. The butler told her none of the family were home. She debated voicing her thoughts, then gave in.

"She was sweet on One Eye Watkins. I warned you."

Lord Morse turned to stone.

"Now I am sure you are pulling our legs, Bess. Enough is enough."

Bess told them about Pudding's infatuation with Sir Lawrence. She had seen them together a few times. There was the lace Pudding had ordered and the vague reference to Africa.

"How could I not see it?" she berated herself.

According to the butler at Ridley Hall, Lady Ridley was in London with her daughters. Sir Dorian and Sir Lawrence were also in London on business and planned to stay overnight at their club.

"That's it, Bess." Richie stood up. "We are going to London."

Lord Morse told them to take the car and chauffer.

"Promise her whatever she wants but bring her back home safe and sound," he pleaded. "Will you stay here with us, Vicky?"

Bess thought they should call the Inspector and let him know their theory. Lord Morse offered to do it himself.

"He is already in London," Bess exclaimed. "He might reach her before us."

The butler handed her a basket of food and they stepped out, dressed in evening clothes. They heard a motor in the distance and a car careened around the final curve and came to a screeching stop outside the castle's entrance.

MURDER AT CASTLE MORSE

A woman in a white wedding dress struggled out, helped by a short man in a safari suit, accompanied by a familiar German Shepherd.

"Pudding!" Bess cried and ran down the steps.

She locked her friend in a tight embrace, cringing at the drama that was about to unfold.

Richie pulled her away and grabbed Pudding by the shoulders, shaking her until she cried out.

"You silly girl. Have you lost your mind?"

Sir Lawrence stood by without saying a word, one hand on 303. Sir Dorian Ridley remained seated inside, refusing to be part of the rapidly unfolding drama. Bess took Richie's arm and coaxed him to take everyone inside.

Lady Morse was growing livid, once she saw that her daughter was back in one piece.

"Do we call you Lady Watkins?" she sniffed.

Sir Lawrence cleared his throat.

"We are not married."

Everyone in the room heaved a collective sigh of relief.

"You worthless bounder," Lord Morse fumed. "What on earth were you thinking? If you have compromised my daughter in any way, I swear to God I will kill you with my bare hands."

Richie added a few choice words of his own.

Pudding burst into tears, mortified.

"It's all my fault, Papa. I thought he loved me."

Lady Morse had recovered some of her poise. She rang for the butler and told him to serve dinner in thirty minutes. Then she sat back to hear her daughter's explanation.

Pudding was madly in love with Sir Lawrence and she was confident he reciprocated her feelings. When she talked about going to Africa, he had encouraged her, telling her it would be a big adventure. She went to London and applied for a marriage license. Then she had sent him a message, asking to meet her in London. Sir Lawrence had no inkling of her plans. He had been dumbstruck when Pudding came before him, dressed as a bride.

"I had no idea." He pleaded with Lord Morse. "Believe me, Clive. I might have mentioned I was looking for a young bride but I meant someone in her thirties or forties. Not a child."

Bess realized he was telling the truth. Sir Lawrence had bundled Pudding into the car and insisted they come back to Castle Morse at once.

"You did not plan to elope with her?" Lord Morse stressed. "I want your word as a gentleman, Lawrence."

There was nothing to be done after that. Nobody said a word when Pudding left the room. Sir Lawrence apologized once again and left, still dazed from the whole encounter. Bess barely tasted her dinner. She and Vicky bid the others good night and went upstairs at the earliest opportunity.

"You had no clue?" Vicky asked Bess as they changed.

"I say." Bess felt overwhelmed. "Let's go home for a bit."

Chapter 30

The twins were welcomed back at Buxley Manor with open arms. Bess admitted it felt good to be home. Clementine thought the girls were looking a bit peaked and sent for the doctor.

"Plenty of rest, fresh air and wholesome food." Dr. Evans prescribed. "You will be fine in a week."

The twins took his advice to heart and slept in for a day, eating everything that was sent up to their rooms from the kitchens. The housekeeper came to meet them on the second day.

"My brother is beside himself, my lady," Mrs. Jones said. "Nobody has ever fallen sick by eating his food."

Bess shrugged off her concerns, telling her she did not need to apologize. It was probably just a bad mushroom.

"Will you go to the Laughing Mongrel?" she asked. "My brother won't feel you have forgiven him until you go and eat there again."

"Capital." Bess promised they would have lunch at the pub one of these days.

They went fishing in the stream with Nigel. Momo and Bubbles were back from London. Mrs. Bird proposed to make roast lamb for dinner, along with mushroom vol-a-vents. The vicar and his mother came. They played records later and danced.

"Mama loved the flat." Bubbles was effusive. "She is looking forward to spending more time in London."

Bess was happy for her. "When do you shift there, Bubbles? I think we have rusticated long enough."

The cold weather was setting in and they were all looking forward to hunting season. Clementine reminded the girls they needed new dresses for the ball.

Bess looked up from her second helping of kedgeree, her eyes wide.

"Thank you for the reminder, Aunt Clem. We will go to Chipping Woodbury today and see if we find something."

"Darling!" Bubbles dismissed the idea. "How boring!"

Bess told her they did not have a lot of time. The Vauxhall had been repaired in their absence and she asked Barnes to have it brought around.

"We will have lunch at the Laughing Mongrel," she announced. "Kill two birds with one stone."

Vicky was quiet on the drive.

"Do we really need new dresses? Mom brought a few more for me from New York. I think they will fit you well."

Bess gave her a wink, telling her she had a nefarious motive in going to the neighbouring town.

"You are adorable, Vicky. So straitlaced. We are going to the jeweller's."

Mr. Newman welcomed them with a smile. Bess produced the bag of gold coins and set it on the counter.

"Can you tell us what these are worth?"

"You are a ray of light in my dull existence, my lady," he beamed. "What do we have here then?"

Bess told him someone had given her the bag on a lark. She was almost sure they were all fake. Vicky's mouth hung open at this declaration. Was Bess trying some new trick on the poor man?

He told them to have a seat, asking a lackey to bring a pot of tea for the ladies. The twins watched him take a leather pouch from a drawer and choose certain tools. He began checking each coin and set it aside. Soon, they could see two piles before him, one a lot higher than the other.

"This is really curious, my lady." He peered at them over his glasses. "Are you sure this is a prank?"

"You don't mean they are the genuine item?"

"Yes and no." He pointed at the big pile of coins on his right. "These are counterfeit. Any expert worth his salt can spot these a mile away, my lady."

Bess asked about the other pile. With a bemused expression, he told her they were real.

"As if that were not unusual, there is one more thing." He placed another coin before her. "This one is very different from the others, although it does appear to be solid gold. I will have to consult one of my contemporaries to find out more."

Bess told him to go ahead and requested he telephone her at Buxley Manor when he had something to report.

They thanked the jeweller and stepped out of the store, looking around the bustling street.

"The Laughing Mongrel is next, I presume," Vicky teased.

The proprietor Jones apologized profusely, bowing multiple times.

"I could never forgive myself if anything happened to you, Lady Bess. You were a babe when I started this pub. Lord Buxley used to bring you two along with him."

Bess assured him she and Vicky were fine.

"Now are you going to starve us, Mr. Jones?"

The famous sausages and mash were produced along with the onion gravy. They could not help but think of Eileen as they began to eat.

"I don't think Eileen tried to poison us, Bess." Vicky looked around. "Is it possible we ate food that was meant for her?"

Bess thought for a moment and nodded.

They went back to Buxley after the meal and headed to the library. Polo yipped and ran toward them. Bess picked him up and settled on the sofa for a nap while Vicky chose a book. Nigel was nowhere in sight. Barnes told them he was in the garden with Annie.

"How long are you going to punish her, Bess?" Vicky sighed.

"Forgive me if I find it hard to trust her. You have been here for a few months. Do you think Papa murdered Philip?"

Vicky shook her head. She would have defended him just because he was her father but once she got to know him, she firmly believed he was innocent.

"We are linked by blood." She set her book aside. "That must be it."

Barnes brought a message. The Carrington girls were coming to tea.

"Jolly good, I say." Bess was pleased. "I wonder what Megan has been up to."

The evening passed in merriment, Bess and Vicky happy to know that Megan seemed to have recovered from the shock of her father's death. Mrs. Bird produced mulligatawny soup for dinner. There was lobster au gratin and roast chicken with turnips and potatoes, followed by bread and butter pudding with custard.

"Fancy a ride tomorrow morning, Bess?" Momo asked. "We haven't gone on a nice, bruising ride in yonks."

Plans were made and they retired early, vowing to meet in the stables at seven.

Bess and Vicky woke up at dawn and dressed in their riding habits, all smiles. They were looking forward to some vigorous activity.

"What do you think about working on our special project today, Bess?"

They nodded in unison. Momo would be at ease, away from the servants and Clementine. Bess thought she might open up more.

The horses were saddled and ready to be mounted when they reached the stables. Momo and Bubbles were as eager as the twins. They set off on a course they had discussed, two grooms following at a distance.

"Do we really need them?" Bubbles frowned.

"Come on." Momo soothed. "You will hardly know they are there."

Bess spurred her mare to a gentle trot and stuck to Momo. Vicky and Bubbles brought up the rear. They picked up speed after some time, galloping across the parkland that stretched as far as the eye could see. Bess reigned her horse in when they reached the summit of a hill.

"Philip and I used to race to this point," Momo shared. "I suspect he let me win."

"You never talk much about him, Momo. How did you two meet? Was it love at first sight?"

They turned their horses and started climbing down the hillock at a gentle pace, heading for a stream.

"Philip was a handsome man." Momo blushed at the memory. "I was always in awe of him, I suppose. Love came afterwards."

He was a man's man, happy among his friends. They rode hard, gambled and indulged in wine and spirits. Life was to be enjoyed to the fullest. There had been a certain understanding between the families so they got married when the earl thought Philip should assume his responsibilities as the heir to Buxley.

"So there was no courting period?" Bess was disappointed. "No rides in Hyde Park and balls and soirees?"

Momo laughed. There was no need for it although Philip turned quite serious after he became the earl. His love for horses did not diminish, however.

"Sometimes I thought he cared more for his horses than he did for me."

Vicky and Bubbles sat by the stream, sipping hot drinks from a thermos. Bess dismounted and joined them, accepting a cup of tea from Bubbles. Vicky was drinking coffee from a smaller thermos.

"Philip loved coffee." Momo could not stop talking about him. "It's all he drank so Cook made sure he had a thermos with him whenever he went for a ride. And that saddle! Remember what a fuss he made over it, Bubbles?"

An artisan from Scotland had come to Buxley and stayed in a cottage prepared for him while he worked on a special saddle for Philip. It had beautiful carvings, including the Buxley crest of arms and Philip's initials.

"He was the golden boy alright," Bubbles agreed. "He was carrying a flask of coffee even on the day he died."

Momo's eyes filled up as she thought of the fateful day. Bess posed the question she had always wondered about.

"You are such a good horsewoman, Momo. Why did you not join them on the hunt?"

She hugged her knees and rested her chin on them, staring into the flowing water of the stream.

"I was expecting our first child. Dr. Evans advised rest and forbid me to do anything strenuous. So a ride was out of the question."

Vicky had been quiet while Bess peppered Momo with questions.

"Surely he must have been at odds with someone? Did he ever mention if anyone hated him?"

Bubbles gave a snort and dissolved into laughter.

"Saint Philip? Not likely, old girl."

Vicky was flustered, unsure how to interpret the statement. Momo stood up, declaring it was time they went back.

"I have worked up quite an appetite," Bubbles nodded. "Good show, Momo. You should get out more often."

Bess asked about their trip to London. Momo admitted she was looking forward to spending some time at the flat, inviting an onslaught of teasing on the ride back.

The family was at breakfast at the manor. They split up, going up to their rooms to change.

"Does Bubbles always talk like that?" Vicky had restrained herself from saying anything until then. "I mean, isn't it crass to speak ill of the dead?"

"That's just how she is, the old girl. Irreverent, ready to have fun despite the situation. Life is one big party for Bubbles. She's the cat's meow, what?"

"So is our Mom, Bess. Why don't you give her a chance?"

Chapter 31

Bess admired herself in the mirror, happy with the way the sequins sparkled on her icy blue dress. Sleeveless, with a demure neckline and a fringe at the bottom, it would send tongues wagging. Vicky wore a similar dress in a soft green. They had come to Castle Morse that afternoon, along with part of the contingent from Buxley Manor for the much awaited ball.

"I plan to dance until the sun comes up," she declared.

Pudding sat on the bed, staring at a spot on the wall.

"Get dressed, old girl," Bess coaxed. "And buck up. Richie promised to invite his friends, didn't he? Time you mingled with boys our age."

Vicky silenced her with a frown. Pudding had been mortified when Sir Lawrence refused to fall in with her plans and brought her back home. Lord and Lady Morse were still in shock and had refused to speak to her.

"How could he not be aware of my feelings?" Pudding was defiant. "I met him in the garden, alone. And we had lunch once in Chipping Woodbury. Why did he think I asked to meet him in London?"

Bess placed her hands on her hips and whirled around.

"You are allowed to be silly once in your life. Now it's time to move on."

There was a knock on the door. A maid came in with a message from Lady Morse. The guests had begun to arrive and she wanted Pudding to come down to greet them.

Pudding let the maid put some finishing touches to her hair and meekly went out. Bess and Vicky accompanied her.

"Mom's here." Vicky spotted Nigel and Annie as soon as they entered the ballroom. They were sipping champagne and talking to Lord Morse.

Richie was in high spirits as he greeted the girls.

"Are you blotto already?" Bess laughed.

"Clock's ticking, my dear. There may be a noose around my neck any day now."

Vicky opened her mouth to protest but Bess grabbed her arm, warning her to say nothing. There had been some developments Richie was not aware of and the twins were hopeful. But there was no point in raising anyone's expectations until they knew more.

The jeweller had called Buxley Manor a few days ago, requesting Bess to go and see him at the store. They took the motor and sped to Chipping Woodbury, sure he had tracked down the unusual coin. It was centuries old, from the Roman era. Very few such coins were in circulation and they cost a lot more than their weight in gold.

"Is this part of those scavenger hunts we read about in the paper, my lady?" His voice was full of mirth. "There is mischief afoot."

Bess thanked him and made a quick exit. They headed to the police station, armed with the new information. DI Gardener was in London, working on another case. The constable protested at first but gave in and placed a call to Scotland Yard.

"You mean you have been withholding information from the police?" The Inspector's anger was palpable. "I can arrest you right now, Lady Bess."

MURDER AT CASTLE MORSE

She ignored his ire and reminded him it was his duty to follow every lead.

"How do you know this will not lead to Richard Morse?" he questioned.

"So be it." Bess responded with a sigh, preparing herself for the worst.

There had been no word from the Inspector after that and Bess was losing hope. It was best they held off on saying anything to him.

"Can I have the first dance with you?" she batted her eyelids at him.

The musicians were tuning their instruments, ready to begin. Richie gave her a deep bow and offered her his arm.

"Shall we?"

To Vicky's surprise, Cedric Ridley, Momo's brother, appeared beside her and offered his arm, asking if she wanted to dance.

Bess ran a quick glance around the room, trying to spot Sir Lawrence. Surely he would not dare to put in an appearance. Pudding cowered beside Lady Morse, ready to burst into tears any minute.

The strains of a waltz began. She placed a firm hand on Richie's shoulder and allowed him to whisk her away to the centre of the room, making up her mind to enjoy the evening. Richie was an excellent dancer and Bess was light on her feet. The couple almost flew across the room, their faces lit up, wreathed in smiles. Then the music stopped.

"I say!" Bess exclaimed, falling against Richie's chest as he came to a sudden stop. "What ... what on earth?"

Similar exclamations could be heard across the room.

Detective Inspector James Gardener tapped the microphone, trying to get everyone's attention. Richie paled when he realized who stood next to the musicians.

"Ladies and gentlemen, I am sorry to disturb your evening. We are here on very important police business."

A team of uniformed policemen was closing all the doors, ushering the guests to a corner of the room. DI Gardener came toward them and greeted Bess and Richie, leading them to a group of chairs by the wall.

"Great timing, Inspector." Bess chided. "Could you not have waited until tomorrow?"

The smile he offered could best be described as devilish.

"You will thank me later, Lady Bess."

Sweat lined Richie's brow and he was shaking with fear. With a pang, Bess realized she could not help Richie if he was guilty. The Inspector grabbed both his hands and pumped them vigorously.

"I owe you an apology, Mr. Morse. It appears you have no involvement in the murders of Joe Cooper and Eileen Harris."

Lord Morse who had been on his way toward them heard him.

"Do you admit you harassed this family for no reason, Inspector? Your superiors will hear about this."

DI Gardener ignored him, waiting for a nod from his seargent.

"Mr. Stephen Ballard," he spoke in a loud and clear voice. "I am hereby arresting you for murdering Joe Cooper and Eileen Harris."

A bunch of policemen held Ballard by the arms, ready to take him away.

MURDER AT CASTLE MORSE

"I did it, I did it," he cried. "I had no choice, you see."

The men took him away. The room was in uproar. Lady Morse and the staff began nudging them to another room where a buffet had been set up.

Richie sat in his chair, staring at his feet, stunned.

"Is that true?" he asked the Inspector. "But why? He was afraid of horses."

Bess gathered what Richie meant. How had Ballard come in contact with the groom?

The Inspector told them to be patient and headed back to the police station. All he could tell them was the Roman era coin Bess found was part of a horde that had previously been discovered on Ballard's estate in Kent.

Richie let out a whoop and grabbed Bess, twirling her around the dance floor. Lord and Lady Morse advised caution.

"Don't count your chickens until they are hatched, my boy," he warned.

Lady Morse was so overwhelmed she wanted to retire to her room.

"Nonsense!" Louise thundered.

Bess and Vicky beamed with pride as their grandmother took control of the situation, assisted by the great aunts.

"Ask those musicians to come back in," Louise ordered the butler. "The guests will follow once the music begins."

She told Lord Morse there was no point in wasting a month's worth of effort. The ball would continue as before.

"Your boy is free. It is no small victory."

Nobody dared to cross the formidable Dowager Countess of Buxley. Lord Morse ushered his wife to the dance floor, soon joined by Nigel and Annie. Other couples followed.

Bess danced with abandon, finally managing to coax a smile out of Pudding. Dawn was breaking in the forest when the guests left. Sleep came at once for Bess. It was an hour past noon when she stirred, prodded by Vicky.

"The Inspector just arrived. He wants to talk to everyone."

"James!" Bess sat up with a jerk and headed to the bathroom to wash.

Half an hour later, she entered the dining room where everyone was assembled. Chef Henri had set up a lavish buffet, mostly comprising of food left over from the previous night. Bess filled a plate and took a seat next to Richie, nodding a greeting at the Inspector.

"Stephen Ballard confessed," he began. "There is no doubt he is guilty." He smiled at Richard, his voice kind. "You are in the clear, Mr. Morse and you have Lady Bess to thank for it."

"Golly!" Richie offered.

"Jolly good, Inspector," Lord Morse roared. "You were wrong to suspect my son." He cleared his throat. "Say, does this have anything to do with the Roman ruins?"

DI Gardener was apologetic.

"In a manner of speaking, Sir. Unfortunately, there are no ruins. At least not on Morse land."

Bess thought Lord Morse took it well. With a stoic face, he admitted he had guessed as much and requested the Inspector to continue.

Stephen Ballard was an eminent archaeologist, well respected in his field. He had become famous when Roman artifacts were discovered at his family estate in Kent, among them, a horde of coins from the 5th century. He enjoyed the limelight for a bit but the subsequent projects he took up yielded nothing.

"He had high hopes for my land," Lord Morse volunteered. "And I believed him."

James told them Ballard had started with good intentions. Maybe his research was correct and the Morse land would still yield something. But he grew frustrated when his team uncovered nothing after months of digging. He planted the mosaic and some bits of gold, making sure his students were the one to dig them up. Joe Cooper saw him.

"Let me guess," Bess interrupted. "And Joe began to blackmail him."

Joe Cooper made increasing demands with every passing day. Ballard promised a big payment, supposedly the last one. They met in the stables at the appointed hour. Joe accepted the money and asked for more in a week's time. Ballard realized the blackmail would never end and grabbed Joe's throat. A scuffle ensued in which Joe Cooper hit his head on something and died on the spot.

"He says he did not intend to kill the man." The Inspector was grim. "But the law does not condone murder based on intentions."

"And poor Eileen?" Vicky asked. "Did she see him commit the act?"

The Inspector told them they could only speculate. Eileen must have visited Joe in the stables. Ballard had seen her argue with Joe and stomp out. She must have come back later for the earring.

"She approached Ballard and asked him to confess to the police. He tried to pay her off with the gold."

Bess told them most of it had been counterfeit.

"That rascal!" Lord Morse spat. "He hoodwinked her too."

Eileen's conscience would not let her accept the money. She gave Ballard an ultimatum. He attacked her in the middle of the night while she was asleep. The girl did not even fight back.

Lady Morse shed tears of relief as she hugged her son. They all mourned Eileen. She had been a rock for the Morse 13, feeding their families during hard times, offering them a shoulder to cry on. The whole village would miss her.

Lord Morse blamed himself. He should never have invited Ballard and his group to dig on the grounds of Castle Morse.

"Will you tell the Royal Society?" he asked the Inspector. "They accepted his application based on what he supposedly discovered here."

Bess saw the Inspector hesitate. She felt he was holding something back.

"What is it?" she pressed. "What else did Ballard say?"

Had he laid the blame at someone else's feet, she wondered.

"It means nothing, of course," the Inspector said. "Nobody forced him to commit these dastardly acts."

"Out with it, Inspector," Lord Morse boomed. "If anyone else poses a threat to my people, I would rather know about it now."

Bess would never have guessed what the Inspector said next.

"Ballard blames Sir Lawrence Watkins."

"One Eye Watkins?" Bess burst out.

"That terrible man!" Lady Morse cried. "He means to destroy us, Clive."

MURDER AT CASTLE MORSE

The Inspector told everyone to calm down. As far as he could tell, the only crime Sir Lawrence was guilty of was grandstanding.

"Ballard was at a low point when he met him. Sir Lawrence was full of stories of his fame and exploits, being the most sought after big game hunter in Africa. Awed by his magnetic personality, Ballard sought his advice."

Bess wanted to know why Ballard would seek help from a random stranger.

"That's just it," the Inspector replied. "Their families have adjoining estates in Kent. Sir Lawrence is something of a father figure to Stephen Ballard who hero worshipped him as a child. They met in Kent earlier this summer and learned that they were both going to be in the same area."

The two men had met for a pint in local pubs, eager to spend time with each other before Sir Lawrence returned to Africa.

"Did he ask Ballard to shoot the man?" Bess grunted. "Or tear him apart with his bare hands?"

The Inspector shook his head and sighed.

"Sir Lawrence told him to go after what he wanted. The only way to deal with obstacles was to eliminate them. Battles were not fought without shedding blood. And more in the same vein, I presume. He was trying to buck him up."

Bess asked about the intruder in Eileen's cottage. Had that been Ballard?

The Inspector nodded. He had gone back to retrieve the gold.

"He also confessed he tried to poison you, ladies."

Vicky gasped, remembering Ballard had been at the Laughing Mongrel with his assistant that day. And they had laid the blame on Eileen.

"She taught me how to properly eat an onion," Pudding sobbed. "Mama, we should rename the Onion Festival. And I will honour Eileen by taking part every year."

Chapter 32

Nigel Gaskins, Earl of Buxley, sat on a bench in the wildflower garden he had planted for his wife, watching her feed the swans in the pond. All his hopes had come true when Annie came home, looking as beautiful as he remembered. After twenty years of separation, neither was sure what drove them apart. They wanted to reconcile for the sake of their daughters but after spending some time together, Nigel realized the old spark was still alive. He had never stopped loving Annie and he wondered if she felt the same.

Annie joined him on the bench, her face aglow and placed her head on his shoulder.

"What are you thinking?"

"What? What, what." Nigel sputtered, never lucid in tense moments.

"We have wasted a lot of time, my darling. I want us to be a family again. You, me, our sweet daughters."

Nigel was of the same mind. But he could not say yes. He had met Bess earlier that morning, right after breakfast. She had been her honest self, explaining what was holding her back from embracing Annie.

"I would like nothing more, my dear, but I have one condition."

"Bess."

"You need to square things with her before we can move on. I believe she deserves at least that."

**

Bess and Vicky had returned from Castle Morse three days ago and had taken some time to recuperate. They were leaving for a week in Paris and they had coaxed Pudding into going with them.

"You are not going to sit around moping, are you?" Bess was stern. "Forget you ever met that buffoon, old girl."

Vicky was a bit more gentle.

"You will meet other men, I promise. And you will fall in love with someone who deserves you."

Lord and Lady Morse had been full of praise.

"We are beholden to you, girls." Lady Morse was emotional. "You have saved our son's life and now you are helping our daughter rebuild hers."

Vicky felt discomfited but Bess lapped up all the praise.

"Pudding is my sister too, Lady Morse. I will always take care of her."

Lord Morse was still smarting from the embarrassment his daughter had subjected him to.

"You might talk some sense into her, Bess. Marry a man older than me? Why, the very idea!"

She would stay at Castle Morse until he saw her off on the train to Paris one week later. Bess thought he was being quite generous, considering the brouhaha Pudding had created.

The twins were glad to be home and slowly settled into the routine at Buxley Manor. They went fishing with their father, had a pint at the pub and rode across the estate every morning. Autumn had ushered in colder weather and it was time for the harvest. Roaring fires were lit in the fireplaces across the manor, creating a warm and cozy glow. Parties and balls were planned as hunts were organized across the various estates in the area. Bess had always loved that time of the year.

The Nightingales assembled in the west wing one morning, ready to take stock. Tea had been served, along with ginger biscuits and cake.

"You have rested on your laurels long enough, girls," Louise griped. "Have you lost sight of our main purpose?"

Vicky assured her they would never let up. Unfortunately, their efforts had not yielded much.

"Update," Hortense nodded.

"Our plan was to learn more about Philip," Perpetua reminded them. "Did you exercise some tact like we discussed?"

Bess told them they had collected a ton of useless information about the previous earl. It had only managed to confuse them.

"Philip was a rum sort of chap. He was nothing like Papa."

Louise agreed with her.

"His mother Beatrice had a part in that, my dear. She was always too big for her boots. Raised him to be proud. I suppose it comes with the territory if you are going to be an earl."

Vicky had sensed the same.

"Was he unkind though?"

Louise did not think so.

"He might have given that impression. We are so privileged, we take many things for granted."

Bess wanted to begin without wasting any more time.

"So Philip was quite wild in his youth. Many of our servants and people in the village have attested to the same."

"And he was mad about horses," Vicky continued. "He rode hard, possibly believed he was invincible."

Hortense told them it was a family trait. Philip's father Percival had been the same, so had his father before him.

"Nigel is an exception, my dear."

Bess told them Philip did have a redeeming trait. He turned over a new leaf when he became earl. Although, it was unexpected, he assumed the responsibility needed for the role. That was why the tenants still worshipped him.

"He died and became a hero."

Vicky sipped her coffee, thankful that the butler and cook always remembered her preference.

"He hated French food but he drank coffee, just like me. They say he carried a flask with him wherever he went. In fact, he did so even on that fateful day."

"Trivia!" Perpetua dismissed.

"Maybe not," Hortense argued, folding her handkerchief into a perfect square. "The tiniest fact can lead us to the truth."

The sisters bickered for a few minutes until Louise prodded Bess to continue.

"We spoke to Momo, of course. And she said the most curious thing, Grandmother."

Vicky explained how Momo had always dreamed about marrying Philip. She was not sure he loved her.

"She kept kidding about how he paid more attention to his horses. There was an underlying bitterness I did not sense before. I don't think Philip was kind to her, Grandmother."

Louise told them the aristocracy always married for convenience. Momo had been chosen for her impeccable lineage and the dowry Sir Dorian conferred on her.

MURDER AT CASTLE MORSE

"Just like Nigel married Annie who was a dollar princess."

"But Papa fell in love with Mom," Vicky protested. "She told me so."

Bess gave a reluctant nod.

"Maybe so." Louise refused to budge. "But her dowry paved the way."

Vicky thought it was a cynical point of view. Bess agreed but said nothing.

"So we talked to every person we could think of, Grandmother. The Harveys, tenants, villagers, Barnes, Mrs. Jones, Mrs. Bird, Momo and Bubbles, even the Morses." She gave a deep sigh, then sat up with a jerk as a thought struck her. "And that rascal Sir Lawrence. Actually, he talked to me!"

Louise admonished her for being disrespectful.

"He is an honourable man, Bess."

"But I bet you don't know this. Philip idolized him, Grandmother. He had promised to go back to Africa with him to hunt for big game. But he cancelled those plans when he learned Momo was expecting their child."

The older ladies finally stirred. Hortense remembered how Philip had followed Sir Lawrence around, even as a boy. The hunter always regaled him with fantastic stories and taught him to shoot.

Vicky asked how he had reacted when Philip got married. Was he jealous of Momo?

"No, he spoiled the Ridley girls too." Louise was thoughtful. "He was happy Philip was not marrying a stranger."

Bess could not take it any longer.

"I say! I am not done yet." She told them about her talk with Nigel. "Papa said Philip argued with Sir Lawrence on the day of the hunt."

This got their attention.

Nigel never spoke about the day of the hunt, always claiming it was all a blur. But the repeated conversations with Sir Lawrence had niggled an old memory. Philip and Sir Lawrence had a full blown argument in the library that morning. The hunter accused Philip of being a cad and a scoundrel who had no backbone.

"What?" Louise's eyes popped.

"I think Sir Lawrence lost his temper. Either he riled Philip up so much that he barely paid attention to where he was going. Or he somehow spooked Philip's horse, intending to teach him a lesson."

Hortense and Perpetua were not convinced.

"No proof," Hortense clucked.

"I agree, Aunt Hortense. But if he is such a gentleman, he will not be able to tell an outright lie."

Louise asked if she planned to confront him herself. Bess told her it was time the police did their job.

"I will meet the Inspector and ask him to question Sir Lawrence. Doesn't that sound like a marvellous idea?"

Everyone agreed it was the only idea they had.

"And it will give you a chance to meet the Inspector," Vicky teased.

"A working man?" Perpetua's eyebrows shot up. "Do we know his people?"

MURDER AT CASTLE MORSE

Bess refused to succumb to their teasing. The clock began to chime and the group dispersed, heading to the dining room for lunch.

Ten minutes before four, Bess got into her motor and headed to the Buxley Arms. She had placed a telephone call to the police station earlier, requesting to meet DI Gardener on an urgent matter. Fortunately, he agreed to meet her at the Buxley Arms that afternoon.

The proprietor welcomed her and inquired after everyone at the manor. Bess thanked him and took a seat by the window, looking up every now and then, trying to spot James. She ordered a cup of tea fifteen minutes later. When the Inspector failed to appear even after she had finished a whole pot, she stalked out of the pub, determined to track him down at the police station.

She heard the growl of a motor and hesitated when the Inspector's Hispano Suiza came around the bend. He jumped out and hailed her, grabbing her arm and ushering her back inside.

"You are late."

"I am sorry, Lady Bess." He closed his eyes and rubbed the bridge of his nose.

"Just Bess. You look tired."

He asked about the urgent matter.

"Is everything alright at the manor? Why did you ask me to come here?"

Bess confessed she had been trying to find out more about Philip's death. She did not mention the Nightingales, afraid he would ridicule them. The Inspector let her ramble on about the different things she had learned, silent until she stopped talking.

"Have you listened to a word I said?"

"Of course. But I don't see what coffee and marriages of convenience have to do with a hunting accident."

Bess revealed her trump card.

"Sir Lawrence Watkins. One Eye Watkins."

"What about him?" He asked sharply.

Bess launched into her latest theory.

"He has been stirring up trouble in the village, asking questions about the hunt, pointing fingers at Papa. We know this man has great powers of persuasion. He convinced Ballard to murder two people. What if he was the one responsible for Philip's death?"

James placed his elbows on the table.

"You are saying Sir Lawrence killed Philip twenty years ago."

Bess nodded vigorously. He had left the country after Philip died and not come back for twenty years.

"He must be confident he got away with it." She banged a fist on the table. "Maybe he just spooked his horse or something, thinking he would teach him a lesson."

James asked what she wanted him to do.

"Bring the man in, of course. Investigate him or do whatever it is you do at Scotland Yard. I may not like the man, but I believe he will confess if he is guilty."

"I agree, Bess. But we are too late."

Bess swore in frustration.

"I say! Don't tell me the rascally man went back to Africa."

MURDER AT CASTLE MORSE

Detective Inspector Gardener of Scotland Yard shook his head, his eyes grave.

"Sir Lawrence is dead. He was found in the woods at Ridley Hall earlier today, shot in the back."

**

Who killed Philip? Will Bess and the Nightingales ever be able to find out and exonerate Nigel? And who murdered poor Sir Lawrence? Does his death have anything to do with what happened at Castle Morse? Read the final book in the trilogy, Murder at Ridley Hall, to find out.

Recipe – Empire Fruit Cake

Ingredients

1/2 cup apricots
1/2 cup Raisins and Sultanas
1/2 cup dried figs
1/2 cup dried cherries
1/4 cup candied citrus peel
1/4 cup Pistachios
1/4 cup Almonds
2 ripe mashed bananas
1 orange juiced
1 cup dark rum
1/2 cup toasted coconut flakes
2 cups flour sifted
1 cup butter
1 cup Sugar
¼ tsp ground cloves
¼ tsp ground nutmeg
1 tsp ground cinnamon
1 tsp ground ginger
1/2 tsp salt
1 tsp baking powder
2 eggs

Method

Chop all the dried fruit and transfer to a bowl. Pour the rum over it, enough to cover. Set aside for a week or more.

On baking day, sieve the flour, baking powder and spices. Chop the nuts and mash the bananas.

MURDER AT CASTLE MORSE

Cream the butter and sugar until light and fluffy. Add the eggs and beat until incorporated well. Now add the juice of an orange, the mashed bananas, the soaked fruit, the coconut flakes and the chopped nuts.

Fold in the flour and mix well.

Bake in a greased, floured tin at 350F or 180C until a toothpick inserted in the centre comes out dry.

Remove the cake from the pan and cool on a wire rack. Cut and serve a day later.

Cook always has a batch of fruit soaking in rum. They get really soft and plump and taste delicious. She uses the best ingredients from the corners of the British empire. Apricots from Turkey are her favourite, so is Jamaican rum and coconuts from the islands. Sometimes, she adds a bit of Ceylon tea to the cake batter, adding another burst of flavour.

Acknowledgements

I would like to thank each and every one who chose to read my historical mystery trilogy. Your encouragement has been a source of great motivation to me and helps me strive harder to bring you stories that will keep you at the edge of your seat.

Many thanks to the beta readers and readers who follow me on Facebook who chose to read the early drafts. Your feedback has been invaluable.

I am forever grateful to my family for just being there for me unconditionally and providing all the support I need.

I appreciate you.

Join my Newsletter

Never miss a new release!

Get access to exclusive bonus content, sneak peeks, giveaways and much more. Also get a chance to join my exclusive ARC group, the people who get first dibs on all my new books.

Sign up at the following link and join the fun.

Click here ⇨ http://www.subscribepage.com/leenaclovernl

I love to hear from my readers, so please feel free to connect with me at any of the following places.

Website – http://leenaclover.com

Instagram – https://instagram.com/leenaclover

Facebook – http://facebook.com/leenaclovercozymysterybooks

Email – leenaclover@gmail.com

LEENA CLOVER

Books by Leena Clover
Pelican Cove Cozy Mystery Series
Strawberries and Strangers
Cupcakes and Celebrities
Berries and Birthdays
Sprinkles and Skeletons
Waffles and Weekends
Muffins and Mobsters
Parfaits and Paramours
Truffles and Troubadours
Sundaes and Sinners
Croissants and Cruises
Pancakes and Parrots
Cookies and Christmas
Popsicles and Poisons
Dolphin Bay Cozy Mystery Series
Raspberry Chocolate Murder
Orange Thyme Death
Apple Caramel Mayhem
Cranberry Sage Miracle
Blueberry Chai Frenzy
Mango Chili Cruiser
Strawberry Vanilla Peril
Cherry Lime Havoc
Pumpkin Ginger Bedlam
Meera Patel Cozy Mystery Series
Gone with the Wings
A Pocket Full of Pie
For a Few Dumplings More
Back to the Fajitas

MURDER AT CASTLE MORSE

Christmas with the Franks
British Cozy Mystery Series
Murder at Buxley Manor
Murder at Castle Morse
Murder at Ridley Hall
Meg Butler Cruise Cozy Series
Sail Away Patsy
Bingo Bashed

Printed in Great Britain
by Amazon